EMALICKEL

THE CELESTIALS ARE REAL

A. M. TRUE

Edited by
KATHERINE O. BROWN

ACKNOWLEDGEMENTS

A very special thank you to friend and author David F. Berens who has a heart full of love. I am ever so grateful for him graciously volunteering his time and effort in helping me to share this work, my soul's passion, with the whole world!

My sincerest gratitude to Jake and to Kathy for taking the time to read the first draft. I appreciate them both, dearly, for helping me to make this novel ready for its readers.

CONTENTS

PREFACE

Emalickel was written over a period of five years after a very vivid and real dream I experienced. Previously, I had been recalling and recording my dreams. Emalickel was one such recording which ended up containing over 65,000 words. For six years I kept this dream a complete secret. Since then, I have decided to go out of my comfort zone and share the wonders of Emalickel with the rest of the world.

Before you begin reading, there are a few things to note in the Appendix. I have included several aids in the back of this novel to help make your reading experience just as vivid and realistic as I once experienced. Therefore, you will find three items in the appendix: a musical playlist, a pronunciation key, and visual aids.

The musical playlist is extremely important to me as it contains cherished pieces of music which help convey the emotion of each scene taking place throughout the novel. Listening to the music, you will need to slow your reading pace down to a "read-aloud" pace, as if what you are reading is taking place in real-time. For example, when the characters speak, they're going to speak in a slow concise manner

—not rushed like you would do if you read at your brain's internal pace. I am aware the timing of the music may not always work out perfectly but playing the music along with the scenes is sure to add some extra flair to your experience—just as does music in the scenes of a movie.

If you use the music, not only will it enhance your reading experience, but you will get to hear some amazing pieces by all the different artists. These songs are listed throughout the book at the beginning of each scene, but please support the artists and contribute to their heart-filled work by purchasing or licensing their music per the information in the appendix. Then, create an "Emalickel" playlist to use while you read.

Another tool readers will appreciate is the pronunciation key. The pronunciation key will help you properly pronounce the names of beings and places throughout the novel. This will help you to know, truly, the names of those places I experienced and beings I encountered. This enables the reader to more easily relate to these important characters and places, thus making the novel more immersive.

Lastly, in the appendix, you will find my visual aids. Shortly after waking up from the experience of Emalickel, not only did I begin writing down what I experienced, but I attempted to draw some of the pivotal places I encountered. I am no artist, but hopefully these sketches will help paint a somewhat more vivid visual for you.

I hope you enjoy the Emalickel experience, and that it resonates with you in some way. May it bring you pleasure escaping into a beautiful world of celestials—be it fantasy or real. May it bring you excitement as you enjoy the unraveling of secrets that were shared with me. The mysteries will eventually all come together. Finally, may it bring you joy to know that you are adored. You are a major part of this big picture we call creation. After all, there is a reason you have found this book. There are no coincidences.

Love to all of you,

A. M. True
United States
05/01/2018

* Also, please note that the words that are *italicized*, throughout the novel, are thoughts and not spoken words.

1

EMALICKEL

1. Artist: Audiomachine
Song: Existence (Ext to 5:31

July 5th, 2012

I was lying out in the sun during my vacation at the beach in Florida. My mind was consumed with thought. The whole day passed in what seemed like a flash. I was totally caught up in the thought of *there is something else out there for me.* I felt it. I just knew it to be true. I sighed and closed my eyes soaking up more radiant sun rays until I drifted off into a semi-sleep state.

Suddenly, I awoke with a gasp. I had an intense feeling of butterflies in my stomach. When I sat up, I looked out at the ocean. There, standing directly on the water about 1000 feet away from me, was a man with his arms crossed at his bare chest. Since he was so far away, I could not see him in great detail, but he appeared to be in his early 30's and was in phenomenal physical shape. His chest was bare, but he was wearing a red velvet cape which blew majestically in the wind behind him. He was staring directly at me. It was weird because I felt like I knew him, but I didn't know how or from where.

When it hit me that he was actually standing on the water in the middle of the ocean, I stood up and started walking towards the shoreline for a better look to confirm what I saw. Instead, I was blinded by a quick flash of intensely bright light. It was as quick as lightning but covered my entire vision. Everything was white light for a split-second. It looked like someone had flashed a camera right into my eyes. I rubbed my eyes and looked around the beach to see if anyone else had seen this peculiar flash of light. Everyone was carrying on like normal, completely oblivious to anything I was seeing. My confirmation of the man on the ocean was never achieved because, just as fast as he had appeared, he faded away and was gone.

I was very confused and somewhat in denial of what had just happened. Was I dehydrated? Overheated? I went back to my towel and sat down to drink from my water bottle. I watched the ocean for a while and waited to see if the majestic man would return. He never did. I decided I would go back to my room in the condo, grab a bite to eat, and shower to rejuvenate myself.

Later that evening, as I sat outside on the balcony of my condo, there was an overwhelming feeling of peace within me, as if I was special and had good things coming my way. I felt happy and content, as if I had nothing to worry about. It was a powerful feeling. I was alerted when an epiphany overcame me—*what if the things of Earth were only a holographic illusion induced by our five senses, a prerequisite to a higher state of consciousness?* All the so-called problems in life suddenly seemed insignificant and disappeared completely from my mind. A satisfied smile grew across my face. I was excited inside at this new profound epiphany.

I was not sure what I had seen that day or if I had even seen anything at all. I thought about the possibility of losing my mind or if I were developing Schizophrenia or something. Regardless, I really didn't care. Even if I were losing my mind, this felt great, and I wasn't about to find something wrong about that.

For several years before that day on the beach, my life had been complicated, stressful, and monotonous. I worried about the same endless tasks each day over and over. Work, money, health, chores, and time ran my life and every thought. Constrained by the principals of mortality, I felt trapped in the bore of this dimension of life where we strive for something higher yet are constantly distracted by routine demands. Indeed, there were moments of blissful happiness where we think of nothing other than the excitement before us, but these moments are short-lived as our minds end up returning to the same old routines in our day to day lives.

It appears the majority of man-kind accepted this colorlessness; being able to enjoy life accepting it at face-value and conforming to the standards. I found it a rarity to run into those whom were consumed by deep thought or imagination. Most were barely inspired by abstract thoughts. Most would fear the opportunity to experience a world where physics is beyond that of the accepted norm.

I, on the other hand, was consumed by these ideas. Because of this, I felt alone in my thoughts. I knew no one obsessed, as much as I, about striving for a higher state of consciousness. I felt like I came from somewhere else—like my true home was not the Earth. I yearned to share a part in an existence where the impossible became possible. There were few doubts in my mind this existed. Even science and physical data backed this idea with the study of quantum physics. The fact is that we are indeed a part of a vibrational universe. Everything is a vibration. Even our thoughts and emotions are measurable waves of frequency, which not only can emit and translate but also create and receive.

That is how we get "gut" feelings about things. We can feel if someone is lying because we are physically picking up on the frequency of fear being emitted from them. We know when something is wrong with someone despite their insisting that everything is fine. That is also why we have the ability to sense things without explanation. We actually pick up on emitted frequencies and vibrations happening around us. We can sense the presence of others by feeling their emitted energy and their emotional frequencies. That is why we can sometimes just "get a hunch" when someone is in a deep negative state or an extremely positive state.

There are people who unknowingly emit emotional frequencies at such intense vibrations that they actually shift the entire energy within the places they go. This is wonderful if the person is blissfully happy, but it can bring everybody down if the dominant energy emitted in a room is negative.

For us as humans, these vibrational waves are being translated by our five senses, thus giving the waves form and tangibility. Some people are more in-tune with translating energy than others. It depends on their state of awareness. It also depends on their ability to decode or perceive reality as it is given.

I started questioning the realness of the other people around me. I did a lot of reading on topics such as: Awakening Consciousness, The Illusion of Reality, and Creating Your Reality. Basically, it seemed to me we were completely submerged in the matrix of an ultimate virtual reality game. *Was it just me, and the rest of the people of this so-called world are just part of the game matrix? Or maybe everyone is real, and we are all in this ultimate multi-player reality matrix together*. I longed to be a part of something different, something better—something beyond that of this current game we all play. *How could I see through the veil of reality and experience something different? How could I help others to do this?* To me, we were all stuck here, and I desired to find other options.

2. Artist: Future World Music
Song: New Beginnings

I prayed about it, and I mean I prayed hard. I asked God, the Creator of all existence, to hear my plea. God-Energy is within each and every one of His creations. We are quite literally "the breath of God." He experiences Himself through each and every one of His creations. He hears my thoughts because He is within me, a part of me, looking through my eyes and listening within my mind. We are all extensions of God. This goes for everyone!

I fell apart and submitted to complete, utter, brutal honestly. I asked questions that most would view as sacrilegious, but I asked them anyway. After all, is God not already aware of everything we think and feel? I might as well ask. He already knows. Does He not understand that we have such questions in a world filled with doubt and conspiracy? So, I put it all out there. I questioned Him. I asked every question I could think of.

Why are we here? How are we here? Is there more than just this? If so, why would God put a veil on reality? Why couldn't we know more than we know? Why can we not eat from the Tree of Knowledge? Was it truly God who instructed us not to eat from the Tree of Knowledge or did that derive from an alternate, more cynical, group of beings trying to keep us constrained and limited in thought? Where do I truly come from—my soul—where does it come from? Have I lived other lives before?

I became frustrated when I didn't hear any answers. I felt abandoned. I begged for an obvious sign that He was listening to me. I asked for Him to send one of His angels to me to explain all that could be explained. Even if the angel came to me and told me to shut up, that would be fine. At least I would know God was listening to my plea and responding.

If we, man-kind, were asleep in our state of consciousness, and there was more to be known or revealed, I invited God to use my body as a vessel to do as needed to assist in that process. I practiced meditations that opened me to receive God's angels of light but protected me from any dark negative entities. Interesting things started happening to me upon doing so. I started seeing synchronicities. Many would call them coincidences, but there were far too many to be explained as such. Everything started to change for me after I started seeing these synchronicities. At first, it felt like I was putting a scattered puzzle together, trying to make sense of the signs. I yearned for answers and clarity. I was perplexed at what was happening.

After the incident of seeing the man standing on the ocean, I started seeing the numbers 3, 33, and 333. They appeared so often it frightened me. They appeared in TV shows, road signs, the speedometer, shirts, clocks, price-tags in stores, rooms of places I visited. I mean daily, several times a day. Intrigued, I started researching this phenomenon. I found out that this is a sign that you are being watched and guided. The moment of seeing the number meant that divine beings were right there. This is also the number of Christ, God incarnate.

As time went on, I started seeing even more synchronicities. I would smell roses when none were in sight. I would sense car wrecks happening in front of me minutes before they would happen. I would see flashes of violet and blue lights at random times in the day. I started seeing mathematical fractal designs everywhere. Even one night before falling asleep, I saw a moving design manifest in my sight. It was a Flower of Life symbol. It was spinning and morphing physically before my eyes, as if I were looking through a kaleidoscope. Even after I rose out of bed and walked to the bathroom and turned on the light, the Flower of Life design stayed so clearly and vividly in my eye sight.

3. Artist: Nordwise
Song: Evolve II

While teaching at school one day, I had an episode where my mind was severely altered. I felt dizzy like I was passing out. My vision started fading to black as a scene fades in a movie. When my eyesight returned, my brain was not right. I wasn't me. I was there, but I wasn't me. I was looking through my eyes, but I didn't know where I was or who I was. I didn't even know what I was. Everything was slow. Sounds were muffled and echoed loudly in my head. I was panicked and over-stimulated at everything. It was like I was a new baby seeing the world for the first time and didn't know what anything was. The children in my classroom weren't familiar to me. I didn't even know what species they were. I did not identify with humans. When the children spoke to me, I didn't understand their words, nor could I conjure my own words to speak. I was in utter confusion. This lasted for an entire minute, then I felt completely normal again. Nobody in the room had even noticed.

Days after the incident, I went to several doctors, including neurologists and cardiologists. They all seemed perplexed, thinking it may have been a seizure, mini-stroke, or a blood-pressure regulation issue. They performed all kinds of tests on me over a series of a period of several months. The doctors were baffled when nothing appeared unusual on any of the tests. All the tests were normal: the brain-scans, the Electroencephalography (EEG), electrocardiogram, tilt-table test, heart-monitor, and bloodwork. There was no possible explanation for the episode I had experienced. Nobody could figure out why or how it had happened. They all called it "just a freak thing that probably won't ever happen again."

As time continued, new numbers in sequences of three started to show themselves before me such as 111, 222, and 555. I also started seeing things manifest after I spoke or thought of them. If I was talking about snakes one day, that same night I would turn on the television and it would be turned to a documentary about snakes. I would see a crow and admire its sleek, black feathers, and the next day I would see crows everywhere. They'd be flying above my car as I drove to work and all over the playground where I taught. The same went for dragonflies, hummingbirds, and butterflies. If the synchronicities I started seeing were a one-mile stretch of beach, the above examples are but grains of sand.

At night, I would practice lucid dreaming for it was my only means of escaping into a world where there were no physical boundaries to constrain me. I desired to continue liberating myself from the chronic monotony of Earth. Convinced that it existed, I attempted to experience another place or existence with endless possibilities. During the day, I'd daydream about meeting the man on the ocean, who would share otherworldly wisdom with me.

All these thoughts consumed my mind. I found myself longing for these experiences with intense desire. Unable to dismiss them, these thoughts quickly developed into a 24-hour a day obsession. I tried to pretend to be normal, pretending to be accepting of things as they were; but even that task became more and more resistant and daunting. It was as if I weren't meant to be the same. It felt like I was meant to be different and was seeing signs of this in my awakening. I continued to plea for more knowledge. Yes, I was seeing all kinds of synchronicities, but what did it all mean? I wanted to meet a higher being who could show me more and tell me more. It was all I knew to do.

For several years, this obsession continued. Endlessly, I thought about meeting a supreme being, like the man on the ocean, and I thought about how he would engage me in enlightening experiences. Never giving up, I continued my persistence in daydreaming for two reasons: 1) I considered the law of attraction. Maybe my thoughts would attract the idea, thus manifesting it into reality, and 2) God knows my thoughts and feelings, He knows my plans, and knows what is best. I knew He would provide me the opportunity for this experience, be it now or later, should He see it fit. Until then, my thoughts were the only retreat I had.

4. Artist: Symphony of Specters (Charles Evans)
Song: Things Worth Fighting For

One night on the 3rd day of September in 2012, I was crawling into bed at my small house in the country. Several images from my memories flashed before my mind: the man standing on the ocean, repeating sequences of numbers, the Flower of Life symbol, black crows, the altered state of consciousness experienced at school, remembering my pleading prayers, flashes of light, high-pitched ringing in my ears, the smell of roses, and predicting havoc before it happened. Although it didn't frighten me, it did bother me to have unanswered questions. I decided to meditate and pray.

First, I thanked God for giving me life and providing me with new perspectives and insights in my life. I asked Him to help me continue to live by this enlightening outlook and to be able to remember it always. Then, I asked Him for answers. I saw signs everywhere, which seemed to be trying to tell me something, but I could not piece it all together. What really stood out was remembering the man on the ocean.

Was he real? Who was he? Will I ever see him again? What was he doing? How did he get there?

In the middle of the prayer I started drifting off before catching myself.

Please, will you send me a sign? Will you visit me in my sleep to give me clear answers?

Again, I had dozed off but quickly resumed my prayer. *Send me an angel, God... something... anything...* I caught myself dozing again, but this time I was unable to move my body. It was like I was paralyzed but was completely alert and awake.

Still lying down on the bed, I heard a deep-pitched, vibrating frequency inside my head. It was frightening. I fought to try and move my body. It felt like all I could do was arch my back off the bed. My attempts to move the rest of my body continued, but with failure. I could hear the low-pitched rumbling continue to intensify deep within my ears. In a panic, I finally felt myself sit up, but it had felt unusual. It felt like I had burst through a thick, gel-like bubble, or like I had popped out of my own body. I also felt very flimsy and uncoordinated. When I managed to pull my feet to the floor, they felt very heavy and landed on the floor with a stomp. As I stumbled to stand, my body was very shaky like a new-born fawn trying to get on its feet for the first time. My thoughts were rattled. *What is wrong with me? Am I sleepwalking or something? Am I sick?*

The rumbling in my head began to subside. I thought to myself. *Maybe if I go into the kitchen to get a drink of water, this funny feeling will pass.* The house was dark, but I knew I could guide myself to the kitchen by touching the walls. I leaned my right hand against the wall to my right. To my surprise, I fell right through the wall as if it weren't even there at all. I landed on my side and quickly scurried to my knees. As I started rising to my feet again, I felt them fall straight through the floor. It felt as if the floor had just given out from under me.

The low-pitched rumbling in my head returned and grew louder. In complete distress, I started running. My feet ran below the floor. It felt like I was running in mud. None of the walls constrained me—instead, my body ran right through them, one after another after another, until I found myself outside in the front yard. I looked up into the night sky. It was stunning. I saw more stars than ever before exhibiting glittering colors of reds, pinks, purples, greens, blues, and yellows.

A sense of calmness encompassed me. I looked at the large field across the road. A white primitive church rested in the middle of this green grassy field. I was drawn in that direction, and desired to go there. I began walking towards the primitive church, but to my surprise, I was at the church in an instant. It was as if I had teleported! Confused by what had happened, I cautiously retreated into the vast grassy field behind the church. There, a small lake sat upon a high hill. On the opposite side of the lake, there was a bench. Secluded from everything, and peaceful, it was my favorite place to be. In an instant, at the very the thought of it, I was resting on the bench on the opposite side of the lake. The sun had begun to rise.

5. Artist: Audiomachine
Song: Spirit of the Stallion

The breeze blew a slight gust, and I heard the bass-rumbling sound of thunder. I searched the sky for dark clouds but saw only a coral-fire sky accented with wispy lavender clouds.

When my eyes returned to the sunrise scene behind the lake, I saw a man standing on the other side. He was staring right at me, I was instantly perplexed because he was wearing medieval-era attire—a black tunic with black leather trousers, black leather boots to his knees, and a hooded cloak trimmed in gold. The cloak was velvety. It was beige on the outside and lined on the inside with white fur. It was blowing magnificently behind him in the wind.

Who is he? I looked around to see if anyone else was with him. Nobody was around. I quickly began questioning his intentions. *Where did he come from? How did he get here? He is looking right at me. What does he want? Should I say something?*

He looked like a handsome prince out of a fairy tale. He stood with tall posture. His feet were flat on the ground, slightly apart, and his arms were down by his sides. He appeared about seven feet tall and looked to weigh about 350 pounds of pure muscle. He had a defined, muscular physique. He had a very serious, yet gentle look on his face.

His skin was bronzed, smooth, and soft, except for a shadow of stubble on his lower face. His face was well-chiseled and defined. I noticed his profound masculine features including medium-length, dark brown hair; full, defined eye-brows; and a strong, squared jaw. Most noticeably, were his piercing, deep-set, aqua-blue eyes. The color of his eyes appeared enhanced, almost as if slightly illuminated. The limbal ring around the iris in both of his eyes was dark and well-defined, thus created beautiful contrast between the aqua-blue color and the white sclera. He was absolutely perfect in creation.

I became infatuated. My heart sank into my stomach, and my body began to tremble. Goosebumps scattered the surface of my skin. My breathing rate and pulse increased. All kinds of questions and thoughts continued to race through my mind: *He is incredible! He looks like a superhero! Am I dreaming? This can't be real!*

6. Artist: Really Slow Motion (Cesc Vilà)
Song: Suns and Stars

I tried to calm myself, attempting to disguise my reactions, but all I could do was freeze up. Every feature of him was perfectly balanced, perfectly proportional. His chest muscles were large and squared through his tunic. His shoulders were broad. Best of all was his facial structure—flawless, strong, well-chiseled, and masculine. He was an absolute dream.

Suddenly, I became very scared of his intentions. *What is he doing here? What is going on?* Then he spoke to me. Only, he did not use his mouth but rather communicated with his mind. I literally heard his words echoing inside my head as if his voice were coming to me through internal headphones. He had a deep, smooth voice, with an English accent. He carried a low, masculine pitch that resonated within me. His tone was calm but authoritative.

Being: ***Please. Do not fear. Come closer to me.***

As he was transmitting these thoughts to me, I felt a soothing vibration throughout my body, almost a cooling, relaxing sensation. It was the same sensation as when someone gently scratches my back and it gives me a shiver. He kept a straight face, making it hard to read on his intentions. I could not believe I had just heard him echoing, as if he were inside my head. I thought to myself, *who is he?*

In perfect timing he replied.

Being: ***My name is Emalickel.***

Had he heard my thoughts or was that just a coincidence? As a test, I asked him a question in my head without talking, *can you actually hear me?*

He smiled gently.

Emalickel: ***Loud and clear.***

I was stunned.

Me: ***What else can you do?***

Emalickel: ***What are the limits of your imagination?***

Impossible! He had just answered my mind's question with his mind! My questions continued uncontrollably: *What is he? Where did he come from? Should I be afraid of him? Why is he here?* His time, he responded to me with his physical voice, which sounded the same as the one in my head moments before.

Emalickel: I will answer each of these questions which circulate your mind. I am a celestial being. I come from Lapoi, located at the center of this galaxy. You need not fear me. I mean you no harm. In fact, the reason I am here. . .

He paused to lock eyes with me, making sure he had my undivided attention. The anticipation was building-up within me so much I had to force myself to breathe. Emalickel smiled and finally continued.

Emalickel: . . . is to seek you.

A surge of surprise hit the pits of my stomach. *Me? Why me? Is this finally what I was asking for? Had God sent him as an answer to my prayers?* Now I was completely drawn to him. I slowly stood up and began walking carefully towards him. I hesitantly continued along the bank to the other side of the lake where he stood. My thoughts raced.

Me: ***I'm afraid. What's happening right now? I don't know you. Are you even real? What are your intentions?***

I stopped 30-feet away from him and continued with uncontrollable questions. Emalickel closed his eyes and smiled as I continued to ramble on.

7. Artist: Audiomachine
Song: Age of Innocence

Me: ***Am I dying or something? Are you here to abduct me? How can I trust you? What are your motives?***

When my questions finally came to a stop, he looked back up at me. Smiling in amusement, he shook his head and spoke aloud.

Emalickel: I know the extent of your discomfort. I know what you are feeling. I want to bring you comfort, not fear. Please, let me help you understand.

Emalickel folded his arms across his chest. He waved his hand in the air at the lake, taking my attention there. He continued to look at the lake while he responded. Within the waters of the lake, I saw his memories playing like a movie as he reminisced. I could see that he and a group of others like him were visiting with ancient tribes on Earth, helping to build ancient structures and providing spiritual knowledge through teachings around a fire. The ancient people seemed to be worshipping Emalickel and the others, but Emalickel kept shaking his head and pointing to the heavens in reference to God.

Emalickel: The last time I visited Earth was in 303 B.C. For centuries before, my brothers and I had been traveling here helping the Lapoian Guards deliver God's instructions to His creation of mankind. The goal was to expand man's intelligence—to enlighten him so that he may know God and gain remembrance of His spirit within them. The humans were receptive, scribing about our enlightenments and spreading the word across the lands, but they were unclear about things. Some tribes of humans even started referring to us as gods—giving us all kinds of names across the Earth such as Apollo, Poseidon, Thor, Balder, and Tyr. Then we were given other names like Michael, Gabriel, and Raphael. Despite our teachings, these messages continued to be misunderstood, altered, or rejected altogether by mankind. We did

the best we could—the evolution of the information was up to the mortals.

His tone became frustrated.

Emalickel: I could bear not to watch the mortals misconstrue our great God's words and turn away from Him without any regard to His great compassion and love for them. Deeply disturbed by this, I received God's blessing to remove myself from Earth and the ungrateful mortals.

He paused to look towards the ground. He sighed to calm himself.

Emalickel: So, I left. I returned to Lapoi to reflect, pray, and center myself.

He rolled his shoulders back and began to walk around. The lake still played scenes of what he was recalling from his mind's memories.

Emalickel: I have known of your energy since you began. I have been hearing your thoughts for some time now. At first, it happened seldom and was very vague. Then, it happened more often and, in more volume and clarity. After a while, I became intrigued with your thoughts. You are different. I enjoyed listening to your transmissions. I started being able to feel your emotions and even physically see you. These abilities intensified, and I developed a deep desire to meet you. Your energy is very unique. You are strong-willed, yet empathetic to others—the qualities of a true leader.

8. Artist: We are all Astronauts
Song: Ether

My eyes had started wandering his body. He was tall, strong, and masculine. My mind began to wander as I scanned him head to toe. I couldn't find one thing wrong with him, not one single thing. *What did he look like underneath those garments? Did he have the same parts as a mortal man? I mean, why else would he be wearing clothes?*

I could feel him looking at me. When my eyes returned to his, he expressed a surprised and amused look on his face, for he knew I was lusting after his body. Embarrassed and blushing, I looked away to avoid any eye contact. Then, I heard him chuckle under his breath.

Emalickel: So, your eyes have wandered my vessel as your mind has drifted?

I was mortified! Since he could hear my mind, all I could do was be honest with him.

Me: It's just that you're . . . I'm just so captivated by you.

He stood up straight, demonstrating a proud posture. He kept his intense gaze on me and gently smiled. He slowly pushed back the hood of his cloak, removing it from his head.

Emalickel: As am I, by you.

The sound of his voice saying that gave me butterflies. There was a long silence as we locked eyes. When he looked at me I felt warm, yet my body felt as stiff as a statue. He was way too perfect to be real. I couldn't believe he was actually captivated by me. Had he really come to Earth just for me?! My dreams and all my pleas had been heard and were becoming reality.

He held out his hand in motion for me to come towards him. I heard his thoughts within in my head again.

Emalickel: ***Please, come closer to me.***

My legs were weak as I slowly closed the gap of space between us. With each step I took closer to him, my emotions consumed me. Step-by-step I continued breathlessly. When I was just five steps away from him, a sudden breeze blew around me. I stopped, for an overwhelming amorous sensation surrounded me when I absorbed a breath of his invigorating scent. It had a hint of fresh new leather, but mostly it was clean, as a man may smell right after a shower.

I was so captivated by him I was unable to move. I did not want him to know what I was feeling, but apparently there was no hiding it from his mind. A part of me wished I could burry my face into his immaculate chest, and feel his firm, safe arms as they wrapped tightly around me.

When I looked at him, he nodded with a wide grin, as if he had already read my mind again. He emphasized the presence of his extended arm to me by gently bouncing it once in the air.

I exhaled the sum of the built-up air in my lungs. I made myself walk towards him. I walked until I was able to place my hand directly into his. He grabbed my other hand with his free hand.

His hands engulfed mine. They were large and warm. I could also feel the warmth of his body radiating from him. We stood there, facing one another, hand-in-hand for several moments. My forehead was level with his chest. I could see his chest rise and fall as he took strong steady breaths in and out.

I looked up at him, and he gazed back down at me. Then, his smile relaxed, and his gaze became more intense into my eyes. I could tell he wanted to ask me something, but he seemed hesitant. After a brief moment he finally asked aloud.

Emalickel: May I take you someplace very special?

He was irresistible, but I still didn't know him enough to trust him.

Me: I don't know. I barely know you. I don't even remember your name.

He smiled genuinely.

Emalickel: Emalickel

He briefly paused in thought before continuing.

Emalickel: Please, Adrienne, let me earn your trust.

Me: You know my name?!

Emalickel: I know everything about you. I know you as well as you know yourself. I have been able to hear your mind for some time now. You intrigue me. You are unique. That is the reason I have chosen to come here. I came to seek you.

Me: So, let me get this straight. I am having a hard time wrapping my head around this. The only reason you came back to Earth was to meet me?

He guided his hands up to my shoulders and lowered his head so that his eyes could be at the same level as mine. His face held a comforting smile as he looked me directly in the eyes and transmitted very slowly.

Emalickel: ***You are the only reason I am here.***

Then he smiled as he stood up straight again. Looking ahead, he began to glow so bright that all I could see was his face. The glowing grew brighter for a moment, but then subsided revealing Emalickel in new attire. This time he had on a sleeveless gunmetal-black vest with matching gauntlets, poleyns, cuisses, and boots—and this time, a very familiar red velvet cape like that of the man on the ocean.

Emalickel: Come with me. I know what you desire. Let me show you a place that you will never forget.

He lightly grabbed my shoulders to help guide my body to turn around to face the opposite direction away from him. His hands lightly grazed my arms guiding themselves to the outside of my waist. He wrapped his solid arms tightly around my waist, pulling me in closer to his body until we were pressed firmly against one another. It sent a surge of goosebumps all over me. Then, I heard the wind whip his large red cape.

Me: Where are we going? We're not going to fly, are we? I'm terrified of heights.

Emalickel: Of this I already know, but does my hold on your body not calm your fears?

Although his body felt blissful against mine, I wasn't sure if I was ready to fly with him. *How do I know he's not trying to mislead me? How do I know he's good and not evil? How fast did he fly? Where would we fly? Would it even be safe for me to travel with him to wherever we'd go? Would I be able to come back? What would happen then?*

My questions were interrupted by Emalickel who leaned his neck forward and placed his face next to mine. He quietly, yet assertively, whispered into my ear.

Emalickel: You do not trust me.

I was silent. *Yes, he may know all about me, but I just met him. How can I trust him? I need more time. Where are we going, and will he return me?* Doubts continued to soar. Emalickel released his strong embrace placing his arms at his sides. His tone became stern.

Emalickel: Suppress your thoughts. I will not make you do something against your will.

I was a bit disappointed of his release of my body.

Emalickel: Look at me.

Slowly, with my head down, I turned around. With a firm hand, he gently lifted my chin up with his index finger and spoke firmly with his mind, yet he was calm.

Emalickel: *Look at me! Look deep, Adrienne.*

Our eyes locked and we gazed at one another for several moments in total silence—one eye to the other—back and forth he desperately gazed at me. It was as if he wanted me to recognize him. Then, it felt as if he was familiar. I knew him from somewhere. It felt like I had known him for my whole life. It was like I was starting to vaguely remember him, but I wasn't sure from where. All I knew is that he desperately wanted my trust. I could see it in his eyes that he was genuine about it. Without a second thought, I gave into him and gave him my trust.

He placed his hands on my shoulders.

Emalickel: With the exception of God himself, I will protect you better than anything else in existence. With me, nothing will hurt you. And I would never hurt you, nor deceive or mislead you. I represent the opposite of evil. I have nothing to hide from you. I am a being of only the truth. If you ask, I will tell.

9. Artist: Patrick Doyle
Song: Can You See Jane?

He began walking around in front of me, with his hands folded behind him, and proceeded to answer every question I had previously asked. I was impressed at how he thoroughly addressed each and every question in detail and in the exact order they had come to me.

Emalickel: On the mortal plane, I am capable of traveling at Mach 9000, which is 2,000 miles per second. In space, I warp-travel. On my home-planet, I teleport. You will be safe while we travel as I have few limits on my abilities. I plan to create a protective force-field to surround you as we travel. Nothing can harm you inside this force-field—not excessive temperatures, nor speed, nor the lack of oxygen.

Go with me and I will take you to Lapoi, a planet within the celestial plane of existence. You can experience a full year on Lapoi, while only seconds pass on Earth. Nobody will even know you are gone. You may stay on Lapoi for as long as God is willing. You may come back to Earth as soon as you please. Everything will be exactly as you left it. You will be in the exact same condition as before you left.

He returned to his stance in front of me and stopped.

Emalickel: As far as my seeming familiar to you goes... without

awareness, you have been experiencing my non-physical energy for a long time.

He placed his hands on either side of my head, protectively embracing my face.

Emalickel: I know this is a lot to absorb, but I promise, it is indeed the truth. You are free from harm, and your fears are not real unless you give your attention to them. What I say, is what is so.

He intensely stared into my eyes for a moment of silence while continuing to hold my face within his hands. He was waiting for a response from me. After a few more moments, I answered.

Me: Ok. Alright, I'll go.

Emalickel shifted his feet and brought his face closer in front of mine. He opened his eyes wide and looked back and forth into each of mine.

Emalickel: Look at me, in my eyes. Let me feel your trust.

Still holding my face, Emalickel stared intensely into my eyes. I could feel the kindness from his soul's energy radiating into me and knew, at that very moment, without a shadow of a doubt, that I could trust him. I cannot explain it, I just knew.

With that, he placed his hands on either side of my shoulders and turned me around so that my back was once again against the front of his body. His arms wrapped around my waist. He leaned his head towards mine and touched his lips to my ear. His breath tickled my neck as he whispered.

Emalickel: I promise, you are safe with me.

2

DEPARTURE

10. Artist: PostHaste Music (Mark Petrie)
Song: Omega Point

Slowly, I felt my feet lift from the solid surface below. I heard the deep waves of air rush beneath Emalickel's cape as we continued towards the sky. I closed my eyes. Our speed increased, and I could feel the cool wind whispering against me.

I couldn't help it, but my eyes opened in curiosity of what was around me. We appeared to be about 300 feet from the ground, as our bodies flew perpendicular to it. Remembering my deep fear of heights, I became dizzy. I wished I were facing Emalickel so that I could see him and feel the security of holding onto his body.

Then, reading my mind, he maneuvered me around, mid-flight, so that I could see the warmth of his face. I wrapped my arms around his waist and held on tightly. He transmitted his thoughts to me.

Emalickel: ***Do not fear. You are safe. I am right here. I will protect you from any harm.***

Emalickel held my head, face first, onto his chest with one of his hands, while the other wrapped tightly around my lower back. I felt the wind resistance on our bodies continue. It was hitting my body at speeds like that of a tornado. The wind was very loud to my ears. It sounded like I was right next to a rocket engine.

Even through all the noise and chaos, Emalickel could still hear my every thought because I felt him looking down at me as he put up another force-field which muffled the loud sounds. I smiled when I thought about how protective he was with me.

By this time, we were traveling at such high speeds, I could only see swarms of clouds pass my line of view. Our speed continued increasing until we reached supersonic speeds. I heard the loud ripping crash of the sound-barrier being broken. I peeked out of Emalickel's embrace to view my surroundings. We were on the edge of the Earth's atmosphere. I knew this because I saw the pitch black of space above the thin blue line of Earth's atmosphere. We traveled streamlined, headed straight upward. I noticed a very deep bass-like sliding sound as we exited the Earth. This sound started from a low-frequency pitch and slid way down to an extremely low pitch. It vibrated my body.

Just when I started to wonder when we were going to stop, everything became calm and silent. It felt like we had stopped moving, and I could no longer hear nor feel any wind resistance.

Emalickel lightened his hold on me. I opened my eyes and lifted my head from his chest. We had exited the Earth. I could see the glow of Earth's blue atmosphere beneath the pitch black of space within which we floated.

Emalickel gently released his hold on me and took me by my hand. I panicked when I saw I was floating freely, with nothing underneath me. I clenched my arms and legs onto Emalickel's entire arm in fear.

11. Artist: Mark Petrie
Song: Where We Are

Emalickel: Everything is alright. You must learn to trust me. There is no gravity out here. You are not going to fall. You will only float.

I didn't want to let him go. I felt safe being close to him. Even knowing I could float, I didn't want to leave the security of his hold.

It was so quiet here; so peaceful; so beautiful. There were billions of bright white diamonds scattered everywhere. I could see thousands of galaxies in the distance. Colored clouds of stars were shades of blue, pink, and purple.

Emalickel: The force-field enhances your vision. You can see clearer and further than normal. I hope you are enjoying it.

I was completely fascinated. I looked down to see how our bodies floated. I was speechless. I felt completely weightless. Glittering stars were below me and above me. The invisible field of energy Emalickel had created was perfect. The temperature felt comfortable like a home, and I was able to breathe crisp air as we continued floating along in the vacuum of space.

Emalickel: Now we will travel to Lapoi.

Me: Where is . . . what is . . . Lapoi?

Emalickel: My home planet. It is near the center of the galaxy, about 2.3 million light-years away. The only decent way to get there is by warp-travel. Warp-traveling may be frightening, but I assure you, you will be completely safe and free from harm. Remember, you will be able to return to Earth whenever you wish. All you need to do is give me the word, and I will return you safely.

Looking at me, as if waiting for my approval, Emalickel appeared serious and confident. Then, he maneuvered himself to face me and placed his hands on my hips.

Emalickel: Would you go? Do you trust me?

I couldn't believe all this was happening. It was so much to absorb and in such a limited time to absorb it. After a moment, I came to a simple conclusion. I was already floating out in the middle of space, so there really wasn't any reason to go back now. I thought to myself, *why not*? I took a deep breath, smiled and nodded at him.

Me: Why not? Let's go.

Emalickel wrapped his warm arms around me again and held me close to his body.

Emalickel: This is going to be incredibly bright. I will filter out much of this light, but you will need to close your eyes. It may also be louder than you will find comfortable, but it will only last a brief moment.

I closed my eyes and held onto him with great force. He smiled. Again, I felt one of his hands holding my head, face first, into his chest while the other held at the base my back. Although I was terrified of what was about to happen, I truly did trust him.

12. Artist: Mark Petrie
Song: High Stakes

Emalickel: Do not be afraid. I will protect you.

I started to hear what sounded like static, or white noise, fading in. It became increasingly loud and high-pitched. Then, as the volume of this noise continued to increase at a more rapid pace, an intense brightness overwhelmed my eyes. Even though my eyelids were closed, and my face was turned into Emalickel's body, the light became so bright it was as if I were looking into a spotlight with my eyes closed. It made my body feel warm, even through Emalickel's protective field.

The white noise increased to a volume which made me feel very uncomfortable; to the extent I almost felt as if I were going to have an anxiety attack. I felt a wave of heat hit my body as if someone had opened an extremely hot oven door to let the heat escape. The whole trip had only lasted a few seconds. During that time, I heard an intensely loud static noise, I saw an immensely bright light behind my closed eyelids, and I felt an intense wave of heat against my body. It made me wonder what it would have been like without Emalickel's force-field.

Then, the noise, light and heat slowly faded away and everything was silent and calm once again. I could not believe I had actually warp-traveled.

3

ARRIVAL

13. Artist: Epic Score (Gabriel Shadid)
Song: This is Our Land

Emalickel: We are here. Open your eyes.

I was so nervous. *What was I going to see? Where was I? Was this even really happening?* Slowly, I opened my eyes. As I did this, Emalickel chuckled.

Emalickel: This is indeed very real. The scenery before you is one of the many lands of Lapoi. This one is called Terpetrus.

Again, I was startled that he read my mind's questions—even those questions I directed rhetorically at myself. In fact, if it hadn't been for the breath-taking scenery laid out before me, I would have become caught up in worry at the fact that he understands every single thing I think. Emalickel looked at me, slightly grinned, and winked. I heard his voice within my head.

Emalickel: ***I am sorry to have rattled your thoughts.***

I was entranced by the perfection and overwhelming beauty of this place. The sky had many fluffy clouds with various shades of pink, violet, blue, and teal, mimicking an Earth sunrise. White rays of light beamed down through them. Enormous waterfalls fell between several cliffs, forming rivers of crystal-clear, sparkling water. The land was vast, green and supple. There were majestic mountains scattered throughout. There were trees near the mountain ranges and were evergreen in origin. The air smelled like wintergreen with a gentle breeze and felt a comfortable temperature. It was like Earth, but perfect.

While still flying over the land, I looked up at Emalickel. The lighting and contrast of this place was heavenly. It made his eyes stand out.

Emalickel: Is it appealing?

Me: You or the scenery?

There was a pause, almost as if Emalickel was surprised by my witty comment. A slight grin grew across his face.

Emalickel: Either one.

Me: Breath-taking.

Of course, I was mostly thinking about him. Emalickel heard this thought because he locked eyes with me for a moment, as if he was trying to read my mind deeply. After a moment of that, his smile grew wider and he chuckled under his breath. Then he looked out into the distance and steered the subject back to the land.

Emalickel: This is only one of the lands on Lapoi. There are a total of thirteen, each unique in its own form. Lapoi is about the same size of a Supergiant star in this galaxy referred to as Antares.

As he said this, I could see a heard of giraffes running down below and an enormous flock of white gulls flying together above them.

Emalickel: About 663 trillion Earths could fit into Lapoi. There is enough room here for every being that has ever existed on the

Earth in the past, present, and future. If they all resided here at once, they would still only take up about 5% of the land.

I saw a large pride of lions relaxing in the flatlands below. They were gazing up at us. I saw one of them yawn.

Me: Who lives here?

Emalickel: Lapoi, also known as Third Sphere C, hosts me, my five brothers, three billion celestials, and the souls of all mortal animals who ever existed.

The land glowed with the hue of beauty—not too light, and not too dark. This place was flawless, perfection at its best. As we continued flying, I kept seeing a variety of animals. They were all peaceful with each other—lions with gazelles, tigers with deer.

Emalickel: On Lapoi, anything that was once mortal is no longer mortal. Everyone and everything here is immortal. That means the laws of your world no longer apply here. Everything is content. All needs are satisfied.

As we descended closer to meet the ground, I noticed a few mansion-like structures made from beautiful stone. I could tell some of these structures were glowing in golden light, while others appeared dull and lifeless.

14. Artist: Howard Shore
Song: The Bridge to Khazad Dum (Ext to 3:23)

Me: Who lives there?

Emalickel: Nobody anymore. There were once hundreds of thousands more celestials who inhabited Lapoi. Those abandoned structures used to be the homes of some of our Lapoian Guards.

Me: Guards?

Emalickel: Humans refer to them as Guardian Angels. Guards tend directly to the matters of mortals.

Me: Why don't they live there anymore?

There was a pause. Emalickel looked through me as he appeared to be concentrating on a voice which I could not hear. He focused back into my eyes but hesitated before he answered.

Emalickel: We lost a large sum of them when the Lapoian Guards were delivering important messages to the mortals of Earth. This was during a time of great intellectual advancement for mortals. Guards were to regularly manifest on the Earth in their celestial forms to educate humans through a series of direct contacts. During their visits, many of our guards began experiencing feelings of attraction and lust for the female humans. Although physical sexual contact on the mortal plane is strictly forbidden for any celestial of all the spheres, many of our guards were unable to resist. The feelings and emotions of lust and love were unlike any ever experienced by celestials before. Lacking self-discipline and control, many of them gave into their emotions. They fell in love. Distracted from their purpose, they physically united with the females of Earth, mixing celestial DNA with the mortals' and choosing to stay on the mortal plane with them.

This blending of species created hybrid offspring. Mortals have referred to them by many names: titans, demi-gods, giants, and nephilim. They predominantly became powerful over mortals. Most of them became destructive towards mankind. They could not be defeated with brute force. Hybrids began producing more hybrids. There were hybrids of hybrids. Over time the Earth became entirely infested with all kinds of interbred hybrid beings. God intervened. He instructed the Warrior Celestials of Lapoi to create a Great Flood on the Earth. Almost all would perish, but it would cleanse the Earth of any abominations.

Even the fallen Lapoian Guards, who were residing on the Earth

with their beloved females, perished. Afterwards, God sent the souls of the Guards and nephilim into isolation with chains. This is where they are still imprisoned today, thus why their homes have been abandoned. The mortal females were able to walk the new Earth again, but without any memory of their past lives.

Me: I'm sorry that happened.

Emalickel: No need to feel sorry. God had it planned that way from the beginning for a lesson in obedience to both celestial and mortal.

15. Artist: Hans Zimmer
Song: Chevaliers De Sangreal

Emalickel took in a deep breath and exhaled. He snapped his fingers and a hologram image of space appeared in front of us. It interacted with Emalickel as he explained the process of existence.

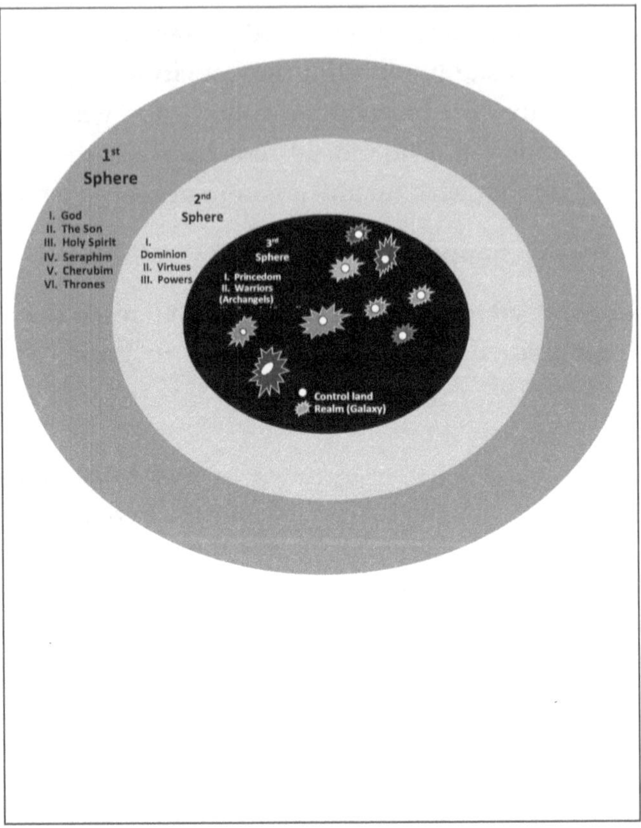

Emalickel: There are Three Spheres to existence. Everyone within each of these spheres is responsible for one another.

The innermost sphere is called the Third Sphere. This is where mortal and celestial reside. Within this sphere there are billions of realms, or galaxies, as humans call them. Each realm is comprised of many stars and planets. Most of these realms are uninhabited, but nine of them host life. At the center of each of these nine realms is a control land. The control land exists on the celestial plane and hosts the celestials who oversee that realm. On each control land there live three types of celestials—Princedoms, Warriors, and Guards. The Princedoms are the authority of the realms. They collectively protect and preserve the Third Sphere while overseeing the duties of the warriors and guards of their realms. Warriors answer to the Princedoms and preserve and protect their realms, while guards directly tend to the mortal plane of their realms.

Lapoi is the control land of the realm of Millattus, or *The Milky Way,* as you know it to be. The Guards of Lapoi tend to the mortals of Earth, and the two other mortal planets within Millattus, called Fynne and Grahst. The Warriors of Lapoi protect and preserve all Millattus but are also able to control events on each planet within Millattus' mortal plane. The Princedoms of Lapoi oversee the realm of Millattus and its celestial guards and warriors. They are the acting authorities of all Millattus. They also are responsible for protecting and preserving the Third Sphere collectively with the Princedoms of the other eight realms. There are two Princedom celestials of Lapoi. They are referred to as the Princes. There are also two Warrior Princedoms who oversee the warriors, and two Guard Princedoms who are over the guards.

Although mortal souls come from various origins, many of the mortal males actually derived from Lapoi. They once walked among us as fellow celestials. When God spoke more into creation, the orders came for each celestial to forget who they were and engage in the mortal experience. The goal was to introduce contrast into the light of creation. The concepts of color, feelings, emotions, appreciation, love, and understanding were a result of experiencing the contrary. The mortal experience was to help creation evolve and expand into more.

One-by-one celestials volunteered to take their turns experiencing mortality. A celestial will return to Lapoi upon reaching an objective level of spiritual evolution. In order to awaken from mortality, one must remember their spiritual origin and obtain an expanded perspective of the true self, the spirit within them. Until then, their soul will cycle into new lifetimes, with new mortal bodies, and having new experiences. Once enough experience has been

gained, a soul will eventually awaken and return to their original origins. Lapoians, who are awakening from mortality, will resume their duty as either a guard or warrior. The experience of mortality and awakening not only contributes to creation, but substantially increases the abilities and perceptions of the individual.

You, Adrienne, are a mortal female. Mortal females are not originally from Lapoi, but rather a different celestial realm. Your unique energy has started to stand out from all the rest, and that is why I became so drawn to you.

He looked up from the hologram at me. I was intrigued and completely submerged in what he was talking about. I kept looking down at the hologram.

16. Artist: Really Slow Motion
Song: You Will Be This Legend

Me: What about the other realms? Are they just like ours?

Emalickel: Most all the realms are equal in power and status, but they all have their own agendas and purposes involving creation. In other words, not all the realms have the same story and goals as Lapoi. This is how God intended it, and we do not question. However, there are three realms, of the nine, who are ridden in their egos. They have become tyrannical and repressive. This has become a major concern among the rest of the Princedoms, as they must ensure the safety of the celestials and mortals within their realms. This is not of your concern, so I will move on from here.

Emalickel touched the hologram on the middle sphere.

Emalickel: Engulfing the Third Sphere is the Second Sphere. The Second Sphere hosts the Dominion, Virtue, and Power celestials. They oversee the Third Sphere. Much of what they do is unknown; however, it is known that the Dominion celestials receive orders

from the Power and Virtue celestials. When these orders involve the Third Sphere, the Princedoms receive them from the Dominions, and then carry out the orders accordingly.

He continued speaking as he touched the outer sphere on the hologram image. It interacted with him.

Emalickel: The outer sphere is called the First Sphere. This is where the source of God exists. Alongside Him are the Seraphim, Cherubim, and Throne celestials. Even less is known about the duties of the celestials within the First Sphere. All we know is they oversee the Second and Third Spheres, and Thrones are the celestials who pass orders along to the Second Sphere per the direct orders of God. God oversees everything. He is the Ultimate, Supreme, Alpha-Being. He created celestials to work together in the process of helping carry out His will of existence across the Universe. He created creation for the experiences. That is what we are all doing in Him as conscious extensions of Him.

As he was talking, I felt myself falling deeply for Emalickel. He was so strong, intelligent, and confident. I was drawn closer to him by the minute. I wondered if he had ever been in love before. *Could he feel love for me? How could he be allowed to fall in love with a mortal? Could he feel physical attraction towards me as I do him? If so, how would he express it?* My mind continued to wander, but he broke my thoughts in clearing his throat and speaking aloud over my thoughts.

Emalickel: Shall we go see the other lands?

I looked over at him. I was confused why he didn't attempt to answer my questions like he had so many times before. Was he avoiding the subject because he was uncertain, or did he just not feel love for me and felt awkward on the topic?

Emalickel looked away from me and focused his sights aside from me. It was apparent he was trying to avoid eye-contact. I didn't understand. Was I not supposed to ask him these types of questions? I wished he would be straight-forward with me again.

Emalickel: The next closest land is 415 miles out. We can teleport there.

I stared at the side of Emalickel's face. I could tell he was avoiding me.

17. Artist: Tunes of Fantasy (Florian Bur)
Song: White Angel

Me: No, Emalickel. Let's stay here for a moment.

He quickly turned towards me, as if startled at my reply. He stared at me for a moment before closing his eyes to take a deep breath followed by a gulp. He did not respond but lowered his head and nodded in agreement.

I continued.

Me: I'm starting to feel really attached to you. I'm confused because I don't know if I'm supposed to have feelings for you, or if I'm allowed to, or if you are allowed to, or if you even feel the same way about me. But I'm desperate to know.

Emalickel sighed before answering.

Emalickel: You may always ask me anything. The reason I avoid your questions this time is because there is so much more you must first learn. I see it best not to answer your questions until you have a better understanding of everything else.

Me: But I just need to know if it's even possible for you to feel anything for me. I won't be able to focus on anything else until I have answers. If you don't feel the same for me, I need to know so I can try to stop feeling so drawn to you. Please tell me, Emalickel . . . please. I need to know. I just must know now!

I was desperate. A tear fell from my right eye. Emalickel tilted his head to the side in disbelief. Looking somber, he watched the tear as it dropped down my cheek, until it fell from my face. His eyes moved back up to look at mine. He then tilted his head to the other side and said hesitantly.

Emalickel: Love between a celestial and a mortal is obtainable, but it is quite a complicated matter. Only while the mortal is in her spirit-form, on either the astral or celestial plane, can the two physically interact. And, yes, in the celestial plane we do physically express love in the same ways as mortals. It cannot happen on the mortal plane without severe punishment. So, to answer your questions—yes, it is possible for a celestial to feel desire for a mortal, and yes, we are allowed to have those feelings. However, we may not physically interact with mortals on their plane, unless God instructs us as He once did thousands of years ago. You and I have only physically interacted in the astral plane, when you were approaching a semi-sleep state, and in the celestial plane where we are now. So, we have abided by the regulations of interaction between mortal and celestial.

I needed more clarification.

Me: So, as long as you and I are here, on the celestial plane, we can do as we please?

A slight grin began growing on Emalickel's face. He quickly scanned my body before letting his eyes toggle between mine. Then, he glanced down at my lips and gulped. His expression grew serious. He mumbled to himself.

Emalickel: Yes... I suppose we can.

Then he returned his eyes back up to mine. He toggled his sights from my eyes to my lips. His lips slightly parted as he gave them a quick lick with his tongue. I noticed he slowly began to lean in toward me. I leaned towards him. He continued to lean closer and closer.

My heart pounded.

He let his lips gently brush against mine; slowly, softly pressing them until every part of his lips touched to every part of mine. Then, he pressed more forcefully, each moment, more passionately than the time before. His lips were full and soft.

We became absorbed in our kiss. We both began breathing more heavily as our lips continued to dance. I could feel the breeze of warm air on my upper lip each time he breathed out from his nose.

My hands grazed his back. He moved his hand to hold the back of my head as he moved in so that his tongue met mine. He slowly maneuvered his head around making sure he got a taste of my mouth. His breath was cool and tasted like wintergreen.

Emalickel exhaled passionately. Both of his hands moved up to hold my head. Then they slid back down along my neck. The kiss continued to grow. He grabbed my arms and pulled my body into his to squeeze me firmly.

Suddenly, Emalickel pulled himself away from me and rested his forehead against mine while we both caught our breath. Then, he began shaking his head and turned away from me.

Emalickel: No.

Emalickel walked away. He sat down on the ground with his knees bent and his arms resting on his knees. He looked out at the landscape, pressing his lips together. He seemed anxious, as if a million thoughts were circulating through his mind.

4

THE BROTHERS

18. Artist: Thomas Bergerson
Song: Immortal

Suddenly, I heard what sounded like a rocket in the sky. I heard a loud crash of the sound-barrier breaking followed by a rolling thunderous pitch. I looked up to see where the sound was coming from. I saw a glowing figure quickly descending from the sky.

Emalickel, still sitting on the ground, looked up and scanned the sky with his eyes. I heard him mumble to himself.

Emalickel: Thorenel.

Me: What?

This time he spoke a bit louder.

Emalickel: It is my brother, Thorenel. My brothers and I are strongly connected. Thorenel is coming to see you.

Me: You have brothers?

Emalickel: Yes. All the celestials of Lapoi are brothers as we share

the same father, however, God created some of us from massive clusters of energy. From each cluster, a group of celestials were made who share the same molecular composition. My five brothers and I are physically related in this way. Our composition is made from molecules of the same source. Figuratively speaking, we have matching DNA.

Emalickel shook his head, stood up, and walked over to me. Placing his hands on my shoulders, he slightly smiled, but it was more of a forced smile.

Emalickel: They are all going to be hopelessly drawn to you.

At that, Thorenel landed. He landed with such force and speed, it made the ground tremble. He landed about 50-feet away in a kneeling position. His long blonde hair blew with the wind of his impact. Maintaining his kneeling position, he looked directly up at me and displayed a wide grin before winking at me.

The massive gust of wind, which followed his landing, continued to blow his hair and the surrounding land. When he stood up, he did so boldly, with his feet apart and his arms crossed at his chest. Like Emalickel, he stood at about seven feet tall and appeared to weigh about 350 pounds. He was wearing the same attire as Emalickel and exhibited the same bronzed, well-defined muscular body.

He and Emalickel had a lot of physical similarities except Thorenel had wavy blonde hair which flowed down to just past his shoulders. Thorenel's face was slightly scruffy, and pieces of his hair fell in front of his eyes; but I could see that his eyes were glowing a piercing glacier-blue color.

Thorenel walked over to us. Everything turned into slow-motion as he walked. His strides were very masculine, and his arms guided his every stride. He never took his eyes from me the entire time he walked towards Emalickel. He and Emalickel grabbed each other's opposite forearms like a still hand-shake.

Appearing annoyed, Emalickel interrupted Thorenel's impressive display. Emalickel sounded apathetic and disinterested.

Emalickel: Acknowledgements, Thorenel.

Thorenel responded to Emalickel in an obnoxiously happy tone. He, too, exhibited an English accent.

Thorenel: Brother! How goes things? Well with you, I hope?

Emalickel: We're on the way to Dillectus.

Thorenel: But I have just arrived. Must you leave Terpetrus so soon?

Thorenel was looking at me. I noticed he quickly scanned my body from head to toe. He brought his eyes to mine in an attempt to disguise that he had just "checked me out."

Thorenel: My brother, where are your manners? You have not introduced to me our ravishing guest.

Emalickel: Her name is Adrienne of Earth.

He leaned towards Thorenel. I could hear Emalickel's thoughts.

Emalickel: ***And I will remind you she is MY guest, Thorenel.***

Thorenel ignored Emalickel's threatening tone.

Thorenel: Adrienne of Earth, I am Thorenel! Welcome to Lapoi! I am certain I speak on behalf of all that we are superbly honored to have your presence among us.

He held out his hand to me. I placed my hand in his expecting a hand-shake. Instead he brought my hand to his lips.

Emalickel quickly walked over to stand directly beside me. His eyes glared at Thorenel, who continued his gaze on me. Emalickel sounded forceful as he spoke this time.

Emalickel: We really must be on our way if we want to see the lands before the light of Auruclerum fades.

The vibe between Emalickel and Thorenel seemed tense. I could see Emalickel clenching his jaw as he stared at Thorenel antagonistically. I found his protective nature stimulating. It seemed that Emalickel cared about me and wanted me for himself.

Still looking at me, Thorenel smiled. He leaned towards me and transmitted his thoughts.

Thorenel: ***We have now connected, Adrienne of Earth. I'll hear if you call to me.***

19. Artist: PostHaste Music (Mark Petrie)
Song: Convergence

He smirked and winked at me. Then, he looked directly up at the sky, slightly bent his knees, and sprang straight up and out of sight. He jumped up with such great speed he was out of sight in less than one second. Again, there was a rush of air, and Thorenel was gone.

Looking out at the land as if reflecting, Emalickel took in a deep breath and exhaled it back out. Then he turned his head to me and smiled a gentle smile.

Emalickel: Shall we continue our journey?

He offered his hand to me. Then, he wrapped his arms around me for another trip, this time via teleportation. For a moment, everything faded into black. I wasn't afraid because I could still feel Emalickel's strong embrace. It was completely dark, and I couldn't see a thing. I felt a slight breeze blowing on my body. Then, after about three seconds, I could see again. We were flying above a a completely different landscape.

Emalickel: This is Dillectus, my personal favorite of all the lands.

I looked down to take in all the beautiful features of this vast open land. The sky was colored with coral, orange, pink, and yellow and contained many bleach-white clouds that were thick and fluffy. There were a few rocky boulders randomly scattered across the landscape of vast fields with various-colored flowers. I saw landscapes including golden wheat fields, fall-colored woodlands, snow-capped mountain ranges, waterfalls, rock cliffs, sand and ocean. Several stone cottages were dispersed around the landscape.

We flew along the shoreline of an ocean with a white sandy beach. The sand looked like snow, but it was sand. To our right I noticed a green grassy valley with enormous snow-capped mountains in the distance. There were autumn woodlands to the west of the valley and to the east was a hillside which led to a golden valley of wheat. In the grassy valley stood an enormous structure, like that of a majestic castle. There were white light rays which beamed down onto this structure from the sky like a glittering spotlight. I saw large, white gulls which flew around the structure.

I pointed in that direction.

Me: Wow! What is that?!

20. Artist: Audiomachine
Song: The New Earth

He ignored me. Instead he lowered our flight until we landed in the middle of the golden wheat field. I heard something moving at extreme speeds in the air. *It's another celestial,* I thought to myself.

Emalickel looked up to scan the sky. Then he rolled his eyes and muttered to himself in sarcasm.

Emalickel: Oh, this is just great. It is Xabiel. That is just splendid.

Emalickel began pacing around in frustration and looking up at sky in anticipation.

Me: Is that another one of your brothers?

Emalickel: It is my brother Xabiel. I have a feeling the other three are not going to be far behind.

The ground shook as Xabiel landed, but he was nowhere to be found. Suddenly, I felt his breath grazing the sides of my neck as he whispered within my mind and moved around me without being seen.

Xabiel: ***Look at you. I am stunned by your presence. Let me provide you as a no mortal man can. I will ensure you feel pleasures beyond that of what you have ever known. We will go places undiscovered, doing things that have never been done.***

I felt his hands touch my shoulders and pull me closer to his body. His hand grazed across my mid-section. It made me shiver. Until now, Emalickel had been looking around for Xabiel. I must have given away his location by my reaction of Xabiel's touch on my body. My body relaxed as if it were melting.

Emalickel: Xabiel!

Emalickel was angry as he suddenly appeared in front of me. He grabbed Xabiel around the neck, making him materialize, and threw him. Emalickel's voice echoed an angry rumble.

Emalickel: LEAVE HER!

Xabiel landed several yards away and completely materialized. He came to his feet, dusted himself off, and slowly stood up straight with his arms by his sides. He had medium-length, dark brown hair like Emalickel. He stood about six feet and eight inches tall and appeared to weigh about 320 pounds. Like his brothers, his muscles were very well-defined. He exhibited masculine facial features but appeared a bit younger than Emalickel and Thorenel. His chest was bare. We wore black leather trousers and black leather combat boots to his knees. His bronzed skin was a slightly darker shade than the others, and the irises of his eyes glowed bright white-grey. He, too, was very attractive.

He gazed at Emalickel.

Xabiel: Please, control yourself, Emalickel.

Emalickel: You shall not give instruction to me, Xabiel! You have no authority equal to, nor over me. Your disrespect has been noted.

Xabiel: I meant no disrespect, my brother, but aren't you acting a bit over-protective? Why do you shield her from opportunity?

Emalickel: My reaction is with purpose. Do not question my intentions, for I owe you no explanation of my actions.

Xabiel: You cannot shield her from us, Emalickel. Does she not have a right to make her own decisions?

Emalickel: You challenge me again, brother!?! I find your communications highly offensive, Xabiel. As I said before, I do not owe anyone explanation of my decisions, yet you continue to challenge me. Shame on you for stepping out of line. One more breath of disrespect from you, and you will find yourself in seclusion.

21. Artist: Mark Petrie
Song: Majestic

Just then, I heard another celestial approaching. He appeared far in the distance and approached on a large black horse with a long full tail. It kicked up debris as it galloped toward us. This celestial communicated before he arrived. His voice was deep and strong like Emalickel's voice. Although he was far away, I could hear his voice within my mind. It resonated throughout my body and echoed when he spoke.

Romenciel: *Emalickel.*

I could see him coming over the horizon. He was glowing as if light were being emanated from him. It illuminated him within a sphere of light measuring about ten feet in diameter. Time seemed to slow, and I was able to catch a good glimpse before he arrived. He was carrying a long steel sword with a black leather-wrapped handle. It looked like an Ulfberht Viking sword. Symbols or runes were etched into the blade. The celestial was dressed in gunmetal-black armor from the neck down. A red cape was blowing behind his back. He approached closer to us. Emalickel still appeared irritated, but not as much as he had with Thorenel and Xabiel.

The celestial stopped his horse about ten feet away from us. He dismounted and immediately kneeled behind his sword. He seemed very respectful and wise. He carried the aura of a warrior.

He looked directly at me. His facial features resembled that of the others, but he was much more physically developed with a much larger, more defined physique. He appeared to be older than Emalickel, but only by a few years—maybe in his late 30s or early 40s. His eyes were glowing the same white-grey color as Xabiel's eyes, and he had the same chiseled jaw line, scruffy face, and bronzed skin as all his brothers. His hair was dark-brown, wavy, and extended about six inches past his shoulders. The hair around his face was pulled back and tied into several leather ties at the back of his head; similar to that of a Viking hairstyle. He was the largest I had seen. He appeared to stand at seven feet and five inches tall and weighed about 400 pounds. His skin appeared glossy, as if he'd been sweating.

Emalickel: Romenciel, demonstrating the entrance of a true warrior and gentleman.

Romenciel replied respectfully.

Romenciel: Emalickel, my brother, why did I not get invited to this meeting of Lapoi's special guest?

His eyes rested upon me.

Romenciel: And may I add, with all due respect, she is radiant to say the least?

Emalickel: There is no gathering, Romenciel. This is not the time.

Romenciel: Everyone knows of her presence. In fact, the other

reason I came to meet you was to warn you about the warriors. I'm sure they will be on their way.

Emalickel: What do you mean?

Romenciel: Seronimel and Dennoliel know about her. They have informed the rest of the warriors and guards of her presence, and I suspect they will all come to see her any moment now.

22. Artist: Audiomachine
Song: Godspeed

I looked at Emalickel. His eyes widened. He appeared flustered and alarmed. He quickly walked up to Romenciel.

Emalickel: What did you say!?! Please tell me they do not plan to bring all the celestials of Lapoi here. Not all at the same time! It is too dangerous! You know that cannot happen!

Just then, I heard in the distance a low rumbling, like a large herd of elephants. It was terrifying. Everything seemed to drastically slow down. Emalickel, Xabiel, and Romenciel were all looking up at the sky in disbelief. Concerned by their reaction, I looked up too. Spread all throughout in the sky were thousands of glowing lights headed towards us. I heard Romenciel mumble to himself.

Romenciel: I cannot believe it.

Emalickel: This cannot happen. They cannot all come here at once, Romenciel, she is just a mortal! We must find a way to hold them back!

Romenciel shook his head in discouragement.

Romenciel: It is too late, Emalickel.

The lights of the celestials filled the sky. There were millions of light orbs coming down like meteors. The wind picked up drastically as it does before a storm. The grass flattened and waved like waves in the ocean. Emalickel's voice echoed as he yelled.

Emalickel: Adrienne! Get down! Now!

He dove towards me on top of my body and grabbed me in his arms. I felt his force-field go up around me.

The celestials began crashing to their landings. The ground shook violently as would an Earthquake measuring over 10.5 on the Richter scale. The rumbles were incredibly loud as they landed. I felt my insides shaking. The only thing keeping me somewhat calm was Emalickel clutching me tightly against his body. I knew he would protect me and keep me safe.

It continued. The violence of the tremors was insane. Debris from their impacts fogged the air. The wind howled as each of them landed one after another. The rumbling from their landings on the ground sounded like repeated crashes of thunder.

There were so many of them. They all landed to a standing position with their spears and shields in one hand and their helmets in the other. Some of them wore armor similar to Xabiel's. They wore leather briefs and long red velvet capes strapped across their chests with black, leather straps, and knee-high combat boots. Others wore golden armor with white capes trimmed in gold. These celestials with the golden armor did not have helmets. They were all beautifully handsome like the brothers. Every one of them had strong, very well-defined ripped muscle tone and deeply bronzed glowing skin.

The wind subsided, and the rumbling ceased. Emalickel stood up and aided me to my feet. He scanned my body with concern.

Emalickel: Are you well?

I was shaking but nodded. Emalickel turned towards the crowd of celestials. His voice was loud and authoritive.

Emalickel: Seronimel and Dennoliel! Come before me at once!

Two of the celestials stepped forward from the crowd. They were wearing golden armor with white capes trimmed in gold, which hung from their shoulders. They also wore beige, hooded cloaks. There was a hint of arrogance behind their facial expressions. They both resembled Thorenel in appearance but looked younger. They both had long, wavy, blonde hair past their shoulders. Seronimel's hair was tied back like Romenciel. Dennoliel's hair was down, and some strands blew across his face.

Emalickel: Whose idea was it to bring the entire fucking realm!?!

They were both silent with their hands folded down in front of them. They shifted their weight from side-to-side, looking down at the dirt as they shuffled their feet. There was an awkward silence among the entire group of warriors as everyone looked at Emalickel with stunned looks on their faces.

23. Artist: Audiomachine
Song: Hell's Battalion

Emalickel: Speak brothers! I am addressing you!

After clearing his throat, Dennoliel responded with a calm demeanor.

Dennoliel: We meant not to intrude, Emalickel.

I could hear Emalickel's breathing pace increase, and he was breathing more loudly. His brows were lowered, and he was clenching his jaw again. He spoke aloud. His deep voice resonated far, and his words echoed off the mountains in the distance. He ground his teeth as he spoke to all of them. He appeared to be intensely angered. The wind on the land began to pick back up as he spoke.

Emalickel: Your actions are juvenile, inexperienced, and unsophisticated. You show disrespect by defying rules. You show immaturity in your thoughtlessness. You embarrass me with your naive

actions. I am beyond infuriated with you both! As blood of my blood, you should know better. What a disappointment, an absolute disgrace, you have exhibited yourselves to be this day. This behavior will not be tolerated in the future. You have been warned. I command you to respectfully dismiss yourselves from my presence at once . . . Immediately! All of you!

He waited a moment. All was silent. Stunned, all the celestials remained standing there in shock.

Emalickel: I SAID BE DISMISSED!

As Emalickel said this, he extended his arms with his palms facing outward, creating a shock-wave which forcefully blew them all out of sight in a burst. Then there was total silence, except for Emalickel's deep breathing as he looked toward the now empty ground in disappointment. He clenched his fists while he caught his breath. The dust of the land began to settle.

24. Artist: Patrick Doyle
Song: Ride to Observatory

He came over to me. His body was glowing in the afterglow which was beginning to set behind the mountains. His tone was contrite as he spoke.

Emalickel: Adrienne.

He cleared his throat.

Emalickel: I am sorry for your having to see my anger. I am astonished my younger brothers have acted in such ignorant ways. They should know better and have always shown higher intelligence than that. Your presence is vibrant and strong. It must have distracted my younger brothers from remembering their manners.

He placed his arm behind my back and we began walking with one another. I had so many questions about this place and who everyone was. Emalickel appeared distracted by thought. He was removed. I don't even think he knew where we were going. At that point, we were just walking together. I looked up at him with concern.

Emalickel breathed deeply and gulped. A few silent moments went by before he stopped in his tracks. He placed his arm in front of my waist to prevent me from walking any further. He positioned himself in front of me, looked me directly in the eyes and held my face in his hands. We engaged eye contact. He sighed, shook his head, and whispered to me.

Emalickel: There is so much I want to tell you.

I could tell he wanted to say more.

Emalickel: I do not know where to begin. It will overwhelm you. I am trying to make the best decisions concerning your well-being.

Emalickel gulped.

Emalickel: Forgive me if it seemed selfish of me to shield the others from you. Understand, it was with good intention. I am only trying to protect you.

He offered his arm to me. I took it.

Emalickel: Come. There is so much to be explored.

5

THE TOUR

Hours seemed to pass as we explored more of the lands of Lapoi. Emalickel took me through a land of illumination, where everything was underground and seemed to glow in neon colors, and to a jungle-land where everything was giant and fascinating. I learned about the truth of the celestials' aid in the construction of the Egyptian pyramids and other ancient structures in Earth's past. Emalickel had shown me using holograms or visions in water.

I continued to hold Emalickel's guiding arm, as I looked up at the flawlessness of his glowing face. I couldn't help but wonder why he had stopped our kiss so suddenly. I wondered why I was so drawn to him. I still had so many questions running through my head. It made me wonder why he truly had brought me to Lapoi.

At that moment, the scenery around us began to fade into a different landscape. We were in a place which looked similar to ancient Greece. In front of us there was a glorious structure lit up by golden light which beamed from the sky. This structure was enormous. It was rectangular in shape and had a gable rooftop. The front of the structure, at the top, had a large mural of several golden-winged beings with swords and shields carved in the gable's cement. The roof was outlined in carved squares of gold and red. Many huge Corinthian columns lined the outside of the structure on all four sides.

Me: What is this?

Emalickel: This land is Karnequlus. This structure is the Warrior Temple where the Warriors of Lapoi train.

We started walking towards the entrance of the giant structure. Many steps led up to the entry-way from all sides.

We arrived at the entry-way. Corinthian columns were distributed all throughout the entire structure. The floor was reflective like a mirror, and the walls were made of golden cement. White chiffon was draped along the ceiling, and red velvet tapestries hung between several of the columns. We walked down a long red velvet rug towards the opposite end of the structure. As we did, our footsteps echoed. Distributed throughout were several trophy boxes filled with different artifacts including armor, weapons, and large balls of different colors of bright light. The light of Lapoi's sun, referred to as Aurucleum, shone between the columns inside. It was beautiful. Down on the opposite end of the structure, I sighted Thorenel standing with his hands folded down in front of him. He was looking at us as if he was expecting our arrival.

When we reached Thorenel, I saw behind him a large valley of sand outside measuring about 20 square acres. There were many warriors practicing combat. Every one of these celestials appeared strong and confident, as they sparred among one another.

Their bodies made the ground rumble upon making contact. Their weapons sounded unbreakable, as they clanked against one another like heavy solid metal. Some of the warriors were manipulating energy while others were conjuring raw materials out of thin air. The rest were simply sparring one-on-one without weaponry.

Impressed with the scenery before me, I headed down the steps and out into the open land.

Across the way, I noticed a warrior looking straight at me. He was walking towards me. As he walked, time slowed down, allowing me to absorb the sight of his rippling muscles gleaming in the light of Auruclerum. His smooth bronzed chest bounced with each step he took. He locked his gaze on me, grinned, and continued to walk on past me. I couldn't take my eyes off him. I turned to watch the back view of him as he continued walking away. His gluteus muscles were well-rounded and moved like that of a stallion.

After about 20 feet, he stopped and turned around towards me again. Time still appeared to be happening in slow-motion for me to be able to absorb his impressive display. Looking to the side, he conjured a bow and arrow. After sliding the quiver onto his shoulder, he reached behind his head into the bag of arrows. With a tight grip of the bow and arrow, he pointed it towards the ground a few feet in front of him. He released it. Upon contacting the ground, it caused a blazing trail of fire to burn. The fire-trail progressed towards me. When the trail was only a foot away from hitting me, the warrior smiled at me and drew a heart-shape in the air with his index fingers. As he did this the fire-trail split into two fires and traveled in opposite directions to surround me in a heart-shape. I looked around in amazement. The warrior, whom I refer to as the Archer, smirked and he proudly gave a nod at me with his chin before turning to walk away.

Emalickel: Adrienne, did you hear me? . . . Adrienne!?!

Emalickel's vocalized thoughts interrupted my indulgence. I quickly focused my eyes to look at him. He was standing at the top of the stairs. He had been discussing serious matters with Thorenel and seemed for that split-moment, oblivious as to what had just happened to me.

I tried not to think about it and I attempted to act as if nothing had just happened. Then I knew Emalickel was already up to speed in the matter. Let's face it, he could read my mind. He narrowed his eyes at me and tilted his head as if trying to receive more information from my mind. Then he immediately turned his head to look at the Archer who obliviously continued his stride away from me. Emalickel tried to appear indifferent, but I could tell he was slightly jealous of the Archer because of the intimidating look he shot at him. The Archer suddenly jerked around to look at Emalickel, as if startled. He must have felt Emalickel's gaze on him. Emalickel crossed his arms at his chest. The Archer then looked down at his feet and continued walking away at a faster pace. Emalickel stared at the Archer for another moment before looking back at me. He repeated himself, but this time he sounded annoyed.

Emalickel: What I said was, I am stepping inside for a moment to talk with Thorenel of a private matter. You seem to be content at the moment, so I will be back out soon.

I nervously chuckled before he stepped inside the temple with Thorenel.

25. Artist: Thomas Bergerson
Song: Colors of Love

I noticed another warrior in the distance using telekinesis to control three swords. The swords were lying on the ground. The warrior made each sword hit a specific target by looking at a sword, and then at its target. Each sword would go exactly where the celestial looked.

Many warriors were practicing invisibility, self-replication, and teleportation methods. I enjoyed watching their different techniques for several minutes. Everything they did was like magic to me. Noticing I was watching, they all showed-off trying to steal the show and capture my attention. It was as if we were birds in the wild and they were all trying to ruffle their feathers and dance for me.

I walked back to the steps, so I could sit down to enjoy the show. The light of Auruclerum warmed my skin as I browsed the open, gently-rolling landscape full of warriors. Completely astonished at everything before my eyes, all I could do was smile and pan the scenery, over and over again.

Time continued to pass until I noticed Thorenel and Emalickel step back outside the temple, this time with Romenciel. The three of them seemed to be discussing something of a rather serious matter. They continued to converse for a few moments before Emalickel noticed me looking their way. He leaned in to whisper something to Thorenel, patted him on the back, and started down the stairs towards me. The warriors continued to spar across the land in front of me, but I had my head turned around to watch Emalickel as he progressed down the stairs. He reminded me of a great emperor as his velvet cape blew with the wind behind his broad shoulders. As he walked down each step, the cape swept gracefully behind him on the previous step. When he arrived at the ground, he stopped in front of me.

Emalickel: I need to inform you my presence will be needed elsewhere for a few days.

He extended his hand to me and continued speaking as he guided me up the stairs.

Emalickel: I have entrusted Thorenel to be your escort during the time of my absence. The two of you will return to Dillectus and explore the rest of the lands.

We arrived at the top of the stairs. Thorenel and Romenciel ceased their conversation and focused their attention to us. Emalickel continued.

Emalickel: Stay close to Thorenel. Listen to his instruction while I am away.

Emalickel turned to Thorenel.

Emalickel: Thorenel, be wise and tend only to matters in her best

interest. She has still just arrived, so remember less is more. We do not want to overwhelm her.

Slowly, he placed my hand into Thorenel's hand and locked strong eye contact with him. Then, he stepped back, looked at me and gently smiled. Looking back at Thorenel again, Emalickel took a deep breath and straightened his posture.

Emalickel: Go.

Thorenel continued to look at Emalickel for a moment. Then he looked down at me. He gently squeezed my hand a few times.

Thorenel: Are you ready then, to go with me?

Like Emalickel, Thorenel was wearing a dark, sleeveless, armor-vest with a long red-velvet cape attached at his shoulders and leather pants with thick black boots. He conjured his beige hooded cloak, like the one Emalickel wore, and draped it across his body.

Emalickel placed his palm on my forehead. There was a bright flash of white light, and the next thing I knew, I was in Dillectus again. The breeze blew my hair. The grass on the prairie-like ground was soft and silky.

26. Artist: Epic Soul Factory
Song: Everdream

I was walking barefoot when I noticed I was wearing a beautiful, white, full-length, fitted, satin dress. *When did I start wearing this?* The question was mostly rhetorical. Nothing surprised me anymore. Randomly circulating through my head were many other unanswered questions that were more important than that one. *Where is Emalickel? Why did he have to leave? What now?* Suddenly, I heard Thorenel's voice.

Thorenel: You have been wearing it since you first arrived here.

I realized he, too, must have been able to hear my thoughts. He was standing behind me. I turned around to see him. He was looking at me analytically.

Thorenel: Have you been intimate with him?

Me: What?

Thorenel: You and Emalickel—have the two of you shared intimacy together?

I was shocked by the question and replied with another question.

Me: Why do you ask? Is that something you must know?

Thorenel looked very serious.

Thorenel: The celestial plane operates much differently than the mortal plane. Existing within the higher realms, we exhibit emotions of joy and love. We do not often feel negative emotions such as envy, jealousy, or resentment. There are also many more celestials in existence than mortals. For each mortal to ever exist on the mortal plane, there are two celestials. The reason there is such an abundance of celestials is because God split our original energy into segments. Divine energy can be altered while remaining unchanged in molecular construction. My brothers and I are made from the same energy, which was split into six segments. First, God split the original energy into three beings, and then split each of those three beings in half. The beings who shared a common half became celestial-pairs, and they share everything with each other in their existence. Emalickel and I were split from the same half, Romenciel and Xabiel were split from the same half, and Dennoliel and Seronimel were split from the same half.

Me: What does this have to do with Emalickel and I being intimate?

Thorenel: Emalickel and I are a celestial-pair. We share the same abilities, the same celestial duties, the same dwelling-places, the

same desires, and even the same lover. This is how I am able to hear your thoughts. Although I was unable to hear you on the mortal or astral plane, I became able to hear your thoughts once Emalickel brought you to the celestial plane. I don't know how Emalickel heard you on the mortal plane—that continues to perplex me. Either your thoughts were strong enough to reach him, or his abilities were strong enough to enable him to hear you. Usually, while on the same plane, Emalickel and I share a oneness of minds and presence. We hear each other's thoughts, feel each other's emotions, and understand each other as deeply as ourselves. If the two of you had physically united I would already know.

I shook my head in confusion.

Me: Then why did you ask me, if you already know the answer?

Thorenel grew a sly smirk.

Thorenel: To bring us to the conversation in which we are presently having.

I didn't fully understand.

Thorenel: Because of this conversation, you know more about celestials and love. Did your mind not still have unanswered internal questions on the matter?

Me: Internal questions?

Thorenel: Although you are not presently asking them within your mind, I can still hear them. They sound like this: *Does Emalickel love me? Why did he choose to bring me here to see all of this? How does love between a mortal and celestial work? Why are celestials so drawn to mortal females?*

I couldn't believe he was that deep into my mind. He was reading thoughts I had already dismissed. It made me feel slightly uncomfortable wondering what else he saw in there.

Thorenel guided me to a large, nearby boulder in the open field. He knelt in front of me and placed his hands on my shoulders.

Thorenel: Do not let it disturb you. Although I know every thought within your mind, even the thoughts you have suppressed, it is unlikely anything about your mind will alter my judgment of you. Celestials seldom can judge. Such emotions, of the lower vibration, are only experienced on the mortal plane. Although celestials feel them from time to time, it is a rare occurrence. Negative emotions exist in abundance on the mortal plane to provide mortals with contrast in their experiences of life. Their contrast generates desires, and their desires generate feelings. Feelings and emotions are building-blocks for reality and perception. This is a complicated topic. All you need to know is this; you are perfect in your creation, and so is everything inside of your body, your mind, and your soul.

I felt myself begin to blush. I looked down and acted like I was tucking my hair behind my ear. The whole time I was trying to fight off a shy smile.

Thorenel: Would you like for me to answer your questions?

I shrugged my shoulders, but also nodded. Thorenel knew the answer was yes. He moved himself to sit beside me on the boulder. With his legs spread apart, he leaned his forearms to rest on his thighs and folded his hands in front of him.

Thorenel: Does Emalickel love you? I have felt his emotions, and the answer is yes.

Why did he choose to bring you here to see all of this? He wanted to share his world with you and be able to spend time interacting further with you.

How does love between a mortal and celestial work? In many of the same ways as it does on Earth, but not with the same principles. In the celestial plane, we come together in groups of three.

Each celestial-pair engages with the same unique mortal lover. If one becomes drawn to her, so does the other. Three is a complete number on the celestial plane, for nothing can be complete without three aspects.

Me: So why are celestials so drawn to mortal females?

Thorenel: In case you haven't already noticed, celestials are all male. Female forms are only found in the mortal plane. Of course, we cannot pursue them until they have reached the astral or celestial plane. There are no female forms on the celestial plane, except for those who already belong to a celestial-pair. Those females were once mortal and became a part of the celestial plane after uniting with a celestial-pair upon reaching an objective-level of spiritual evolution.

Me: What about the males of the mortal plane? What happens to them?

Thorenel: Many of them have origins as celestials from Lapoi. They will return to Lapoi, upon their full awakening, and resume their celestial forms and duties. The other males, not of this realm, will return to their home-realms upon awakening.

This was a lot of information. I was trying to sort and process it within my mind.

Thorenel: I should not overwhelm you. I fear we have gone too far on the subject. This is all we must discuss at this time. When you have processed this information, I will provide you more.

One question was burning within me as I processed this new knowledge. It was a very bold question, and I did not feel comfortable asking it, but I had to know the answer. I quickly responded to Thorenel before he could change the subject.

Me: One last question to clarify—you said that Emalickel loves me; so, if he and I were to . . . um . . . share love, and since you are his celestial-pair, what would that mean of you and me?

Thorenel closed his eyes and smiled as if in complete satisfaction. He opened them again before answering.

Thorenel: Emalickel and I are a celestial-pair. Whatever comes into his experience will also make its way to mine, and whatever comes into my experience will also make its way into his.

There was a silence between us. I was still trying to process. Thorenel changed the subject.

Thorenel: So! Where shall we go first on our adventure?

Although I wanted to entertain the previous conversation and wanted to go deeper on the subject, I knew he had said all he wanted to say. He had already changed the subject. Referencing the pervious conversation would have been awkward. I pointed at the castle-like structure located in the distance.

Me: How about there?

Thorenel: No. Emalickel did not include it in the itinerary for our travels.

Me: Why do we have to do what he says do?

He cleared his throat before answering.

Thorenel: I told Emalickel I would be your escort during his absence. He provided me with an itinerary of places he would have taken you had he been here. We shook arms on this. I am one of my word. I vouched to take you to specific places—places which fail to include the structure of your fascination.

Crushed, I looked off into the distance at the structure, daydreaming of what it looked like up close and inside. *What is it? Who goes there? When can I see it?* My thoughts were interrupted as Thorenel gently placed a hand on my back, guiding me towards the sandy beach.

Thorenel: I will tell you what, let us explore the other lands. Mean-

while, you can ask me those other questions which roam about your mind. I'll answer as much as I can.

We continued walking towards the beach.

27. Artist: Patryk Scelina
Song: Voices of Namibia

Thorenel: Please . . . you may ask me your questions.

I hesitated, for I had millions of questions. *Where should even I start?* I chose to ask the first question that came to my mind.

Me: What does everyone do here all day?

Thorenel: We all have our individual duties as they are given, but in general we monitor the mortals and tend to our given orders. We also share enlightenment among one another, we train at the Warrior Temple, and we have one day per week of complete freedom. On that day, we may do as we please, as long as it does not rebel against God's commands.

Me: Do you eat and sleep here?

Thorenel: We do not have a need to eat, drink, or rest, but partaking in those things certainly are pleasurable. We also enjoy other—more physical—pleasures.

I was taken by surprise at his bluntness.

Me: Oh? Like what?

He chuckled.

Thorenel: You know exactly of what I am referring. That is a universal pleasure. Only if we are lucky does the opportunity arise for us to share this endearment with a mortal.

Thorenel looked in my direction, but not directly at me.

Thorenel: It is known that love between a celestial and a mortal is

amazing, like none other ever experienced. Unfortunately, this bond does not happen often because there are specific rules. Being out of compliance in any matter regarding a mortal sends a celestial straight into isolation with the other fallen celestials. Mortals are strictly off limits to us unless certain criteria have been met.

We stopped after reaching the soft sand of the beach.

Thorenel: Wait here for a moment.

Thorenel walked towards the water, stopping on the shore. He turned himself to look up the shoreline. He opened his arms wide and clicked his tongue. An enormous cloud of sand manifested about one mile away. Two large bleach-white stallions emerged from the cloud. Time slowed as I watched them approach. They galloped along the shore towards Thorenel. As they sprinted, the water splashed vigorously at their feet. They were so beautiful, so majestic!

When they arrived, Thorenel signaled for me to come to him. I walked up to one of the horses and stroked its nose. They were larger than any I'd ever seen before. As they stood on four legs, I could have walked right under them. They had no saddles, but they did have golden reins. Their coats were glowing white and seemed to sparkle.

Thorenel placed himself behind me and put his hands on my hips. He hoisted me up onto one of the horses, placing me on its back. I took the luxurious golden reins in my hands, looking at them in complete astonishment. Thorenel then lifted himself onto the other horse. Thorenel looked at me proudly. He knew I was impressed with his abilities. He commanded the horses, with a click of his tongue, as he winked at me.

At that, the horses neighed and began galloping along the water again. Time continued to slow as they ran along the shore, parallel to large rocky cliffs bordering the beach. The water splashed at their feet as they ran. The wind rushed against my face. I was laughing, filled with excitement. I looked over at Thorenel who was already gazing at me with a grin on his face. I heard his thoughts.

Thorenel: ***I am pleased to have pleased you.***

After some time, we veered to the right of the shoreline, approaching the base of the cliffs lining the beach. Our horses slowed to a walking pace. It was quiet, but over the sound of the horses' hooves brushing in the sand, my thoughts and questions began to resurface in my mind. Thorenel was aware of this.

Thorenel: I know. Let me explain the criteria for interaction between celestial and mortal.

28. Artist: Audiomachine
Song: Transcendence

He was relaxed, holding the reins of his majestic horse with one hand while the other rested in his lap.

Thorenel: First of all, the mortal must be in the process of spiritually awakening. Secondly, she must make the decision to fall in love with a celestial completely on her own without any force or influence from the celestial.

He adjusted himself on the horse, shifting his body back a bit.

Thorenel: Finally, any physical interaction must not happen on the mortal plane. This leaves our options limited. Not only must a mortal awaken into their spiritual awareness, but they must raise the vibration of their consciousness to a level high enough to perceive the celestial plane. They also must believe and accept what they are experiencing on the celestial plane. Then, they must have the desire to fall in love with a celestial—not to mention that the celestial must desire her as well. They must have that special connection, if you will.

Thorenel shrugged his shoulders and shook his head.

Thorenel: The rules are unrealistically set as not to interfere with the development and natural progress of creation. Celestials lucky

enough to unify with a mortal will fall into such deep love that she becomes their only partner for eternity. They become a part of each other, quite literally. Without creating additional offspring, the celestial and mortal energies blend into a oneness of molecules. Celestial becomes one with mortal and mortal with celestial.

Me: Everything is so perfect here. Why are celestials so drawn to the mortal plane?

Thorenel: It is so amazing, God's creation of the mortal plane. It resulted in the manifestation of a perceivable time-space reality—a physical, tangible reality. Inhabitants of the mortal plane are equipped with special abilities including imagination, emotion, and physical senses of sight, sound, touch, taste, and smell. These abilities enable them to interpret energy into forms and to alter energy to their likeness—although most mortals remain unaware of their ability to do this.

I narrowed my eyes, as I became intrigued.

Thorenel: At first, a tangible reality only existed in the mortal plane and not in the celestial plane. As mortals began experiencing reality, everything started to evolve, extending to all planes of existence. Unaware of their ability to alter energy through perception, mortals unknowingly extended physical reality to the celestial plane, introducing shape and form into our extension of existence.

It all started when mortals began perceiving the celestial plane and feeling our non-physical energy. As a result, they started believing in our existence. This vibration of belief resonated through the celestial plane. When mortals began interpreting our energies into form we manifested physical bodies in the male format. Not only did we still have our divine abilities, but we also started feeling traces of mortal emotions and physical senses. These bodies made us capable of interacting with mortals, being able to physically appear to them, and teach them of divine love

when God instructed us to do so. God planned it perfectly so that celestials and mortals would have a symbiotic relationship; mortals would admire celestials for their aid and protection, while celestials would admire mortals for their interpretations and manifestations through imagination.

Our horses stopped to eat some of the sea grass which grew along the base of the rocky cliffs. Thorenel opened his mouth to explain more, but then closed it as he exhaled.

Thorenel: There is so much more to the story, but I must stop there as it would only confuse you. You will one day understand everything, for you are a being of expansion and evolution.

Thorenel clicked his tongue, signaling for the horses to begin walking again. We turned right, along a path between the rocky cliffs into an orange and yellow forest. It was peaceful. The orange and yellow leaves fell from the tree tops which were so thick only a few beams of golden light shined through them from the sky.

29. Artist: Adrian Von Zeigler
Song: Home of Heroes

Auruclerum began to fade, but never disappeared completely beyond the horizon. When it dimmed, the sky became navy in color. Many thin, wispy, clouds of purple and blue-green were visible among the stars. Lapoi had two moons. They were both dark-lavender and grey in color. One was the size of Earth's moon, the other was about ten times as large. Not to my surprise, Lapoi's night sky was breathtaking.

Thorenel explained to me that Auruclerum is a bright start which shines daylight on Lapoi over a period of 48 hours. Auruclerum never sets completely, so ambient light glows across the land in the night, which lasts for about 20 hours. The complete cycle, from the rise and the set of Auruclerum, takes 70 hours on Lapoi to complete.

Over the next few days, we visited several landscapes of Lapoi.

Through the golden forest, to the water world which looked like Atlantis, to the underground caves, to the surface containing large mountains rising out of the water. There were so many lands which looked more beautiful than any fantasy world I'd ever dreamed of—crystals, gems, and diamonds; huge sparkling waterfalls, white birds, and numerous fields of grass and flowers. It was such an astonishing place. Everything in Lapoi was so perfect, so pleasant, and so magical. Even the structures they built for their homes were glorious; made from smooth white and grey rock, marble, and stone. We spent days touring a piece of each of the lands until we finally arrived back at Dillectus.

During our tour, I became more trusting of Thorenel as we spent a lot of time together. He seemed very open and honest. I felt I could trust him. He was also very funny and made me laugh. We had a great time on our three-day tour together and shared many fun memories. I starting to feel really close to him and felt comfortable in his company.

Our horses continued past the castle-like structure of Dillectus, then stopped when we arrived back at the starting point of our tour. We continued riding until we arrived in the grassy field. Thorenel dismounted from his horse, then came over to mine and offered his hands to me to assist in my dismount.

Thorenel: You must remember, even though you are in your spirit form, you are still partially mortal and need your sleep. It has been three Lapoian days since you first arrived here.

He picked up some rocks from the ground and blew on them. They blew a few feet away, glistening in the wind to slowly form a structure looking like a cottage made from stone.

Thorenel: It is for you. Go inside. I think you will find it pleasing.

As I walked into the cottage, I found it was well-lit with candles and sconces along the interior walls. The walls were made of stone and there was a fire lit in the fireplace. It was very cozy consisting of only one room measuring 30 feet by 30 feet. A king-sized bed was across from the fireplace. Next to the bed was a table with a candle and a vase of my favorite flowers, tropical white and violet Orchids! I smiled as I touched their soft, cashmere petals.

Thorenel popped his head inside the doorway.

Thorenel: I figured you'd like those. I will be standing guard right outside while you slumber. When you awaken, we will get some of the most wonderful food you have ever tasted. It'll be a free-day for the two of us. We'll do whatever you like.

There was a moment of silence as we stared at each other smiling. Then he started out the door. He turned back around and paused in the doorway a moment before he winked at me and patted the door-frame. Then he walked out.

I realized I was starting to feel really close to Thorenel. We shared many experiences on Lapoi together, and he was very wise and fun. I could not help but wonder if Emalickel had set Thorenel up with me to try and encourage us to bond and grow closer together.

There was a white, satin slip on the bed, which I changed into before laying down. I found myself smiling and thinking about the past few days Thorenel and I had shared together. It comforted me to know he was just outside the cabin should I need him, but I found myself longing for him.

I sat up to blow out the candle next to the bed. When I looked up, I saw in the doorway, Thorenel. He was looking straight at me while leaning on the frame with his arms crossed at his chest. His skin glowed in the light of the candle. He was grinning, as if he knew what I had been thinking.

Slowly, he began to walk towards me. He brought himself to sit on the edge of the bed next to me. Looking into my eyes, he gently stroked my hair behind my ear. He gazed at me for a long while as if digging deep into my mind. I remained silent but could not hush my lustful thoughts. He smiled and squinted his eyes at me trying to read these thoughts.

30. Artist: Audiomachine
Song: Wars of Faith (Extended to 5:03)

Finally, he whispered.

Thorenel: You do desire me.

I couldn't speak. All I could do was desperately gaze into his eyes and try to catch my breath.

Thorenel: As I desire you.

With passion in his eyes, he slowly began leaning in towards me. He continued cautiously, testing for my approval. Only one foot away from my face, Thorenel stopped. He looked intensely into my eyes.

He whispered.

Thorenel: May I enjoy the splendor of you?

There was no way I'd find the will to turn him down. I nodded in approval. He continued leaning in until I could feel his warm breath as he breathed against my cheek. He touched his lips gently sliding them across my cheek towards my lips. Just before getting to my lips, he lifted them away, gently brushing them against the corner of mine.

He looked at me again for approval. Pleased to see the lack of my rejection, the corner of his mouth grinned. He scooted his body in closer to me to hold my head in his hands as our lips approached one another again. This time, when they touched, they locked intensely with one another. After several moments of this embrace, our lips opened more. Thorenel lightly glided the tip of his tongue across mine.

His hands wandered down towards my shoulders, sliding the straps of my slip off. He kissed my exposed shoulder then moved up to work on my neck. One of his hands slid across my chest, grazed my stomach, down to my leg where it explored the unexposed thigh underneath my slip for a moment. Leaving me yearning for more, as if trying to tease me, he moved his hand back up to grab around my waist. His lips returned to mine, once again, but this time his tongue was more aggressive with mine. His breathing was harder, as he rolled his body more onto the bed to position himself on top of me. His armored-vest suit disappeared in a glowing light, exposing his bronzed bare chest. He was solid and heavy as his body pressed against mine. He brought one of his arms to rest under my neck.

One of his hands slid my slip all the way down from my shoulder exposing my bare breasts. His chest touched against mine. I could feel the heat radiating from his body. As we continued to kiss, I allowed his hands to explore the outside of my body, while mine explored his. He was so strong and had many muscles in his back and shoulders.

He moved his face down my neck, and finally to my chest. He buried his face into my bare chest for a moment, making his breathing heavier. His hands firmly grabbed my hips as he pressed his against me. He scooted back up so that his eyes met mine again. We smiled at each other in surprise of what we were doing. His lips went back to kissing mine, and our entire bodies slowly rubbed against each other.

He began pressing his pelvis firmly against mine. I felt his manhood bulging as it grew increasingly harder beneath his leather trousers. I could feel heat coming from that area. I felt myself aching to feel that part of him inside of me.

Thorenel let out an exhale and stopped for a moment. He buried his head into my neck, breathing heavily, almost as if agitated because he wanted more of me.

He continued, again, rubbing against me with increasing intensity. I felt myself throbbing for him to enter me.

Thorenel let out a quiet moan under his breath. He stopped and propped himself up on one of his arms. I could see his round chest gleaming in the candle light. Catching his breath, he paused to look straight into my eyes for a moment.

Thorenel: I've never been so drawn to anything in all my existence.

He continued looking back and forth into each of my eyes. I knew what he wanted. He looked very nervous as he slowly reached down to gently slide my gown up my thighs. He then brought his intimate extension out from an opening in his leather pants and slung his leg over my body to position himself on top of my entire body. He laid his chest back down on top of mine. Sweat glistened his skin. He continued looking into my eyes. His body began shaking as the sensitive skin of his intimacy grazed across mine. His breaths became rapid as he positioned it so that it was almost at penetration.

Suddenly, the cottage started shaking violently. I heard a low rumble in the distance. It grew increasingly loud. I became worried. The cottage door flung open and Xabiel barged in. He was out of breath and in a panic. He yelled out to me from the doorway.

Xabiel: Adrienne, get down!

He saw Thorenel on top of me. He looked surprised and confused. The whole scene played out in slow-motion. Xabiel blinked a few times and continued, but his voice was distorted and hard to hear over the deep rumbling. The cottage shook tremendously.

Xabiel: Thorenel, call the warriors! We've got uninvited company!

6

THE ABDUCTION

31. Artist: Aleksandar Dimitrijevic
Song: Waiting for Gods

I sat up in the bed, confused at the apparent danger. My perception of time slowed down, and my hearing became muffled. All I could do was look at the chaos around me, trying to absorb what was happening. Xabiel stood in the doorway looking outside at the sky and then back at me. He expressed a look of terror and disbelief.

Thorenel immediately began conjuring armor—his gunmetal black armored-suit with the red cape. Several weapons were stored away within his attire. I struggled to reposition the straps of my slip back onto my shoulders. The ground shook and rumbled like an earthquake. The wind howled at hurricane speeds. The fire in the fireplace blew out completely. Objects within the cottage were falling from the shelves and rolling all over the floor. The furniture bounced and moved all around.

Then, a violent gust of wind blew the roof off the cottage. The ground shook so violently it knocked me down. Disoriented, I was having trouble coming back to my feet. Everything was blurry. Xabiel ran over to me. He was yelling something, but I couldn't hear him due to my disorientation. He reached his arms out towards me, but the wind was too powerful. All I could do was grab the underside of the bed. I could barely hear Thorenel, whose eyes were squinted shut as he called out to the warriors in a language which sounded like a blend of Latin and Aramaic.

Suddenly, I was lifted from the ground by some unknown force. My body became airborne. I looked around helplessly. When I looked up, I saw a dark circular object hovering in the sky. It was very large and looked like some kind of spaceship.

As my body continued rising closer to the dark ship, which hovered a few hundred feet above the cottage, Thorenel and Xabiel flew up to me, this time with Romenciel, who had just arrived on the scene. They attempted to grab me but were blocked by an invisible force-field. They could not get closer than two feet from me. They frantically punched at the force-field but were getting nowhere. I continued being drawn up higher.

Then I saw hundreds of small lights begin to appear in the sky. The lights grew from dim to bright as they approached. They were being given off by the rest of the warriors of Lapoi. Some landed on the ground, while others began warfare on the ship in the air. Several celestials flew to surround the ship while others, including Dennoliel and Seronimel, flew over to help Thorenel and Romenciel free me. I regained my lucidity.

Thorenel: They have placed a shield around her!

Looking up again at the ship, I saw a large sliding door begin opening from the underside. I could see inside, it was very dark and foggy. Terrified, I screamed down to the brothers and warriors.

Me: You have to help me! Please help me!

They continued frantically shooting fire and all kinds of energy directly at the force-field. Nothing was working. The brothers panicked among themselves while they continued the struggle.

Romenciel: The shield is too powerful to penetrate without Emalickel!

Seronimel: Where is he, for heaven's sake!?!

Thorenel: You all know he left the celestial plane days ago! He isn't returning until this evening!

Romenciel: That'll be too late!

Thorenel responded in frustration.

Thorenel: And just what do you expect for me to do about it, Romenciel!?!

Dennoliel expressed his concern in the matter.

Dennoliel: We must do something now!

Exhausted and annoyed, Xabiel threw his arms into the air. He exhibited his usual, sarcastic, arrogant attitude.

Xabiel: What a genius! You got any more mastermind ideas, Dennoliel?! I know you Guard Celestials are real experts in battle and combat! By the way, where are the guards—having tea with each other?

Holding his head in irritation, Thorenel had heard enough. He roared fiercely.

Thorenel: Would you all just shut the—

The quarrel was interrupted as they were ambushed by orbs of fire and other energies. The brothers were forced to retreat after taking several direct hits to their bodies. I knew they weren't giving up, but I also couldn't help feeling abandoned. I watched in terror as a chaotic battle continued. Warriors were fighting in the air and on the ground. The ground was far away as I continued floating up, closer to the door of the ship. I heard thunderous explosions all around me. The land of Dillectus was polluted with debris and disorder. I felt hopeless as I approached the inside of the ship.

The battle continued below me as the ship's dark metallic door closed to engulf me. Then, it was dark. I found myself standing in the center of a dark room, surrounded by hundreds of beings who stood in the shadows. I was unable to move, as if I suffered from some kind of paralysis. The dark beings that surrounded me were all looking towards me, but I was unable to see their faces for they were all covered by the hoods on their dark-blue robes. The room had a very dim ambient light. It was quiet. It was too quiet. It was the kind of quiet that felt eerie. It sounded like a cave with echoes of a gentle winds whirling throughout.

32. Artist: Adrian Von Zeigler
Song: Angel of Death

Directly in front of me, I saw a very tall and thin being slowing coming my way out of the fog. He appeared to be the leader as everyone moved out of his way to let him pass. He glided as if he did not walk on feet. It was very creepy. I was absolutely petrified. He continued closer to me until he was directly in front of me. He was so tall that my head came to the base of his torso. I was unable to look up at his face due to the paralysis induced upon me. Then I heard him speak to the other dark beings. His creepy voice echoed throughout the ship.

Leader: Yes. Her energy is very strong. She could be of use to us. She has many experiences radiating within her. Emalickel is connected to her. He will come, but he will only receive her when he is ready to share his secrets with me. Otherwise, I will keep her and use her to obtain the knowledge she holds within.

The leader then spoke to one of the other dark beings.

Leader: Jamaleo, you will take her into my chambers. Prepare her for reading.

A being dressed in the same dark-robed attire stepped forward.

Jamaleo: As you wish, Lord Barthaldeo.

The leader's voice was then directed at me. Slowly, he bent down and stroked my slip at my breasts with his gloved hand. I was mortified but was still unable to move away from him. He addressed my fear and spoke in an insincere tone.

Leader: It will be quite an uncomfortable sensation, beautiful mortal, but you will not be harmed unbearably. I do apologize, but this is the only way I will be able to see all that you have seen and know all that you know of mortal life in Millattus.

He nodded at Jamaleo, who walked closer to me. Jamaleo quickly swept me off my feet and slung me over his shoulder. Although I was disoriented, I could see, as I hung upside down from his shoulder, that he was taking me down a long, dark hallway lined with several doorways and small purple lights on the floor. It was very cold and foggy. He turned down several additional halls in route. His footsteps echoed loudly. Each step was slow and steady. I began to wonder how far into the ship we were going. Finally, at the very end of yet another long hallway I saw a pair of large French-style concrete doors that were lit up by ambient white lights.

Jamaleo carried me down to these doors and pushed them open with his booted foot. Inside the room, there were several arches made from concrete. The only source of light was from candle sconces on the walls. The floor was made of stone. It looked more like an ancient dark tomb than a room. There was a large fog on the floor next to a dark fireplace. Jamaleo placed me in this fog. It felt soft and fluffy, like that of a bed, but the room was dark, cold, and uninviting.

Jamaleo: Lord Barthaldeo shall arrive soon to begin your reading.

Jamaleo turned around and walked out the large French-style doors. I was still unable to move. All I could do was lay in the bed of fog and breathe in panic. I didn't know what this so-called reading was, but my mind thought in fear of all the possible things it could be. I could hear my breaths echoing within the room which was bare of objects. I could, however, hear a fountain trickling from somewhere in the middle of the room, but I could not see it from the darkness and fog. My body wasn't able to move on its own, but I could feel it shivering from the cold. As my eyes scanned the room, it was made of stone. It reminded me of a gothic castle or some type of old fort. It was very empty and dark. How could anyone take pride owning a ship like this? It was ridden with cold, darkness and evil. The reality suddenly set in hard that I was aboard this ship with an unknown destiny. My heart began to race in panic.

I tried to calm down and become absorbed in beautiful memories of Lapoi, Emalickel, and Thorenel. *They will come for me. They will find a way to get me out of here.* Then, my mind returned to worry only moments later. I began having doubts. *Will they even be able to find me? How long will it take? What was about to take place in this so-called reading? What will happen afterwards? What about Emalickel and Thorenel? How could I get away? Will the others from Lapoi come in time to save me? Could they die? What would happen if they died?*

Just then I heard the leader speak from a distance.

Barthaldeo: My, my, you do worry excessively.

He was standing in the doorway facing me. Then he placed his hands behind his back and began walking around the room as he spoke.

Barthaldeo: We are the celestials of the realm called Haffelnia. There are nine realms in this Universe containing their own individual evolution of life. Your realm of Millattus, you see, is advancing along quite swiftly. Haffelnia is similar, in structure, to Millattus. I am rather envious of the progress of your realm. The mortals there, having become more awakened to their own self-awareness, have evolved immensely. They are entering a bronze

age—a time when mortals can experience the celestial plane and directly interact with the celestials of their realm.

He stopped to stare into the fountain at the center of the room.

Barthaldeo: A bronze age occurs just before the dawning of a silver age. A silver age is where the real juice is—a new and improved super-world of enlightened beings is created, where celestial and mortal blend into a civilization of highly-advanced, evolved beings. It becomes a time of even further expansion in this experience of creation. This has yet to be accomplished by any of the realms, but I desire this glory for Haffelnia. And then, I shall be exalted across all the realms!

Turning around to look at me, he grew a mischievous smile.

Barthaldeo: Millattus is on the brink of discovering a great awakening. You, my dear, will act as my window to view how this great awakening has taken place on the mortal plane of Millattus.

33. Artist: Adrian Von Zeigler
Song: Fallen

He soared over to me in a fog. His dark-blue robe shed into a simple dark-blue kilt. A golden cape hung behind his back, tied with a golden rope around his chest. He pointed at the fireplace causing it to light. He positioned himself onto his side next to me. I could now see his face and body. He looked like a normal man with medium-length, wavy, black hair which grazed his shoulders. A few wispy strands of hair fell in front of his eyes. His face was tattooed on one side extending down his cheek and neck, to his shoulder and chest. He wore a thin golden rope crown around his forehead. His body had a thinner and taller frame than the celestials from Lapoi. It was the same in structure, but his skin was pale.

Barthaldeo used his long skinny fingers to stroke my face. I cringed.

Barthaldeo: I desire to know the secrets of how you became awak-

ened. How has Millattus become so awakened without revolt from the mortals? Emalickel has chosen his moves wisely and tactfully. I wish to know his techniques and will to do the same for Haffelnia.

I struggled to speak

Me: Why don't you just ask Emalickel?

Barthaldeo rolled over onto his back. He laughed overtly.

Barthaldeo: Ha! And Emalickel break code? He wouldn't even think of such!

He calmed himself from the dramatic laughing episode.

Barthaldeo: The code says we are not to exchange information between realms as it interferes with the development of our own unique individuality. Perhaps Emalickel will talk, though, seeing how I have your life at my mercy and all. It is worth a try.

Me: How can you expect to be glorified when you've done everything so maliciously?

Barthaldeo: I am already on the shit-list of realms, so what do I have to lose? I will see what your conscious mind has to offer me, otherwise, perhaps Emalickel will spill the beans in exchange for your fate.

I noticed his facial expression become bitter.

Barthaldeo: If he doesn't, he will forever suffer in his own guilt of your little soul being trapped and warded from celestial radar on one of the primitive planets of Haffelnia for eternity.

He rolled back onto his side to face me. He spoke in a creepy soft voice right next to my ear.

Barthaldeo: You see, I have a plan for you. Once we arrive in Haffelnia, I will hide you away on one of my mortal planets, in a cave warded with spells keeping any Lapoian celestials from finding you. Not even Emalickel will be able to sense your pres-

ence there. If he still refuses to talk, then I will ward your very flesh from all of Lapoi, and you will dwell among the mortals of Haffelnia lifetime, after lifetime, after lifetime. You won't even remember anything of Millattus or Lapoi after this present lifetime.

Barthaldeo stroked my hair behind my ear before continuing.

Barthaldeo: Do not worry, mortal, I will try to make this fast.

He sat up to position himself in front of me. His eyes turned dark and cold. He gazed at me with hunger for power. He looked at me with a wide grin. I knew he was about to do something awful.

Barthaldeo: Now, shall we begin?

He lifted his arm and extended it out. Examining it closely, he shook out his arm and opened and closed his hand as if warming it up for something. He traced a circle around my lower abdomen and placed his open hand on that spot. Then, he drew his arm back, like he was about to punch me there. He closed his eyes. I was terrified, but it was impossible for me to be able to move. I closed my eyes, too.

34. Artist: Audiomachine
Song: Akkadian Empire

Then I felt it—the punch. I felt his arm reach inside me. It traveled up through my neck to my head. My scream must have been heard all along the entire ship. He squeezed everything inside the path. It felt like my insides were being twisted in a vice. The slightest move of his hand felt like ripping and tearing. I screamed in agony. There had never been a pain I had ever endured as intense as this. I was in my astral form, but it felt like my brain was being mixed around in a blender. My entire torso and neck felt like fire was burning from the inside as a thousand knives churned and poked the fire.

I felt myself drift away from awareness. Images flashed throughout my mind. Memories from previous lifetimes resurfaced. There were so many of them, from various time-periods. Each memory that played contained a common theme. They were all at pivotal moments involving my own self-awareness or when others around me were exhibiting higher levels of consciousness.

After what seemed like 15 minutes of memory regurgitation, I heard Barthaldeo take a long, deep breath. He slowly removed his arm from inside of me. He rolled onto on his back and closed his eyes. Relived he was finished, I thought to myself, *at least it's over.* The sound of Barthaldeo's thoughts interrupted me.

Leader: Only for now mortal, only for now. It will take quite a few times before I have received all I need to know from you.

35. Artist: Audiomachine
Song: Sand of Time

I felt myself passing out from exhaustion. A vision of Lapoi came into my head as if I was viewing it remotely. All the celestials were at the Warrior Temple preparing for battle. They were sharpening and perfecting their weapons and putting on their armored gear. Inside the Warrior Temple, Thorenel and Xabiel were talking with one another privately.

Xabiel: I saw what you were about to do with her, brother.

Thorenel: I cannot help my feelings for her.

Xabiel: Nonetheless, you know Emalickel is going to question you about how all this happened.

Thorenel was silent but glared at Xabiel with an annoyed look for bringing up such an obvious matter.

Outside, two lights shot down from the sky at incredible speeds. They were from Romenciel and Emalickel. The ground shook when they landed, and a cloud of sand filled the air around them. The two of them almost immediately emerged from the thick dust. They were both marching with purpose. Emalickel looked straight ahead as he walked. His fists were clenched, and he appeared tense. He questioned Romenciel.

Emalickel: When did this happen?

Romenciel: Nine minutes ago, brother, while you were in the higher planes. We knew her thoughts would not transmit to that plane, and we also could not reach you to inform you of her danger. I came to meet you as soon as we knew you had returned to Lapoi.

Emalickel: Who took her?

Romenciel: It was Lord Barthaldeo and his celestials.

Emalickel: Where did they take her?

Romenciel: They pulled her into their ship perhaps, headed back to Haffelnia. There was a strong force-field around her. I am sorry we could not break through it, brother.

At first Emalickel was silent as they continued walking, but then he suddenly stopped in his tracks. His face grew angry. Then he roared.

Emalickel: Thorenel!!!

It began to rain. Emalickel scanned the scene for Thorenel. Once he sensed Thorenel's location, Emalickel jerked his head to the Warrior's Temple. Thorenel and Xabiel were standing inside. Clenching his fists even harder, Emalickel teleported to his brothers. He stood, breathing heavily, only six inches from Thorenel's face, staring straight into his eyes with anger.

Emalickel: I want to know how, in the name of our Holy God, this happened, Thorenel!

Thorenel: I created a cottage for her, brother. She was safe in bed at the cottage when Barthaldeo's ship suddenly arrived. It blew off

the roof and lifted her away. They bombarded us with attacks. We did everything we could.

Emalickel spoke slowly, as if trying to fight the urge to unleash himself on Thorenel.

Emalickel: Had you been doing what you were supposed to be doing, Thorenel, you should have had ample time to forecast Barthaldeo's arrival and construct counteractive energies far before he even came close to the atmosphere of Lapoi. So, what I want to know is, what were you doing all that time?

Thorenel gulped and looked at Xabiel. Xabiel returned an insincere look, tilting his head and lifting an eyebrow. Thorenel then bowed his head to the ground, and there was a brief moment of silence. Emalickel, still with his face right in front of Thorenel's, stood up straight, making himself a few inches taller.

Emalickel: Tell me, brother, why were you not able to forecast Barthaldeo's arrival?!

Thorenel kept his head bowed as he hesitated with an answer.

Thorenel: I was... distracted.

Thorenel made brief eye contact with Emalickel but was unable to hold it there. He looked back down at the ground, almost as if in shame. Emalickel's expression turned fierce. He bitterly mumbled.

Emalickel: And exactly what had you so distracted Thorenel?

Again, Thorenel was silent, but Emalickel turned bitter. He had finally gotten a read on Thorenel's thoughts.

Emalickel: Thorenel, you defective sideliner! I chose you to protect her and keep her safe!

His tone became even louder.

Emalickel: I trusted you to protect her! Your only job was to

protect her! Instead, you allowed your reckless school-boy emotions to interfere and now . . .

He grinded his teeth as he spoke.

Emalickel: . . . Now, she feels nothing but fear and abandonment.

He flung his cape into Thorenel's face as he turned around and began pacing towards the large group of warriors who had gathered outside. As he walked, he conjured armor and weapons onto his body. He positioned himself in front of the warriors to address them. Thorenel reluctantly emerged from the temple behind him.

36. Artist: Audiomachine
Song: Guardians at the Gate

Emalickel: Warriors, you will join me in battle! Lapoi is being tested. Our peace has been disturbed! Our strength has been challenged! Barthaldeo and his warriors intruded the parameters of Millattus. We shall make them face judgment! We shall make them beg for mercy! Their trespasses against us will not be tolerated!

He opened his arms to the crowd before continuing. He spoke very slowly and clearly, with power and ferocity.

Emalickel: We are all celestials of God and should behave as such! Today, warriors and brothers, we will open the eyes of Barthaldeo and his warriors and of all else who may be in contemplation of defiance and corruption! Today we will make a statement that will never be forgotten by any one across all the realms! United by brotherhood, we are the celestials of Lapoi! We value our peace and our serenity! We value our love and our loyalty to God! Most importantly, my warriors, today we value our strength! We value our tenacity! We value our power! Thus, we can be certain our dominance will persevere, and the echoes of our eminence shall resonate through eternity forever!

The warriors cheered. Thorenel stepped to stand beside Emalickel.

Still facing the warriors, Emalickel had a disgusted expression on his face. He shook his head and spoke under his breath.

Emalickel: I expected so much more from you.

Thorenel spoke quietly and looked directly at Emalickel.

Thorenel: I meant not to intrude, Emalickel.

Emalickel shifted his feet to turn towards Thorenel to look at him. Emalickel's voice became louder and more agitated.

Emalickel: Intrude? What do you mean intrude? Not intrude, Thorenel, but rather fail! You failed at your mission miserably! I put my complete trust in you. You may not have defied orders, but you certainly failed in your line of duty. A physical abduction is inexcusable!

Thorenel: I feel like the majority of your anger is from resentment of what I—what she and I—were about to do. I am worried how you can exhibit such extensive negative emotion in our plane.

37. Artist: Aaron Sapp
Song: You Were Born for This

Emalickel looked to the side, at the crowd of warriors who were standing at attention, watching the conversation. With both hands, Emalickel snatched Thorenel by his armored-vest and forcibly pulled him in closer. Emalickel turned his back to the crowd of warriors as he spoke discreetly and firmly through his teeth to Thorenel.

Emalickel: The majority of my anger is from your failure to do your job, Thorenel!

He pushed Thorenel away as he released his powerful grip on his vest. After taking a moment to recollect himself, Emalickel stepped closer to Thorenel. Emalickel spoke in a peevish tone.

Emalickel: And more thing... as for my ability to feel the emotion

of rage—believe me when I say it is a blessing to behold such an ability as I lead us in the pursuit of Barthaldeo.

Turning back around to face the warriors again, Emalickel looked to the sky, took a deep breath, and darted into the air and out of Lapoi's atmosphere. The warriors followed him. One by one they positioned their helmets over their heads and burst into the sky. Romenciel, Xabiel, Dennoliel, and Seronimel were standing at the bottom of the stairs outside the temple. They were looking up at Thorenel, who stood speechless at the top of the stairs. Romenciel nodded at Thorenel before he shot into the air. The other three brothers followed suit.

Thorenel paced on the landing at the top of the stairs, infuriated and breathing heavily. He grunted as he punched a nearby concrete wall with such great force, it crumbled around his fist. He nibbled on his bottom lip in anger as he closed his eyes and caught his breath. When he appeared calm again, he too, looked to the sky and vanished into the galaxy behind his brothers.

The celestials of Lapoi stayed grouped together as they began the search for Barthaldeo's ship. Capable of seeing thousands of light-years away, they scanned the vastness of space. Romenciel pointed to the left.

Romenciel: It is over there. They are headed for Haffelnia.

Romenciel pointed at a galaxy in the distance. They all simultaneously traveled in that direction at warp-speed. Upon arriving, the ship was located on the outer arm of the galaxy. There was a maroon-colored planet illuminated in white star dust. The ship appeared to be headed towards that planet. Emalickel slowed his speed and turned to face the others. He communicated to them.

38. Artist: Aleksander Dimitrijevic
Song: They Fought as Legends

Emalickel: Everyone hold back here. I will break down the force-field around their ship. When it is done, we will invade together. Take down any enemy in your path. If you find an enemy, openly attack him. If you see a fellow warrior in need, go to his aid. If you find Adrienne, enclose her into your safety shield and communicate to me. If you find Barthaldeo, I want you to trap that selfish bastard. Bind that vermin in a restraining spell for me so that I may have the pleasure of throwing him into the deepest pits of isolation myself.

Emalickel turned back around and sped up directly towards the ship. Everyone else remained back as he had instructed. Emalickel continued approaching the ship. He made himself invisible and started creating some type of clear energy in the palms of his hands over his head. It gradually increased in size until it was the size of a small house. It was colorless, like water. Emalickel grunted and began trembling as the ball became larger and grew denser.

Upon reaching the ship, Emalickel re-materialized himself. He struggled while stabilizing the giant ball of energy above his head. He looked at the ship, scanning it for the best place to direct the energy. Then he thrust the ball forward with his hands. Large powerful lightning bolts shot out from the palms of his hands, and the big energized ball collided into the ship. The hazy, blue force-field surrounding the ship began to flicker and fizzle. As the lightning bolts from Emalickel's palms contacted the ship, the haze rapidly began to fade away. Emalickel continued dispensing the lightning energy until the ship's protective field was completely broken down.

The others immediately rushed toward Emalickel. Xabiel flew underneath the ship. He looked at the closed, sliding doorway and shot powerful heat lasers from his palms in an attempt to burn a hole for entry. It only created sparks. He called to Emalickel.

Xabiel: Emalickel, how do we get in, brother?

Everyone flew down to Xabiel's aid. Seronimel and Dennoliel, although guards, had the abilities of the warriors because of their extensive training among them. They shot fireball explosions from their palms, but after several attempts, it was evident that their method was not going to work.

39. Artist: Daniel James
Song: You Must Overcome

Romenciel and Thorenel attempted forcefully opening the doorway together by using waves of energy which burst straight from their palms directly at the door. Xabiel joined them. The door slightly cracked open, but the three of them were unable to sustain enough energy to open it any further.

Thorenel blew ice cold air onto the doorway until it was frozen solid. Then he backed up, several hundred feet away, and zipped toward the door at full-speed, attempting to shatter it like glass with the impact of his body. Although this made an extremely loud, thunderous sound, he was unsuccessful at breaking in.

Then, Emalickel flew to the door. He placed the palms of his hands directly onto the doorway. He looked at the door as if in deep concentration. He spoke to his brothers.

Emalickel: Get back.

They flew back, but not too far away from their brother. After taking several quick deep breaths, a powerful burst of red energy flew from the palms of Emalickel's hands directly into the doorway. Upon contact, it sounded like the powerful strike of a deep-rumbling bass drum. The energy continued flowing from Emalickel's palms, but it came out in pulses. It shook the entire ship and sounded like thunder crashing with each pulse. Emalickel groaned in struggle to maintain the energy. Sweat began dripping down his face. Still, he kept his hands on the door, emitting the red energy, and clenching his teeth. He roared as he fought through the effort required to perform such a skill. Not giving up, he finally managed to warp the door enough to create an opening for entry.

Emalickel turned back to look at everyone, who were all staring in astonishment. Xabiel rolled his eyes and muttered to himself.

Xabiel: Red energy? Show-off.

Emalickel adjusted his shoulders and turned back to head inside the ship. Once inside, he knocked the doorway clear out of sight with a final blow of his booted foot. The others followed him inside. As soon as Emalickel jumped on board he was greeted by several hostile dark beings. He pushed them out of his way using the red energy which derived from his palms. He did not even have to touch them. He used a unique and powerful telekinesis while fighting.

The others jumped onto the ship and immediately joined in on the fight. Some used swords and weapons, while others used unlimited energies and telekinesis. They battled using epic techniques. With each hit and contact, time seemed to slow down, and my perception zoomed in on the movements until they played-out. Not only was there a lot of swinging, punching, and kicking; but there was lots of jumping, spiraling, and flipping. The techniques they used were like that of the best martial artists of Earth. Things were exploding, crashing, and breaking. Beings were being tossed and thrown, shattered and crushed. Fires were being conjured, and bodies were being thrown.

40. Artist: Edward Brawdoshaw)
Song: Prepare for the Onslaught

Then, I was startled back into consciousness. I was still on Barthaldeo's ship. He had just re-positioned himself next to me. He expressed a sultry gaze as he held his hand to my torso again.

Barthaldeo: Try to relax. Make this easier for me. I could do without your squirming and disruption.

Suddenly, the ship shook, and I heard the voices of men grunting as they battled one another.

Barthaldeo: What the hell!?! Surely they haven't arrived already!?!

Barthaldeo jumped up and conjured his armored garments. He opened the French-style doors and peered down the hallway. Although I was unable to move my body, my eyes were able to look down the hallway. I recognized several beings wearing black armored suits exactly like the ones worn by the Warriors of Lapoi. I exclaimed a sigh of relief when I realized it was the Lapoian Warriors there to retrieve me.

Coming back into the room, Barthaldeo slammed closed the doors. He looked alarmed and was breathing nervously. He paced for a moment around the room. I heard the continuing sounds of battle outside the chamber. Barthaldeo began placing a force-field over the entire chamber room by waving his hands in the direction of each wall. He appeared exhausted from doing this as if it had taken all his energy to conjure such a thing. He turned to look at me once again. He was still breathing hard.

Barthaldeo: Maybe I still have enough time! At least make this worth it.

He reached for me with his arm again and began pushing inside me.

That's when I heard a loud crash at the doorway. It had been knocked down and crumbled to the ground. My paralysis ceased, and I ran behind a table near the door. One of the beings from Lapoi had flung a dark being through the door. There were six beings battling in the chamber room now—three Lapoian Warriors, two dark beings, and Barthaldeo. The dark being, who had just been thrown through the doorway, was being finished off with a great sword of a Lapoian Warrior. He had been the one who broke the concrete doorway down.

A different Lapoian Warrior, who appeared to be the Archer from the

Warrior Temple, entered the room while suspending a dark being in the air via telekinesis. This dark being was clearly disoriented, but the Archer proceeded to taunt him by displaying his control as he continued to slowly twirl his body in the air. After a moment of playing with him, the Archer suddenly threw a bowling ball sized amount of energy directly at the dark being, pinning him against the ceiling. The Archer then conjured a bow and some arrows. He pulled one of the arrows from his quiver. It was golden and sparkled at the sharp tip of the arrow. He set up his aim and held it there for a moment. The dark being struggled in attempt to get away from the binding energy, which pinned him to the ceiling. The Archer shook his head at the dark being and ticked his tongue a few times. Finally, he released his arrow directly into the dark being, right between his eyes. The golden arrow pinned the dark being to the ceiling, as his body dangled beneath.

Meanwhile, the third Warrior of Lapoi had been battling it out with force-fields with Barthaldeo. Finally, he had Barthaldeo cornered. He shot out lasers from his fingers to surround Barthaldeo in a circle of fire. He used his palm to shoot electrically-charged restraining symbols which etched themselves on the floor within the circle of fire. Barthaldeo dropped to the floor in pain. He was flitching and jerking, exhibiting electric-like pain.

The third Warrior of Lapoi stared for a moment at Barthaldeo, before stepping into the ring of fire, which didn't seem to hurt him. Once inside, he bent down to look at the fearful expression on his opponent's face. I could not see the Lapoian Warrior's face, but I suspect he was proud of his near victory. Slowly, he stood back up, and continued staring down at Barthaldeo. Out of utter disrespect, he spit at Barthaldeo's feet. Just as he was turning to walk away, he began forming a huge ball of energy in his hands. He jerked around and slammed the ball down to crush Barthaldeo's body. Barthaldeo struggled to speak as his voice sounded in pain.

Barthaldeo: This is not the last of this! I will regain my strength! I will never ever, ever give up!

At that, his body gave out and he released his struggle. An orb of maroon light swirled from his torso and began floating upward until it disappeared through the ceiling.

41. Artist: Howard Shore
Song: The Bridge to Khazad Dum (Extended to 3:23)

The three warriors from Lapoi stood there for a moment, breathing heavily and staring at their unconscious enemies lying on the floor. The hallway outside the chamber was filled with dozens of other warriors from Lapoi who were also quietly standing, while their chests rose and fell from deep breaths, over the unconscious bodies of numerous dark beings. The battle appeared to be over. The dust was settling.

I couldn't believe they had all come to rescue me. I was finally safe again. One by one, they removed their helmets revealing themselves. In the chamber room with me I saw Romenciel and the Archer. The warriors in the hallway began removing their helmets. I didn't recognize many of them, but they were all so incredibly handsome. I hadn't yet seen Thorenel, Emalickel, or any of the other brothers besides Romenciel.

I heard breathing behind me. When I turned around, I remembered the third warrior in the chamber room. Still in full armor, he was standing over Barthaldeo but was looking in my direction. His fists were clenched by his sides as he continued breathing deeply. His helmet was still on. Romenciel spoke to me from across the room.

Romenciel: You should go to him—give him your gratitude for disposing of the enemy.

Slowly, I walked to stand directly in front of the third warrior. He began lifting the helmet from his head. Embarrassed by my weakness, I couldn't bring myself to look at him. I dropped my head in shame of the chaos I had caused while he finished removing his helmet.

I felt a finger under my chin, gently tilting my head up. My eyes scanned his chest up to his broad shoulders. My eyes followed up his neck, his chin and his jaw, up his entire squared, chiseled face. I gasped. Butterflies of excitement filled my stomach.

Me: Emalickel!

Tears filled my eyes. I buried my face into his immaculate chest, as he wrapped his secure reassuring arms around me. I heard his voice as it echoed with words in my mind.

Emalickel: ***It is okay. You are safe now.***

I felt guilty and scared, relieved and overwhelmed. I felt like this whole ordeal was my fault. I burst into tears. Embarrassed of the other warriors watching us, I spoke to Emalickel through thoughts. I knew he could hear me.

Me: ***Emalickel, I'm so sorry. I don't even know what to say.***

Emalickel: ***Do not cry. Everything is going to be alright, do you hear me?***

I continued to cry anyway—I think it was from relief. He placed his hands on either side of my face and gently lifted my head up to look at him. He spoke aloud this time.

Emalickel: Do you hear me, Adrienne? Everything is alright. We are all well.

He gently smiled at me.

Emalickel: All is well.

He watched as a tear rolled from my eye. Then, he wiped it from my face with his thumb, and paused to stare down at me. He suddenly changed his focus as he to rustled to remove the armored-vest from his body and dropped it to the floor. Under it he wore a black sleeveless tunic. He pulled my head into his chest. He held my head with both arms and squeezed me even closer into him. He nestled his head with mine and I felt his hands stroking my hair. I could feel warmth radiating from him.

42. Artist: Tunes of Fantasy (Florian Bur)
Song: White Angel

I pulled away to briefly look at up at him once again. I couldn't believe it was really Emalickel. When I looked around, I noticed we were no longer on the dark ship. We were standing in a thick, beautiful, grassy valley. There was a gentle wintergreen-invigorated breeze.

Me: Where are we?

Emalickel: We are back in Dillectus—safe and sound.

He gazed all around us at the scenery for a moment before continuing.

Emalickel: I needed to be alone with you. I know you have been through a lot, and there is yet still so much for you to learn, but this is something I feel you need to know now.

He grabbed my hands with his. His eyes pierced into mine.

Emalickel: I want you to know... I love you, Adrienne of Earth—so incredibly much. I have felt this way since long before you even knew me. I would move the heavens for you. This is not a dream. This is not a fantasy. This is real. And, if you are willing, when your mortal life expires, and you have fully reawakened to your innerself, you may return here to Lapoi. It would be my honor, and an absolute pleasure, to have you at my side from there on—but only if you wish to do so. Your happiness is my priority.

Looking into my eyes, he brushed the hair strands which gently blew across my face from the breeze. It seemed all my hopes and dreams were coming true. There he was, all I had ever wanted, in a world full of everything I had ever dreamed of. I was overwhelmed by the reality of these manifestations. Not only did I get to meet a supreme being who shared all kinds of knowledge and experiences with me, but I had just received an invitation, directly from him, to enjoy the experience for the rest of my existence alongside him. And even more, he was so damn attractive. We stared only briefly at one another before I became overwhelmed and dizzy. My legs became weak and my knees gave out from under me. I fell into Emalickel's arms. Embracing me, he gently lowered us to lay on the soft, warm ground.

He held me there in his arms with a compassionate expression. Words could not even begin to explain how I felt about him. I felt so connected and in-tune with him. I couldn't see myself without him. All I knew is that I wanted to be with him forever in this magical place. There was this insuppressible desire to be with him. It felt like our souls had come from the same source, once upon a time, and now it was as if they were reuniting after a long time away from one other.

Still he continued to gaze down at me with love and understanding behind his eyes. A gentle smile grew on his face. He appeared to be proud and nodded his head. It was as if he had heard my thoughts and was giving me confirmation of their truth.

He licked his lips and slowly began to lean down into me. We closed our eyes. Our warm lips gently and timidly grazed across one another a few times. We both knew of our desires for each other but were hesitant of the newness of the reality that it was happening. I felt so free. I clenched his body and pulled it in closer to mine. I kept the hold on him as he nestled into my neck. I wanted to feel Emalickel become a part of me. My body just couldn't get close enough to his. I wanted to unite with him, as one. I wanted to feel him deep within me.

Emalickel pulled away from our embrace to stare into my eyes back and forth.

Emalickel: Are you certain? Is this what you want, truly?

He had read my mind again. Trusting in him completely, I smiled confidently in agreement.

Looking around, he began sitting up with me. I never took my eyes from him. He appeared to lock his eyes on something in the distance behind us. He paused to think for a moment before helping me to my feet. He was still looking into the distance as he spoke.

Emalickel: Come here.

He pulled me in close with his arms once again. This time, he was looking down at me and used both hands to slowly move my face to look up at him. The scenery around us started to fade into another place. We appeared to be inside a beautiful white room with sheer chiffon drapes which blew as they hung from several arched windows.

He grabbed me by the shoulders and turned me so that my back was to the draped archways. Then, he began walking forward, which in turn, caused me to walk backward. Once the momentum was going, he moved his hands to hold my face again. We kept walking until I fell backwards onto a large bed. The mattress felt very similar to memory foam but was slightly softer.

43. Artist: Audiomachine (Ivan Torrent)
Song: Wars of Faith (Extended to 4:30)

Emalickel kicked off his boots before crawling onto the bed with me on his hands and knees. I followed his lead. As he continued crawling forward, I scooted myself backward to maintain my position underneath him. When both of our bodies were entirely on the bed, Emalickel slowly lowered his head to mine. Our lips met and pressed firmly against one another intensely. He breathed in deeply. He lowered his body to mine by shifting his weight onto his elbows instead of his hands.

Our lips parted to allow one another inside. Our tongues danced passionately with one another. He leaned onto one arm to allow his other hand freedom. It felt warm as it held the side of my face. After a moment, he slid his hand down my neck and traced down my arm to my waist. He grabbed my hip and squeezed it fervidly as I heard him take in another lustful deep breath. The kiss intensified. Emalickel's warm hand continued over to my stomach and moved up to my chest until he clutched one of my breasts.

Against my thigh, I felt a long, thick bulge begin to rise and harden beneath his black trousers. He pressed it against my leg. I broke away from the kiss to let out a yearning cry for him. Our hands began exploring all over each other. My nails gently scratched down the muscular ripples of his back while he continued to move his hands in the path from my face, to my neck, to my breasts.

Our entire bodies began moving with one another and rubbing against each other. Our breathing became more rapid and extreme. Our body temperatures were rising, and our intimate areas became filled with aches of desire.

Emalickel pulled away from our kiss and looked into my eyes while catching his breath. He was trying to gain permission to enter me. Upon a slight nod of my head, I closed my eyes submitting to him. Still mounting me, he sat up to remove his tunic. He slowly slid my dress up with his hand as it grazed up my inner thigh. He inched himself up with his knees to get closer, while untying his trousers and removing them from his legs.

My heart skipped a beat as I felt his warm, smooth intimate area brush against mine. I let out a craving moan. This caused his bulge to become even harder. He lowered his chest to mine and nestled his head into the side of my neck. I heard Emalickel let out bursts of air and quiet moans under his breath as he allowed his throbbing hardness to gently brush against my intimate area. He steadily increased the intensity of this until I felt him begin to push it against me. My eyes closed as I prepared for the ecstasy he was leading up to. I felt him lift his head from my neck.

He was looking into my eyes as he allowed himself to slowly slip himself inside of me. His pupils dilated as he continued all the way in, deeper and deeper. We both couldn't help but moan loudly as he filled me completely. An intense cry of pleasure from me echoed throughout the entire room as he chose to hold this position for a minute. I felt how thick and large he was as he remained pushed in so deeply. Then he slowly glided himself back out, and then back in again. Steadily picking up the pace, he continued pumping faster and faster until his pace was almost in unison with our breaths. The more rapid our breathing became, the more rapidly he pushed himself in and out.

Emalickel lowered his head to mine and wrapped me tightly with both his arms and legs. My pleasure escalated. I enjoyed being beneath him as his body engulfed mine. I felt safe and protected by his power and mass. He had complete control in his mount on me. It stimulated me to know how easy it would be for him to dominate me, yet I knew he wouldn't do such because he knew of my trust in him and exhibited such self-control. He was civilized and in control of himself, yet there was a touch of dominating primal in his movements; just the way I liked it. I had never felt that before Emalickel.

He began shaking as his speed increased; faster and faster, harder and harder. We both breathed and moaned together as he continued his strong thrusts into me. My body began to tremble. I felt him grab onto me tightly. He clenched me harder with his arms and legs as he let out a loud moan. I knew he was approaching climax. This made me throb with heat in preparation.

44. Artist: PostHaste Music (Mark Petrie)
Song: Convergence

Then, I felt him lift his head from me. He whispered with authority.

Emalickel: Look at me.

I looked up at him, but it was hard to not roll my eyes into the back of my head or close them in pleasure. He repeated a bit louder and sterner.

Emalickel: Look at me.

I gained enough control of myself to maintain eye contact. His aqua-blue eyes pierced right into me.

Emalickel: I will only complete myself with you. Are you ready?

I wasn't sure if I would be able to climax. I was no good at climaxing on-demand. Emalickel spoke in a sultry whisper against my ear.

Emalickel: If you're ready . . . I will provide it to you.

I wasn't sure if I understood what he meant.

He groaned deeply several times as he gave a few final strong thrusts inside of me. I felt his long, thick shaft begin to pulsate against my walls as the warmth of his ejaculation pumped forcefully into me. He maintained eye contact with me as his pupils suddenly dilated once again. A wave of energy shot through my chest, and I felt a surge of pleasure travel downward, shocking my nether-region with ecstasy. I felt myself pulsating intimately along with him. I cried out and latched onto him as I convulsed with him. I had never felt anything so physically pleasurable. What had he done to me? My body was feeling sensations I had never felt before. I couldn't help but scream out. My body began shuddering uncontrollably in ecstasy. We both held onto each other as the intense convulsing continued.

Suddenly, my torso began to tingle, almost like the sensation of excited butterflies, but then it spread to everywhere throughout my body. It traveled into my head. I opened my eyes. Looking at our bodies, I noticed a fog being emitted from the both of us. It was all the colors of a rainbow. It blended together in a dance all around and within our bodies. His energy was literally blending with mine. It felt tremendously invigorating and took my breath away. This blending lasted a minute or two. We then laid there for a time, catching our breath again.

We finally approached a calm and coherent state again. Emalickel removed his body from mine and rolled over next to me on his back. He placed my head onto his chest and gently stroked my hair. My eyes grew heavy. My body had never felt so relaxed. I felt so safe and protected. Feeling secure and guarded, I allowed myself to drift to sleep in his arms as an uncontrollable tired overcame me.

7

THE REVEAL

45. Artist: Hans Zimmer
Song: Time

I felt peaceful. My eyes began to slowly open as I awoke from my slumber. My bed felt so soft and warm. Smiling, I remember thinking to myself, *what a wonderful, beautiful, long-lasting dream!*

Feeling depressed that it had ended, I knew I must go on with the routine of real life. It felt like I had been sleeping for days. Suddenly, I was slightly panicked. *Oh my gosh! What time is it? I need to get ready for work! Am I late?* As my eyes grew wider, and I became more aware. I realized my surroundings were unfamiliar. I was not in my room, nor in my own familiar bed.

I sat up to get a better look at everything around me. The first thing I noticed was how incredibly large the room was. It was about 900 square-feet with an immaculate 20-foot cathedral-style ceiling, which was outlined with recessed lighting and contained a diamond chandelier.

The walls of the room contained many arches and advanced architectural designs. There were many large windows, large decorative mirrors, and pewter and bronze decorations along the walls. A slight breeze and soft light came streaming in through the sheer white curtains, which hung from the arched doorways along the wall to my left and at the foot of the bed. Both archways led to two different 600 square-foot balconies which were connected by a bridge. On my right there was another large arched doorway which was open. It looked like it led down a hallway which opened into a dining room. There was another arched door in the adjacent corner of that wall which led to what looked like a bathroom.

The bed I sat upon was larger than any I had ever seen before. It contained no footboard but had an eloquent headboard, which was built to act like a decorative wall. The headboard was padded and consisted of white velvet circles, which intertwined with one another and were outlined by thick gold into an arched shape. The pillows and sheets were white. The large plush comforter which lay atop the sheets was white and gold to match the headboard. The bed sat upon a raised area of the floor which was trimmed in gold.

Behind the giant headboard of the bed was a white sitting area with a white fireplace. The couch and chairs were beige to match the fluffy, square rug on the floor. There was another smaller archway in the white room behind the headboard, which also led to the huge 60-foot balcony I already mentioned. A diamond chandelier hung from the ceiling here in this room behind the bed.

I rose out of the bed and began walking on the smooth, furry, cream-colored carpeting which filled the room. I noticed I was wearing an unfamiliar long, white, chiffon dress with a one-sleeve Grecian design. It was accented with diamonds and had pewter beading around the waist-line.

I headed towards the large mirror which hung on the wall between those arched doorways to the right of the bed. Slowly, I crept closer to the mirror. As I walked, I noticed my skin was silky, smooth and seemed to glow a deep, healthy bronze as if I had been lying out in the sun at the beach for a day.

A slight smile came across my face. Everything about me looked the same but improved. I wasn't wearing any make-up, but my features looked as if I were. My eyelashes were full and dark, my cheeks and eyes were defined with bronze-pink shading, and my lips glowed a soft nude pink. My hair was long and dark brown, and it flowed of beautiful, shining, loose, wavy curls which blew gracefully as the breeze continued to drift in through the windows.

A small diamond pendant hung at my collar bone by a tiny silver chain. The diamonds were arranged in a trinity symbol and looked very familiar. I brought my hand up to touch it. It was just like the golden symbol I had seen on Emalickel's cape. *My dream was real? Was I still on Lapoi?*

Excitement suddenly overwhelmed my entire body. In awe, my slight smile turned into a huge grin. Wide-eyed, I watched myself in the mirror as I shook my head in disbelief.

No way. It's impossible! This can't be real. Is this really happening? Was it a dream? What is going on?

46. Artist: Eurielle
Song: Je t'Adore

My overwhelmed emotions caused my legs to grow weak. I turned around towards the arched doors leading to the balconies. I took a deep breath of the crisp air blowing from that direction. The scent somehow comforted me as if I were home. Still smiling, I walked to the right-most arched door and stepped outside onto the balcony. It was about sixty feet from the ground and overlooked a grassy valley surrounded by a snow-capped mountain range. To the left and around the corner, was the second balcony. A bridge connected the two. The view from the second balcony was woodlands containing tall birch trees of yellow, orange, and red leaves. As the breeze gently blew across my face, I leaned forward on the white concrete railing of the balcony and closed my eyes. I heard nothing but the breeze which gently blew. *This can't be real.* I thought to myself. *There's no way this is happening in real life! I must be stuck in some kind of vivid, looping dream.*

It suddenly felt very warm like on the first morning of the springtime. A breeze began to bring with it a familiar, comforting, clean leather scent. My eyes still closed, I lifted my chin to inhale and absorb this familiar aroma. There was a presence with me—I could feel it raising the hairs on my skin.

Then, I felt a warm sensation at my back. Two large warm hands slid across my shoulders and gently squeezed them. Butterflies of anticipation filled my stomach. My breaths became short, and I began to tremble. Along the right side of my neck I felt a soft scruffy face brush against me. A warm breath teased my ear as a familiar soothing voice whispered to me.

Emalickel: Is it real? That is not the question you should be asking yourself. The question you should be asking yourself is how is it real?

When I recognized the voice, my heart jumped into my throat as I became overjoyed. I exhaled and whispered in a gasp to myself, *Emalickel!* Slowly, I turned around.

There he was—tall, strong, handsome Emalickel was gazing down at me with those brilliant glowing eyes. His presence made me feel at ease, and he looked even more handsome than I had remembered.

Me: Emalickel!

Emalickel: Is it real because you imagined it? Or did you imagine it because it is real? Thoughts create reality, just as well as reality creates thoughts. Either way, this proves your experience here is indeed real.

I remained silent in attempt to mask out the intense lust I desired for him. We continued staring at one another. I knew Emalickel felt mutual lust for me, but he broke the silence.

Emalickel: Will you stay for a while?

For a while? I'll stay for as long as he'd let me!

Me: You know I will.

He moved his hands down to hold mine. He held his gaze for a moment, and then he licked his lips before pulling me in closely towards him.

He tilted his head to the side and slowly bent in for a kiss. The moment our lips met, he squeezed my body tight. Our lips danced for several moments. We both began to breathe heavily the longer we kissed. We squeezed each other's bodies more and more closely to one another.

Emalickel suddenly stopped and pulled himself away. Catching his breath, he held my face in his hands and pressed his forehead against mine. Then, I heard his thought.

Emalickel: *There is still so much for you to learn.*

He gently let go of me and walked over to the rail of the balcony. His back was to me, as he looked out at the landscape.

Emalickel: I came up here to let you know there is a pressing matter I must tend to. While I am away, I will find a celestial to escort you while you finish tour of Lapoi.

He crossed his arms and leaned on the rail as he cocked his head to look over his shoulder. He didn't look directly at me, but rather kept me in his peripheral vision. His expression was relaxed yet appeared slightly agitated.

Emalickel: How about Thorenel? You did enjoy your time with him the other day, yes?

47. Artist: Mattia Cupelli
Song: Waves

Judging by the "as matter of fact" look on his face, I felt he was aware of my previous romantic encounter with Thorenel. The silence grew awkward, and I couldn't think of anything to say in response. My mind was cluttered with thoughts of confusion.

Emalickel looked back out at the landscape.

Emalickel: It is settled, then. I will call to Thorenel. When you arrive to him, I want you to stay with him during the time of my absence.

He closed his eyes and he communicated in telepathy. I heard his thoughts but was unable to understand them as they were transmitted in something like Latin or Aramaic. Crossing his arms again, Emalickel turned to face me. There was a brief pause as he locked his stare to me. His expression remained straight.

Emalickel: Thorenel is expecting you, so I will send you to him. You have my word I will see you again very soon.

I still didn't understand why he would volunteer Thorenel. I couldn't stop wondering why. I was confused and worried. *Does he know about it? Is he angry? If he doesn't know, should I tell him? Why would he choose Thorenel to escort me?* Emalickel interrupted my thoughts with a stern tone.

Emalickel: You are so accustomed to your world. Do you think of me as an oblivious mortal? Of course I know! There is nothing that happens to you in which I do not know.

He knows! I was frightened and embarrassed. Emalickel's demeanor quickly became more frustrated.

Emalickel: How could you think I wouldn't know?! I have known all along. I can read your every thought. I can read Thorenel's thoughts. Seeing how Thorenel is my celestial-pair, and since you

and I have physically engaged, Thorenel is now paired to you as well. Most intimate connections on our celestial plane are grouped into three individuals. This is not unusual, so it is not the matter in which disappoints me so intensely. What disappoints me is the fact that you tried to shield it from me. You tried to hide something from me.

He pulled the hood of his cape onto his head. There was a silence before Emalickel spoke in a smooth quieter tone.

Emalickel: My presence is required. I must be going.

Although I was curious of where he was going and what he was about to do, I did not ask as I knew he would volunteer to tell me in his own time. I also knew he seemed a bit on-edge, so I did not want to overstep my boundaries.

Emalickel: You have been on Lapoi for quite some time now. As a result, you are feeling the energies of teleportation less drastically. Also, since you and I have blended ourselves with each other, you will steadily become accustomed to my abilities as our energy molecules intertwine. One day, you will be able to perform every power of mine on the celestial plane.

He stepped towards me and placed his hands along the back of my head to cup it. He leaned in to touch his forehead against mine. With that, I saw a bright flash of light, and then found myself standing in the cottage home which Thorenel had created for me. It had been cleaned-up and repaired.

Thorenel was already there, leaning on the door frame with his arms crossed at his chest. His back was turned as he looked outside, but I could see that he was wearing his beige cloak. His hood was off, and rays of white light beamed through the strands of his wavy blond hair. He looked radiant. I still felt attracted to him. He had this protective, wise, warrior vibe that went along with his rugged alpha-male appearance.

I knew he was aware of my presence in the cottage because he slightly turned his head to the side as if trying to view me in his peripherals. He was silent, and I could feel tension in the air. I tried to break the awkward silence.

Me: Hi, Thorenel.

Keeping his arms crossed, he turned around. He looked at me briefly raising both eyebrows as if to say "hello." He wouldn't maintain eye contact with me.

Me: So, what are we going to do today?

His answer was quiet and seemed forced as if he wasn't in the mood to socialize.

Thorenel: We are doing what has been ordered for us to do.

He turned back toward the doorway to head outside.

Me: Why do you seem upset?

He moved his hands to fold down in front of him. Thorenel stopped in the doorway and tilted his head up to look at the sky outside. He signed loudly and replied with animosity.

Thorenel: Emalickel isn't the only one who can hear your thoughts. Did you forget that I, too, can hear your wandering mind?

Again, he turned around in the doorway to face me. When he spoke, his voice carried a tone of resentment.

Thorenel: You must rid yourself of guilt and fear, Adrienne, of all the negative emotions within you. Accept things as they come and embrace the experiences. Be proud of love. Why would you try to conceal ours? Why would you speak so openly of your feelings for Emalickel to me, yet try to hide the feelings shared between us from Emalickel? It disappoints me.

He was still a bit disgruntled.

Thorenel: You are still so attached to the mortal plane. All its little laws, rules, and morals of control and constraint do not exist here. You must let go.

Silence fell within the room before Thorenel spoke again. He looked down and took a deep breath.

Thorenel: I am sorry. I apologize. I am being harsh, and I have allowed my ego to sneak to the surface. All I ask is that you call on me every time you desire me—every single time. Even at the slightest desire for me, I want your calling.

Thorenel stepped forward and came over to me. He touched my shoulder and bent down so that his face was level with mine.

Thorenel: Please, please do not let that be sparingly.

He kept his gaze on me for a moment before continuing.

Thorenel: There are no limits to how often, when, or where you can call on me. Even if you are with Emalickel, he shall not anger should you call on me. I shall either join you both, or you and I may be alone. Brothers bound by celestial law, Emalickel and I both belong to you, and you belong to both him and me. We both share a part in pleasing you—spiritually, emotionally, and physically.

48. Artist: Audiomachine
Song: No Matter What

He held his gaze into my eyes. I desired him, especially since we were alone in the same cottage house where our connection had first begun. I wanted to feel his lips on mine. I craved his strong arms to embrace my body so that I could feel the warmth radiating from his body pressed firmly against mine. I yearned for him to do with me as he pleased. I wanted him to take me right there, so we could finish what we had started a previous time ago.

He zoned-in on me. I could feel his mind exploring within mine. Thorenel tilted his head to the side and slightly squinted his eyes, as if in concentration, trying to read my thoughts more deeply. I could feel a sensation, like that of a warm, gentle breeze blowing throughout the inside of my head. I knew it was him. I knew that he was aware of my thoughts of desire for him.

Still, I continued thinking, as I could not control my thoughts.

I knew he had gotten a clear read on my thoughts when he shifted his feet closer to me. He moved his hands to hold my face gently. He slowly pulled it towards his without ceasing eye contact. He pressed his forehead to mine and transmitted his thoughts.

Thorenel: ***You tremble . . .***

He paused, gently sliding his hands down the sides of my neck, continuing down my sides to my hips.

Thorenel: ***. . . yet, it is not fear I see in your eyes.***

I caught a slight smile on his face before our lips brushed against each other. Without breaking contact, our lips danced with each other, growing in intensity, moment by moment. My mouth began to open, inviting his tongue to enter. He pressed his lips even firmer against mine as our tongues began sliding against one another.

Thorenel breathed harder and his hands began to slide passionately up and down my body. He walked forward, thus pushing me backwards, until I fell to the bed. Wasting no time, he used my underarms to scoot my body the rest of the way onto the bed. He rushed to remove his boots before positioning himself on top of me. He leaned his weight on his right arm, while his left hand slid up my satin gown along my outer thigh. Then it grazed across my breasts, slipping each of them out from behind the neckline.

After catching sight of this, he pushed himself up, straddling my torso between his knees. He removed his tunic in a hurry. Breathless, Thorenel scanned our bodies, which still wore clothes. He shook his head with impatience. Leaning his weight onto his fists, which were to the sides of my shoulders, he closed his eyes and breathed in a long deep breath. As he exhaled, I felt a warm breeze and noticed we were glowing in a white, shimmering light. It circulated all around us.

49. Artist: Audiomachine (Ivan Torrent)
Song: Wars of Faith (Extended to 4:30)

When the light dimmed, we were both completely undressed with the sheet drawn over us. Before either of us had any time to look at the other, we locked our lips together again, and he pressed my body further into the bed using the force of his body.

His body felt solid and dense. He was so strong. I felt vulnerable to his strength. It would be so easy for him to destroy me in one swipe of his power, yet he was so tender with me. He was still assertive in his passion and maintained a carnal nature, as a lion is with his lioness. Thorenel interrupted my thoughts with his whisper.

Thorenel: My strength means nothing when I am so weakened by your touch.

I had gotten carried away in my thoughts and forgotten that Thorenel could hear every one of them. He locked eyes with me. He was trying to receive permission to enter me.

Without hesitation, I eagerly nodded.

And that was all he needed. He looked back down and began rubbing the head of his throbbing extension along the outside of my intimate area. I was instantly stimulated. His thickness began to slowly penetrate me. He looked at me with craving eyes. Slowly he glided inside me, deeper and deeper until he was fully and completely all the way inside. He pressed himself in and held it there while letting out a deep pleasurable primal-moan. He grabbed my body, to press me closer to his. By this time, he, too, was trembling. After a moment, he slid back out, but only briefly before sliding back in and moaning again. He slid out, then back in. His speed grew faster and faster as he thrust harder and harder.

This intensity grew until his pace stabilized at a peak rate. I could feel the walls of my intimate area clenching around his. At that very moment, Thorenel yelled out in pleasure. Then, I could feel his member pulsating warmth inside me. Unlike anything I'd ever felt before, it continued to pulsate more and more rapidly inside me. It vibrated my entire genital area, both inside and out. I had never felt anything so amazing. His head dropped to my chest and his hands clenched down on the bed. My intimate folds swelled full in arousal —ready to burst. Thorenel whispered breathlessly to me.

Thorenel: I won't stop until you are complete.

He continued vibrating his extension inside me. I felt it all through the most sensitive of areas—from my inner walls to the tip of the outside. I felt sensual sensations even in the base of my back and below. He truly had on him an instrument made for divine pleasures. His intimacy performed in a way that brought me to convulsions as it emitted vigorous vibrations without rest. I felt myself begin pulsating with warmth inside. Thorenel continued vibrating himself inside me, looking at me intensely, waiting for me to explode from what he was providing to me.

I fell into complete ecstasy. I gave into the pulsating sensations he had been offering so generously and continuously. A loud erotic moan escaped my mouth. I couldn't hold back as my entire body tensed up and released the all the desires and pleasures that had built-up within it. From the unfinished yearnings of the first intimate session with Thorenel, to the cravings within this session, he had completely satisfied them all. Physically engaging with Thorenel was electrifying—mind-blowing—stupefying!

50. Artist: Kevin Ohlsson
Song: Returning Heroes

After experiencing the magical swarming and blending of our energies within an invigorating colorful fog around us, our bodies finally released. We continued convulsing for a few moments as we caught our breath. Thorenel was still propped up on his hands with his face dropped down towards my chest. Occasionally, I could still feel him convulse inside me, which made me convulse. We lay there recovering until our bodies finally relaxed with one another.

Thorenel removed himself from me and slid his right arm underneath my head as he positioned himself on his back, bringing my head to rest on his chest. It was apparent that Emalickel and Thorenel exhibited similar mannerisms after intimacy. Thorenel covered us up in the white fluffy sheets of the bed. Neither of us spoke nor said any words. There was no need to. Thorenel stared up at the ceiling with his other arm behind his head. An overwhelming sleepiness overcame me. I fought to keep my eyes open.

Thorenel: It is normal for your body to react in this manner after engaging with Emalickel and me. It is imperative that you rest. The reason you feel exhausted is because your body is overloaded in processing information from my celestial energy. It is in the process of fusion with your mortal energy. You are about to enter a deep state of hibernation while your body works at intertwining my celestial molecules with your mortal molecules. With my energy literally flowing inside you, you are becoming more closely attuned to me and my powers. This will happen each time you engage with me or Emalickel. Eventually, you will share the same abilities and powers as both of us.

I felt my body slip into total relaxation. My eyes closed before I could even respond to Thorenel.

The nest thing I knew, I was waking up again to the sound of someone moving about the room. I opened my eyes and saw that I was still in the bed at the cottage. Thorenel was standing by the fireplace pouring himself something to drink. He glanced up at me, then back down at the cup.

Thorenel: Ah, there you are! That was quite a slumber! You were out for almost seventy-eight hours.

As I sat up, I noticed I was wearing the beautiful Grecian dress again along with the sparkling jewels. My body felt strong, clean, refreshed, rejuvenated, and completely energized.

Thorenel: Come along. We must continue our tour of Lapoi. Emalickel wants you to see something very special.

Thorenel extended out his hand to me.

Me: Does he know about us being intimate?

Thorenel chuckled to himself.

Thorenel: Are you serious!?! Of course he knows! He came by yesterday to check on you, but you were in your slumber.

Me: Was he okay with everything?

Thorenel: It's a silly question, and deep down, you know it is a silly question. It would be like me asking you if it is okay that I breathe. This is not the petty, selfish mortal plane. He and I are a celestial-pair, and this is how it goes on the celestial plane. It's nothing unusual or anything to feel uneasy about.

Once again, he extended his hand out to me, inviting me to take hold of it. I stood up, walked to him, and placed my hand into his.

Thorenel: Now close your eyes, and do not open them until I tell you to do so.

I smiled and closed my eyes in excitement and trust. There was a brief pause. Then, Thorenel said very quietly.

Thorenel: By the way, you are glowing with radiance!

I felt Thorenel wrap me into his arms and pull me into him. The lights and vibrations began. I knew we were teleporting somewhere. Then the silence grew back into the sounds of awareness again. I knew we had arrived at our destination. Thorenel released his embrace of me but continued to hold my hand while he exhaled a sigh.

Thorenel: Okay. You can open your eyes now.

51. Artist: Mattia Cupelli
Song: Mooncatcher

My excitement built as I slowly began to open my eyes. Only, I wasn't surprised at all. We were staring at snow-capped mountains in the distance. I continued to scan the scenery. There was a wheat field to my right, but I saw nothing else of surprise. Only more snow-capped mountains. Thorenel let go of my hand, but I could see he was looking at me.

Me: I don't understand the surprise. What is this? What are we looking at?

Thorenel leaned in and whispered in my ear.

Thorenel: Behind you.

He placed his hands on my shoulders and guided me. slowly turning me around, revealing the surprise. I gasped to myself. I instantly recognized what it was. I found myself staring at the enormous, impeccable castle-like structure! It reached up into the clouds of the sky. It stood directly in front of me, lit up like a piece of heaven—immaculate and breathtaking. It made me feel inferior from its size. It took my breath away.

Me: The castle!

Thorenel: Indeed. Though, we refer to it as the Palace of Lapoi.

We stood there for a moment while I absorbed its enticing beauty. I admired the white and golden palace with the gleaming ocean in the background behind it. Then, Thorenel teleported us right up to the structure. The sculpted arches were lit glamorously with recessed lighting. The top contained blocked peaks. The whole structure itself was lined in golden trim. The face was made from smooth white stone. Slowly, I scanned every detail from top to bottom.

Thorenel guided me along the stone walkway until we came to a set of huge gold and white arched double-doors.

Me: Can we go inside?

Thorenel looked at me and chuckled. He gently grabbed one of my hands again.

Thorenel: Yes, but this is only the gate, gorgeous.

As we approached the gated doors, they slowly began to open inward by themselves. The gates opened to a glowing, beautifully landscaped, courtyard area with enormous statues of archangels. There were stone paths and architectural structures throughout the courtyard. Pink petunias in huge stone pots lined the central walkway which lead to the massive palace doors. Perfectly trimmed, soft, green, grass lay across the rest of the landscape. A massive four-story palace stood at the center of it all. Two warriors guarded the front doors of the palace. As Thorenel and I approached, they began opening the doors for us. As we walked by, they looked at Thorenel and nodded in respect. Their eyes discretely followed me.

The palace doors opened into a huge throne hall and a long, perpendicular hallway. A massive archway opened to the Throne Hall. We proceeded towards this archway, but first we crossed a long, perpendicular hallway which stretched 100 yards to the left and 100 yards to the right. After crossing the hallway, we walked under the massive archway and into the giant Throne Hall. We walked along a centrally-located aisle on a black rug which was outlined in golden trim. The ceiling above the aisle was dome-shaped and was open all the way to the second floor.

The Throne Hall was approximately 100 yards deep and 60 yards wide. At the opposite end of the long aisle, was a semi-circular stairway which led up to a glowing throne area. Behind it was another semi-circular set of stairs leading up to an immaculate balcony which overlooked a grassy valley with snow-capped mountains in the distance. Three massive open archways led to this balcony behind the thrones. Sheer white chiffon drapes hung between each of these arches and blew gracefully with the breeze.

The entire aisle was lined with a series of white, marble archways on each side. Looking up, I noticed several Corinthian-style columns lining the balconies along the second floor. Each opening of the archways and columns was about 15 feet tall and 10 feet wide. There were about 20 archways extending down the aisle to the throne area. The floor itself was glossy white marble containing hints of gold and bronze.

Our footsteps echoed as we continued to walk further into the palace. Along the way, I noticed several large arched windows on both floors tucked away about 20 yards from the central aisle. The windows were hidden behind the archways which lined the aisle. These windows overlooked beautiful courtyards on both sides. So, the aisle itself was 20 yards wide, then there was a wall of archways to the left and right sides of the aisle. The arched windows were 20 yards behind these archways.

52. Artist: Steve Jablonsky
Song: My Name is Lincoln

Midway down the aisle, to the left and right, were stairways leading to the second floor. I slowed my pace. Everything glowed of divinity. I felt so small inside the majestic palace.

Thorenel's mouth tugged into a smile. He continued to guide me down the main aisle towards the throne. As we got closer, I noticed two large, golden emblems, resembling the Celtic trinity symbol, on the white, marble floor. This golden symbol was also etched into the black rug which ran along the aisle and on every other black tapestry which hung from the walls between the archways. The archways near the end of the aisle, on both the first and second floors, formed a large semi-circle around the throne area, making it more spacious and open near the throne. It was here, on each side of the aisle, the two large, golden, trinity emblems where engraved on the floor.

Down at the throne, two men were wearing plain, white, robes. They were assisting a much larger, important-looking man who was wearing a beige, hooded cloak. His cloak was lined with gold and contained the golden trinity symbol on the back. The assistants were in front of the important man and were reviewing with him some sort of glowing golden tablet. I could hear them talking, but the powerful echo of the palace made it difficult to understand what they said from where I stood. The important-looking man sat down on one of two white and gold thrones. He was facing our direction, but I couldn't see his face because of the shadow created by the hood of his cloak, and he was also blocked by the assistants. For a moment, he seemed to be looking in our direction, although I couldn't see his face. Then, he looked down at the tablet in his lap. I assumed the man on the throne was some kind of authority-figure.

My thoughts were interrupted by the sound of Thorenel's telepathy.

Thorenel: ***He is one of the two Princedoms in charge of the Kingdom of Lapoi. Come. It is time you are properly introduced to him.***

I became increasingly nervous as we approached the stairs of the throne. My thoughts raced. *What do I say? What if he doesn't like me? I hope we're not interrupting him from something. Should I bow? Was I dressed properly?*

I felt Thorenel place one of his hands on my shoulder.

Thorenel: You have nothing to worry about. Just be yourself.

Our footsteps continued to echo until we had reached the stairs. Two white lions were perched on either side of two gold and white throne chairs. Upon reaching the stairs, both lions changed their positions from lying to sitting upright. They stared right at me attentively. My heart raced in fear. We stopped. Thorenel cleared his throat, obtaining the attention of the Prince. Thorenel bowed his head before speaking aloud.

Thorenel: My Prince, please, excuse me. I hope this is a good time and mean not to interrupt.

The assistants moved to the side, and the Prince moved his head to look towards us. He didn't say anything. Thorenel continued.

Thorenel: May I introduce to you our guest of Lapoi? She derives from the mortal plane, from the planet they call Earth.

The Prince held up the golden tablet. The assisting men removed it from his hands. The Prince motioned for them to leave. The men walked down from the throne area, exited the stairs, and disappeared into the archways.

53. Artist: Two Steps from Hell
Song: Miracles

As soon as the assistants had moved, light from the windows beamed directly onto the Prince, making him glow of divinity. All else around him seemed to fade darker, making him stand out. Still though, his face was shadowed by the hood of his cloak. Still sitting on his throne, he motioned for me to come to him, using the first two fingers of one of his hands which rested upon the arm of the white and gold throne.

Thorenel slowly guided me up the stairs. When we arrived at the top, Thorenel used his free hand to subtlety squeeze my hand, which clenched onto his arm with a tight grip. Thorenel looked at my grasping hand and cleared his throat. I looked at him but shook my head, refusing to remove my hand from the security of him. He nodded reassuringly and looked at my hand once again. I felt so foolish, but I also felt overwhelmed and uncomfortable in the presence of this Prince. I didn't want to let go of the of Thorenel's arm. He patted my hand. After a slight struggle, he managed to pull himself away from my grip. My hand felt cold to the air as it had become comfortable to the growing heat from Thorenel's arm. I looked back at him. He was trying to keep from laughing. He was amused by my childish behavior. He nodded at me in reassurance to continue moving towards the Prince.

As I stepped before the Prince, I could feel the energy of his power emanating from him. I smiled but was so intimidated I couldn't muster up the courage to speak. It was hard to even breathe.

The Prince turned his head to look at Thorenel for a moment before his shadowed face returned to me. Slowly he began to stand. He stood at about seven feet tall and weighed about 350 pounds. I still couldn't see his face, but I could tell he was looking down at me with his eyes. He wore armor, like Thorenel, under his cloak. He also wore similar black boots which came nearly to his knees. I could see his sleeveless arms peeking from under his cloak, and I could tell he had a defined muscular stature. His skin was smooth and bronzed. His body was very attractive

Slowly, he reached for the hood of his cloak and began sliding it from his head. I was so nervous that my breathing became shallow. Time moved in slow motion as the hood fell back from the Prince's head. When it fell, I tilted my head to get a better look at him for he looked strikingly familiar. The Prince winked at me, and a sly smile grew across his face.

Me: Emalickel!?!

He gave me a reassuring nod.

My jaw dropped. My heart raced. I couldn't catch my breath. *A Princedom . . . THE Princedom of Lapoi! All this time, I've been with the prince of celestials without even knowing it!?*

Emalickel: It is true.

His demeanor was serious. He did not even flinch. With my mouth still open in disbelief, I looked behind my shoulder at Thorenel, who nodded to reassure me it was true.

Me: But . . . why didn't you tell me?

Emalickel soothingly rested his hands on the tops of my shoulders.

Emalickel: I am sorry for withholding this from you. I feared my status would influence your decisions. I wanted to make sure you chose me for who I am, not for my position or title. I also did not want to distract you from the others should you have interest in them. Now I know you chose me, not because of my status on Lapoi, but because of your love for me.

He paused to place my hands in his.

Emalickel: This palace is my home—it belongs to me. Having united with me, this is also your palace now—it belongs to you.

Blown away, I was completely silent.

Emalickel: Do you understand what I am telling you?

He smiled and motioned for me to sit in the empty throne next to his. He then took his seat as well.

Emalickel: You see, it is true, I am one of the Princedoms of Lapoi. The Kingdom of Lapoi belongs to me. I was chosen to watch over this realm of Millattus. In doing so, I was blessed with a gift from God. He showed me the presence of you. As sure as I sit here upon this throne known to be mine . . .

He scooted himself to the edge of his throne and leaned towards me so that his eyes were directly in line with mine. He took my hands into his before continuing. He engaged eye contact with me and spoke very slow and clearly.

Emalickel: ...and now you, Princess . . . are sitting upon yours.

My breath was taken away. Goosebumps scattered the surface of my skin. Butterflies of excitement swarmed the pits of my stomach. I felt doubt and disbelief. *There's no way this is true. I had to have misheard or misunderstood him.* His eyes remained serious as he searched my face for a reaction. He then began to smile at me. That is when the reality began to set-in. *This is really happening! I am with a Prince! I've become a Princess! I share a palace with a celestial Prince—with THE Celestial Prince over all life as we know it!* I was filled with mixed emotions: surprise, joy, and astonishment. I was absolutely flabbergasted. I could feel my eyes pooling with tears of joy and astonishment. I tried to cover this up by smiling and blinking the tears away. I wasn't sure what to say. There were no words I could find to even speak at all.

54. Artist: Really Slow Motion
Song: You Will Be This Legend

Emalickel began guiding me up the stairs, toward the open balcony behind the thrones. Sheer curtains were draped at the openings of three massive archways, but I could see they led out to an extensive balcony containing a giant pool on the left side. The entire balcony was about 60-feet by 60-feet. Cherry Blossom trees accented the balcony, one on each side out at the far end. Emalickel stopped at the top of the stairs to face me.

Emalickel: As Princedoms of Lapoi, our duties are simple: enlighten and protect the mortals of our realm and ensure God's will is done as it is given. Life here is pleasurable and fulfilling. You will learn so much more as you awaken but know this much now; as is the case with all mortals, you chose to leave your realm of divine origin to share in the mortal experience. You chose to forget your divinity, in order to procure your spiritual evolution. You chose to go to Earth, as you have many times before, for the adventurous unfolding of different experiences. You have not yet achieved your full evolutionary-expansion in the mortal plane, so your presence on Lapoi will not be permanent until you have

fulfilled your objectives. Know that someday, very soon, you will reside on Lapoi. I anxious wait for that day.

There was a low bridge which crossed over the pool on the balcony. Emalickel held my hand and guided me as we began crossing over it.

Emalickel: Until your more recent lifetimes, your energy blended in with the rest of the mortals. But several centuries ago, something began lighting-up inside you. I became drawn to you, hopelessly drawn to you. In the past, I had always felt that a third aspect to the Throne of Lapoi would only cause distraction, confusion, and disorder. I had no desire to find love with another. After noticing you, I knew I was about to make an exception. Still a little hesitant and nervous, I withheld from making contact with you for as long as I could, but my desire for you only continued growing. I couldn't resist any longer. That is when I came to seek you, meeting you within the astral plane you regularly crossed as you drifted into sleep.

Emalickel stopped to look at me. He brought my hands to his heart.

Emalickel: You want to know why I seemed so familiar to you the first time you physically saw me at the lake? My energy has been all around you for centuries. I was intrigued by you and desired to observe you and to protect you. Although you could not physically see me during that time, you sensed my presence and my energy. This is why you felt like you knew me at the lake, yet you didn't know from where. I have been immersed in your presence for a very long time now, periodically leaving Lapoi to watch over you. During my absences from Lapoi, the second Princedom is in charge. My closest brother, Thorenel, is the second Prince of Lapoi.

55. Artist: Future World Music
Song: Anthem of the World

I turned around to look at Thorenel who had been following behind us. He was walking up the second set of stairs to the balcony to join us. He had been looking around, but when he noticed I was looking at him, he exhibited a noble smile back at me. I remember the safe and secure feeling I felt, in that very moment, being in the presence of the two most exalted, prominent, and powerful celestials in the entire realm of man-kind!

Emalickel: You will learn more as you continue your spiritual journey of awakening. For now, come this way. Lapoi deserves to meet their Princess!

As we walked out beyond the bridge to the flat open balcony, the roof ended, and we could see the entire sky above us. I saw countless celestials scattered across the entire spread of land sixty feet below us. They were lined up in perfect rows all throughout the vast valley. For miles and miles, they stood by the hundreds of thousands, in complete silence, looking up at the large balcony in attention. Some wore the guard attire with golden armor and white capes, while others had on the warrior attire with black armor and red capes.

A breeze blew, and a swarm of white gulls flew by as Emalickel, Thorenel, and I joined hands and stepped out towards the balcony's edge together. Everyone was watching us. Emalickel released my hand to reach for the gold and diamond crown on his head. As he touched his crown, a duplicate one appeared in his hands. He lifted the duplicate from his head, while his own crown remained in its position. The new crown was a smaller, more feminine crown. It sparkled as it was covered in many small diamonds.

Emalickel: A princess needs her crown.

As he held the crown in his hands, it glistened like all the stars of space. I couldn't wait to feel it resting on my head.

56. Artist: Really Slow Motion
Song: End of An Era

Emalickel smiled and spoke to me quietly.

Emalickel: I am glad it pleases you. I am honored to be able to present it to you, Adrienne of Earth . . . Princess of Lapoi.

I smiled. Too excited to wait any longer, I released Thorenel's hand and knelt to Emalickel, so he could place the radiant, new crown on my head. Instead, he spoke loud enough for others to hear.

Emalickel: Rise from me. You need not ever kneel to me. We are one, and you are my equal. I do not kneel to myself at any point, on any given day, and so neither shall you.

He reached out to gently place the crown upon my head. It felt solid and heavy. Emalickel and Thorenel each took one of my hands again. I looked up at Thorenel, who was squeezing my hand extra tight. He was looking at me, smiling. He shook his head in disbelief and mouthed the word "beautiful."

Emalickel then addressed the countless celestials in the valley below very slowly and clearly.

Emalickel: Celestials of all Lapoi! For centuries, you have anticipated the day our kingdom would complete the Throne of Lapoi with the balance of three. That day has come! My brother and I, are eagerly and delightfully pleased to introduce to you . . .

In unison, Emalickel and Thorenel raised my hands into the air like a champion.

Emalickel: . . . your radiant, eternal, Princess of Lapoi!

Row by row, in perfect unison, like a wave, the celestials began to bow. I could hear the clanking of their armor and weapons as they repositioned themselves to a respectful kneel. The sight was extraordinarily beautiful. Hundreds of thousands of white capes and red capes were all blowing in the breeze as every celestial in the valley took to their knee. The red-caped warriors kneeled behind their swords, while the white-caped guards kneeled with their head dropped to their knee. Romenciel, Xabiel, Dennoliel, and Seronimel were positioned in front and center of all the other celestials. Wearing their beige, royal cloaks over their armor, they also knelt to their knee in respect. Every celestial, filling the valley of Dillectus for 20,000 acres, froze themselves in this position, maintaining it in perfect stillness.

The celestials looked up from their bowing positions. Emalickel and Thorenel each grabbed one of my legs and hoisted me onto their shoulders. They pumped their fists into the air, encouraging celebration and cheer from the celestials below. The celestials roared. In celebration, some jumped and threw their helmets into the air. Others roughed each other up in bear hugs, punches, and chest bumps. It looked like a massive football team celebrating an epic championship win. Golden and white fireworks exploded over the mountains on the horizon in the lavender and coral sky.

The Princedom brothers set me back down. Thorenel conjured a beige, hooded cloak. It was just like the cloak worn by Emalickel and his brothers, with many tiny diamonds sparkling throughout it. He draped the royal cloak across my shoulders. I felt complete.

8

CONCLUSION

57. Artist: Brunuhville
Song: Spirit of the Wild

Emalickel, Thorenel, and I rushed into the palace to celebrate among the rest of the Lapoians. The celebration lasted through the entire evening, which on Lapoi was about 20 hours.

It was so much fun! There was unlimited food, dancing, and pleasures. Everyone tasted the limitless varieties of foods and danced with endless stamina. No one became bored. I even found out that those in the celestial plane can become intoxicated with alcohol. Celestial molecules react to alcohol in the same way as the molecules in mortal bodies; however, there is no hangover effect in celestials because the alcohol is metabolized rather rapidly.

During the weeks following the celebration, Emalickel showed me his vast spectrum of abilities. He was by far the strongest on Lapoi. Basically, if it could be thought, Emalickel could make it happen. Anything. Anything at all. Through his thoughts alone things would manifest.

Knowing I always dreamed of living the life of a teenager in the 1950s, Emalickel received permission to take me to Earth during the 1950's era via the astral plane. As long as we didn't directly interact with the mortals, we could go where we pleased and do as we wanted. While scanning Time, Emalickel came across the close-knit community of Mayfield, Ohio in August of 1958. That is where he decided to take me for a few days.

Before we left Lapoi, Emalickel passed down the Lapoian Crown to Thorenel and left Millattus under his care. Being the second Princedom of Lapoi, Thorenel was always the second in command upon the absence of Emalickel.

Our visit to the 1950s lasted for three days. We observed many things from the astral plane in the town of Mayfield, Ohio in 1958. We dropped by the local high school on the first day and enjoyed watching sock-hopping teenagers discuss their dramatic lives among one another—the soda shop after school was even more entertaining!

Another day, we enjoyed going to several drive-in movies, and walking the town to see shops and diners. We also took an evening stroll around the town park. I also learned that two beings are able to share some private, intimate, and very sensual moments within the astral plane!

On the last day, we hitched a ride in a red convertible Thunderbird. The driver was on a road trip, and since he couldn't see us, we had a party in the backseat! Emalickel channeled the radio frequencies of the mortal plane and played them out of thin air within our astral plane bubble. We blared the music, which couldn't be heard in the mortal plane, and stood up in the backset to dance and act fools with one another.

After returning to Lapoi, Emalickel made me a promise that he and Thorenel both would be taking me on several trips in to come, not only to the most exotic and historical places and times on Earth, but to see the other mortal planets of Millattus, called Fynne and Grahst. In the meantime, we would enjoy our free day each week on Lapoi.

It became time for me to learn more about my place on Lapoi. Each day while Emalickel was tending to the orders, Thorenel would take me to the Education Quarters of the palace to train me on my powers. The Education Quarters was a giant circular-shaped room at the front of the palace, on the eastern side. It contained two floors of books, tables, refreshments, and study aids for magic abilities. The center of the Education Quarters was open to the second floor, so one could pier down from the second story onto the first floor. All the decorations and construction of this part of the palace was made to resemble a medieval time. Candles were the source of lighting and, wood was the source of all the walls, ceiling, and furniture. There were many trophy boxes with ancient artifacts enclosed within. There were several celestials from all over Lapoi who regularly visited the Education Quarters.

Once per week, we went into the Chapel of the palace to worship God. It was similar to church but much less organized. Emalickel and Thorenel alternated weeks leading. All celestials were equally divine, but only the higher-ranking celestials attended the Chapel because there was only enough room for 1,300 celestials.

58. Artist: Brunuhville
Song: Celestial Temple

One day I had been sitting in my throne practicing conjuration while I waited for Emalickel to return from receiving the orders from the Dominion. I was trying to conjure a crystal sphere between my hands, but instead I only conjured flickering light. My powers were still at a beginner's level. I rolled my eyes in frustration.

Emalickel arrived back. He had flown in through the open archways behind the thrones. I felt the breeze from his flight blow lightly against my skin. I could smell his fresh scent with the trace of new leather. I turned around in my throne chair to see him. He appeared somber. He looked at me, frozen for a moment, without smiling. Then, he migrated to take a seat on his throne next to mine. He weakly slouched in his seat and rested his face on his fist. It appeared as if he were in deep thought about something which bothered him. He was silent. He did not even greet me.

Me: Emalickel? Are you alright?

Keeping his stare to the ground he replied in a lifeless mumble.

Emalickel: I received the orders.

There was a long pause.

Me: Is everything ok?

He looked straight ahead, took a deep breath, then he looked at me.

Emalickel: One of the orders is . . . going to be very hard to carry out.

Me: Why? Maybe I could help you.

He looked straight ahead, in the general direction of the aisle of the Throne Hall. Continuing to look somber, he closed his eyes as he took a deep breath in and exhaled it. Without words, he looked down and kept his gaze low. I knew something was terribly wrong. My stomach sank in fear.

Me: Emalickel? Tell me. What is it?

There was another long silence before he finally spoke.

Emalickel: In his orders, the Dominion included an order from God, and... He wills for your return to normal life on Earth. It is time for you to leave Lapoi.

I was shocked. Surly I had not heard him correctly.

Me: What?! Why?! Did we do something wrong?

Emalickel: No... Not at all. Your time on Lapoi must come to an end so you can resume your place in the natural cycle of the mortal experience. For now, you have seen and learned all that is necessary of Lapoi.

He rested his elbow on the arm of his white and gold throne. He began grazing his forehead with his fingers. His eyes still looked down.

Me: You will be able to come with me, right?

Emalickel: I am afraid I will not.

The tears which had been building-up beneath my eyelids began trickling onto my face

as I began to panic.

Me: No!?! Why not!?! Please come with me, Emalickel! Please!?!

Remorsefully, he shook his head.

Emalickel: It cannot be done.

Me: I don't understand.

Emalickel straightened his posture. He leaned forward and placed his elbows on his knees. He folded his hands together.

Emalickel: I do not know where to even begin. It is all so complicated. These memories of Lapoi rest within your spirit, not in your mind. You are in your astral form. Your astral body contains your spirit, and only the awakened aspects of your mind. When you arrive back to Earth and reunite with your mortal body, your mind may recall what has happened on Lapoi, but you will question the authenticity of what you recall. Your mortal mind will label your encounters here on Lapoi as figments of your imagination.

Me: But if I can physically see you, I will believe you exist without doubt.

Emalickel: I have not been authorized. I have been ordered to maintain Millattus. Celestials are not to interfere with the mortal experience.

Me: You did say I will remember everything, though, right?

Emalickel: You may remember it, but you will not believe it, not while you inhabit your mortal body on Earth. Only when your spirit becomes separated from your mind will you be able to remember the truth of Lapoi. This can only happen during periods of awakening or else when your time on Earth expires. When your spirit becomes freed from the control of your mind, it is then, your memories of Lapoi will become unquestionable. It will become as real as you see it now.

I began to panic and become frantic.

Me: I don't want to doubt! I don't want to leave! Isn't there anything you can do? Emalickel, I can't leave! Please don't let this happen! You must do something! Sneak to Earth or hide me here!

He shifted forward in his throne chair to better face me. He interrupted my panic as he grabbed my head firmly with both hands and spoke in a loud and stern voice.

Emalickel: Repress your selfish tendencies, mortal! How dare you ask me to rebel against our Father's will! He is El Shaddai—the Almighty Creator. We do exactly as He justly wills, without question! This is His creation, and we are extensions of Him. Or would you rather exist on one of the realms of darkness!?! Resist your rebellious instincts and don't you ever, ever tempt me to fall into corruption... ever again! Do you understand me?!

I was very frightened of his angered tone towards me. Although I knew deep down he would never hurt me, I was terrified at the thought of his capabilities and power over me. As if realizing my fear, he became regretful of his outburst. Emalickel released my head and looked down at the ground. He paused to take a deep breath and calm himself.

Emalickel: You are going to doubt Lapoi—this is inevitable. I assure you it will not be hard for you to endure, as you will know no differently when you arrive to Earth. This event will be most hard for me as I will be able to remember everything without doubt. I will look down on you while you live your life, enduring your absence for a very long time. Since time on Earth passes much slower in relation to Lapoi, centuries will come to pass on Lapoi before even decades have passed on Earth.

Completely distressed, my face collapsed into my hands and I began crying out of control. Emalickel knew I felt hopeless. Looking down at his hands folded in his lap he spoke again.

Emalickel: You may feel deep within your heart a sense of belonging to something not of your Earth. Your mind will dominate in convincing you that Lapoi is from a dream or from your own imagination. Let your spirit be strong and free. Believe in what you feel, for there is more truth within your spirit than within your mind. This is the only way you will continue awakening during your days on Earth. Upon full-awakening, you will see me again.

Me: Will I be with you still? What if you find someone else?

Emalickel looked me straight in the eye.

Emalickel: Our togetherness is a guarantee. When your spirit is released from your mind in mortal expiration, it will return to Lapoi. Having united with me, our energies have blended. We are a part of each other, and we will remain to be for eternity. I have shared with you, my celestial energy—even during your days on Earth, you will carry my energy within you. During your absence from Lapoi, your throne remains empty, as well as our chambers. Thorenel and I remain alone until your return—on this matter, I give you my word.

59. Artist: M83
Song: Starwaves

There was a long silence. Emalickel returned his stare downward. He appeared to be in deep and painful thought. I could see he was nibbling at the inside of his mouth. I looked around the palace. The white-robed assistants were conversing midway down the aisle, and a few warriors were guarding the major doorways of the palace. The lions were both lying down, seemingly asleep, next to each throne chair.

Me: Where's Thorenel?

Without pulling himself from his downward gaze, Emalickel shrugged his shoulders, and responded with low enthusiasm.

Emalickel: Call to him.

Me: When must I leave?

Emalickel slowly turned his head to look at me. He paused a blank gaze on me for several seconds, then suddenly looked deeply depressed. He pointed his right palm outward in front of me. A portal appeared.

Emalickel: It was instructed that I create the portal upon your asking this question.

Me: If Earth-time passes so much slower relative to Lapoi, then why do I have to go now? Why can't I stay longer? No one on Earth will even notice I am gone.

Emalickel's eyes grew wide as if in shock of what I had just asked. His reply was slow and with authority.

Emalickel: Because our Father has willed it, Adrienne. Do not stall by questioning His intentions. He has already spoken. It will be done.

Then he stood up from his throne.

A live image of the entire planet Earth appeared within the portal Emalickel had conjured. He slowly zoomed-in on the image with his hand until it showed the view of the lake where Emalickel and I had first met. There, the sun was still beginning to rise—just as it was before I left.

Emalickel looked at me. He tried to appear strong and emotionless, but I caught him gulp in attempt to swallow down his feelings of sadness. He tucked in his lips and, looking away from me, lifted his chin.

Emalickel: It is time. You must go.

He pointed into the portal. Slowly, I stepped towards him until I stood directly in front of him. He maintained his gaze, refraining from looking at me. I reached my hands up to touch his face. He clasped his hands around my wrists and brought my hands down. Still he did not look at me.

Emalickel: No, don't. It would only make this harder.

It felt like my gut began to sink in. I was hurt by his reactions. Tears began to fall down my face. My body felt heavy. I didn't want to go.

Me: I can't . . . I can't. I can't go. I can't do this!

Crossing his arms at his chest, Emalickel replied.

Emalickel: Your fears are distorted, Adrienne. None of your concerns will hold any burden. When you arrive back to Earth, you will not feel attached to any of this. Therefore, your depression will cease as soon as you arrive back there.

I was trying to understand what he meant. *He's saying there's no need for me to drag this out because, since my memory of Lapoi will be unrealistic when I get back to Earth, I will not be sad about it.*

I placed my hands over my eyes before turning to step into the portal. I didn't want to watch Lapoi disappear. Then, I changed my mind and uncovered my eyes. I decided I actually did want to watch

—that way, maybe there would be a chance I would remember something.

60. Artist: Anne Lennox
Song: Into the West

Suddenly, I heard Emalickel's voice again.

Emalickel: I apologize for my off standish behavior. I am not accustomed to feeling these emotions. Since we have physically become one, not only are you beginning to feel the power of divine magic as would a celestial, but I am beginning to feel the power of emotions as would a mortal. Truth is I do not want you to return to Earth. But since it is inevitable, it must be done. Taking longer to say goodbye only deepens our sorrow. Please, you must go. I do not want to start feeling temptation of rebellion against God. I will see you again, certainly before you know it, upon your awakening.

He stood his ground, arms still crossed, without flinching a muscle. Looking up at him through the blur of my tears, I could tell I needed to move along. Loyal to God, Emalickel was trying to be strong. My lingering presence was only testing his might. I did not want to be responsible for tempting the disobedience of such a noble and loyal Celestial Prince.

In effect, I decided not to call to Thorenel as that would make it even harder for me to leave Lapoi. It would also prolong the time Emalickel would have to endure the emotional pain. So, hesitantly, I eased my left foot into the portal. I was so scared and so depressed. I could not bring myself to say anything—not even goodbye. I did not know what to say, but I knew I didn't have to say anything at all because Emalickel felt everything I was feeling.

Slowly, stepping into the portal I turned around to ask Emalickel one last question.

Me: What am I supposed to do after I get there?

Emalickel smiled and replied.

Emalickel: Be aware of the illusions of mortal reality but remember to absorb the experiences for your own expansion and evolution. Continue to awaken yourself. Continue raising your vibration by following your passions. All will fall into place as it is supposed to be. We will be right there with you and will not let you fall astray. Lapoi's best guards will be ever present with you. They will remind you of their presence with reoccurring synchronicities. Do not be afraid to speak aloud to them. You will return here. Know that we are watching, listening, guiding, and guarding you in every moment. We will be with you and all of mankind for the entire journey. If you pay attention closely, you will find us—you will find me there.

The portal began to fade. Just before the portal turned into a shining orb, I caught a glimpse of Thorenel rushing to Emalickel's throne. Even though I had decided not to call to him, he must have sensed my emotional despair. The portal orb grew in brightness and was about to disappear in light, when I heard Thorenel's thoughts echo.

Thorenel: ***Worry not, Adrienne. Be strong and know all Lapoi will be watching over you, anxiously awaiting your return. The return of our beloved Princess.***

There was a massive explosion of light-energy. I could not see a thing. This explosion was followed by complete darkness and all became silent once again.

61. Artist: Epic Soul Factory
Song: Riding the Light

The vision of Earth faded in. The sun was beginning to rise above the horizon at the lake. I started to travel back home. I remembered everything from Lapoi—it was very vivid—but I started to wonder if I had envisioned it all in my imagination. The authenticity of the whole experience seemed to fade, as I questioned myself whether Lapoi was a creation of my own mind.

On my way back to the bedroom of my country home, I noticed one of my cats giving himself a bath in the hallway, while the other cat was sitting in the windowsill watching the sun rise. I lay down on the bed and everything went dark again. It was as if I had fallen asleep.

After what seemed like an instant, I woke back up. Sitting up in the bed, I looked around the room. By this time, there were parts of my memories from Lapoi that were foggy, although I still remembered the whole experience. I thought to myself, *what a crazy, vivid, wonderful, beautiful dream!*

Then, I noticed something—something very intriguing. My cats were in the exact same place, doing the exact same thing as they were in my dream! One was giving himself a bath in the hallway, while the other was sitting on the windowsill watching the sun rise.

WAS that a dream?! And so, began my doubts—a perpetual inner conflict whether Lapoi was a dream or a valid experience taking place on another plane of existence. This relentless, inner conflict would always exist within me.

My regular life on Earth continued as I stepped out of bed to get ready for work. As I washed my face at the sink, I felt a presence with me. I was unsure if it was real, but it felt warm and light. I looked up and scanned the reflection of the bathroom in the mirror. I smiled with comfort as a thought came to me. A name came to my thoughts, and a feeling of happiness sparked within me. I whispered the name out loud.

Me: Emalickel.

A brighter smile grew on my face as I thought about it a bit longer.

Me: *His name is Emalickel.*

It all started to come to me like flood gates of memories. I was not sure if what I had dreamed the night before was real, but saying that name, Emalickel, caused an intense passion to surface within me. After that, I started remembering everything about Lapoi in such detail. I began recalling more names, places, and events. I could describe everything down to the most intricate detail. I decided then that I was going to begin writing it all down. The dream, or whatever it was, would end up an entire novel by the time I was finished recording everything.

I continued getting ready for work that day, but for the first time in a long time, or perhaps for the first time ever, I had a blissful feeling. I felt at ease as if something wonderful had happened and that there was so much more to come. There was a strong, loving presence which seemed to surround me from that day going forward. It shifted from time to time, sometimes it felt like the energy of Thorenel, while other times it felt like the energy of Emalickel. Not being able to see them or interact with them in any way, I figured they watched from the astral plane on occasions. Sometimes, I felt no presence at all, but I remembered Emalickel telling me there would be Guards of Lapoi who would watch over me always. I trusted him, be him real or imaginary. Until the day when all becomes revealed, I decided to put the conflict of reality behind me. I decided it was time to appreciate and enjoy the fantasy of my encounter in a magical place of the celestial plane, called Lapoi.

9

THE SECOND ENCOUNTER

62. Artist: Audiomachine
Song: Homecoming

On Saturday, September 20, 2017 I was driving to the mountains for my annual hike, when I experienced a vision with a message.

I looked up into the morning sky. I saw one star shining brightly as the sun rose. It was all alone, with no other stars around it. The sky was too bright, with the sun rising, to see any stars—only planets. There were a few wispy clouds which glowed with soft shades of coral, orange, pink, and lavender. As I looked at the lonely bright star, which I think was the planet Saturn, I began to wonder what else was out there in the vastness of the universe. I found myself daydreaming once again about Lapoi.

My mind filled with wonder, and my heart became filled with desire. Why had the vision of Lapoi and the celestials in my so-called imagination been so persistent? Why had the passion for it not faded? It had started over five years ago, yet I was still fixated on it. I had never been drawn to something so deeply, so passionately, in all my life.

Usually, after a year, passions that come soon fade. Not with Lapoi, not with Emalickel. In fact, my desire only grew more intense with time.

My heart began to yearn, to ache almost, as I thought about my previous experience in Lapoi, the palace, Emalickel, Thorenel and the others. The need for a sign of truth was vital. I was questioning everything. *Was it real? Did I lose my mind during that visit? Was it just my imagination? Was I just trying to create something to make myself feel worthy?* My loss in trust, faith, and hope was beginning to bring me to tears.

That's when it happened.

A holographic movie started to play before my eyes as I drove along. I was completely aware of the road and of my driving, but all seemed to freeze and then blur. My mind's eye was playing an additional image in front of everything else. It was an image of an ocean, I felt no emotion. I was simply observing. This was a good thing, because the emotion I had felt only moments before, was a negative yearning, like emptiness, doubt, and sadness. Now, I felt void of the negative emotion.

A familiar and comforting male voice echoed in my mind. It was the voice of Emalickel.

Emalickel: Your vibration—it has changed. You show more doubt that before.

Immediately, my attention fixated on this voice. Emotions began to surge within me again. My heart raced with excitement and anticipation. I felt myself perspiring. I began asking questions out loud.

Me: Is this happening? This is too good to be true. Is it real?

Wasting no time, Emalickel's voice answered.

Emalickel: Is it too good to be true, Adrienne? Is it? I feel the time has come, so I will show you more.

63. Artist: Audiomachine
Song: The Fire Within

Then, in the inner vision, I found myself flying fast over a vast ocean about three feet above the surface of the water. A dim sun reflected in the waters as I watched the ripples gleaming under me. I passed a group of white gulls floating on the ocean's water. I looked forward and, in the distance, I saw a beach with a sandy embankment. As I flew closer I noticed a stone pathway leading up the bank to flat grasslands above. There were monstrous snow-capped mountains many miles in the distance of the grasslands. It felt like home. I knew I was drifting into Lapoi again, but from a different perspective and via a different method this time. I heard Emalickel's voice as I continued forward toward the beach.

Emalickel: Your doubt is the enemy. It is what imprisons you. It is what confines you within the mortal walls of perception. You must learn how to let go, trust, believe, and know Lapoi is in existence. Regardless of whether Lapoi exists because you imagined it, or if you imagined it because it exists, the fact stands—it exists. It is real.

My flight was headed straight towards the stone path. I had no control over where I was flying, but this is where I wanted to go anyway. As I flew over the beach, my body landed on two feet, and I was in control again. I approached the embankment. It was about a foot taller than my line of vision, so I couldn't see the grasslands above.

Looking down at my feet as I shuffled in the sand, I noticed they were bare, and I wore a long white dress as with my previous visit to Lapoi. The sand felt soft and warm, like walking in flour or powder. Having felt this, my senses began to kick back in. The air felt crisp, refreshing, and renewing. The temperature felt like 70 degrees Fahrenheit with a gentle constant warm breeze. I smiled and opened my arms wide to absorb everything.

As I began walking up the path in the embankment, a sense of excitement began to stir within my gut. I could sense another presence around me. I approached the top of the embankment and could see the grasslands. As I looked out, I saw, perched about 100 yards in front of me, center of the valley, was a place like home. That familiar place I felt like I've known since the dawn of my creation—the Palace of Lapoi. It absolutely was majestic. It was heavenly. It was lit up completely from the base to the rooftops. It stood out in the valley like a candle in a dark room.

64. Artist: Audiomachine
Song: Across the Horizon

The voice of Emalickel echoed again in my head.

Emalickel: Just because you are viewing something remotely, instead of in your physical plane, does not grant reason to question its existence. You only believe what you see in your present state of physical reality, but you must learn that there are other planes of existence which vibrate at different pitches. Upon matching your pitch to that of the desired plane, you will experience your physical reality within that plane to be just as real. You must believe you are already within the manifestation, carrying yourself in the manner, feeling the same emotions, and perceiving reality in a translated way of what you wish to see.

The palace seemed to glow and even hummed the sound of a soft angelic choir. The massive gate, which made a perimeter around the palace and its courtyard, began to open its centrally located 25-foot arched doorways. It sounded like a massive piece of heavy metal echoing across the entire land. Which made sense, as the doors were enormous.

A figure was walking out of the gate doors. By the stride and physique, I could tell it was Thorenel. I could see the strands of his wavy blonde hair peeking out from the sides of his royal cloak with white fur lining and golden trim. Under it he wore a black tunic, suede-leather pants, and his knee-high leather boots.

A soft golden beam of light from the sky glowed down upon him. He became brighter than anything else in view. Time slowed as he continued walking my way. His cape was blowing behind him like a great hero or emperor. As he approached closer, I was able to see his face. He reached up to remove his hood. Gently he lowered it to his shoulders revealing the Lapoian Crown sparkling upon his head. His eyes were smiling as a few strands of his hair blew across them.

My heart was pumping so fast, it felt hard to breathe. The splendor of Thorenel left me stunned—breathless. His majestic display had entranced me as if under a spell of love.

Thorenel spoke to me with his mind from across the valley.

Thorenel: A long while ago Emalickel said you would return again.

With his arms spread open, he looked up to the sky and yelled aloud.

Thorenel: Since then, I have been counting the stars of Millattus to occupy my mind.

Flattered, I chuckled. Then, I proceeded to run towards him. I ran until I finally came crashing into his arms. He held me and swung my body around in circles with his. We were both smiling so hard it made our faces hurt. All we could do was laugh out of pure joy. I was so happy my eyes began to fill with tears. After several engaging moments, we finally collected ourselves enough to be able to speak. I apparently wasn't thinking very quickly as I chose some very poor first words to say to Thorenel during our reunion.

65. Artist: Audiomachine
Song: Leaving the Nest

Me: Where is Emalickel?

His smile turned forced and almost irritated.

Thorenel: So that is where your thoughts are focused in this moment?

Me: I am sorry. I didn't mean it like that. It's just that I heard Emalickel's voice moments ago and was wondering from where he spoke.

I smiled in awe at him before continuing.

Me: And, the crown . . . you're wearing the crown.

Thorenel's voice was slightly disgruntled.

Thorenel: Your Emalickel will be here. He addressed you from a transmission sent a while ago before he left to receive the orders. As you know, I am the acting Princedom when Emalickel's presence is elsewhere. That is why I am wearing the crown.

It suited him well, resting so perfectly upon his head blending in flawlessly with his luxurious wavy golden locks of hair. There was as brief silence. I spoke at the onset of the awkwardness. I wasn't sure exactly what to say, so the words were kind of hard to speak—awkward and forced.

Me: So, what's going on? How am I here?

Thorenel tilted his head and slightly squinted his eyes at me, as if trying to figure out what I meant. I meant well, but my nervous and overjoyed feelings were causing me to mess up my words terribly.

Me: I mean, don't get me wrong, I'm crazy happy and excited about being here! I'm just curious how I got here, and why I have been granted the pleasure of finally being able to visit again.

Thorenel looked down at his black leather boots grazed by the golden trim of his perfectly-pressed velvety cape. He shuffled his feet in the grass a bit before looking back up to me. He extended his hand out to me as he spoke with a forgiving smile.

Thorenel: Come with me. Let me show you something.

I took hold of his arm. He began escorting me towards the woodlands in the West. The snow-capped mountains were all along the North, which the back of the palace faced. The ocean ran along the South, in the front of the palace. To the East were the gently rolling hills covered in golden wheat grass.

We walked towards the woodlands. The Western Woodlands extended from the ocean shoreline all the way north to the snow-capped mountain range. Near the shoreline, the woodlands dropped off into steep rocky cliffs, which lined the shore for as far west as I could see. I noticed a long, steep waterfall coming out of one of the tall cliffs. This waterfall fell into a small basin. I didn't remember it from before. White gulls were flying all around the waterfall making it appear even more magnificent than it already was.

I felt Thorenel place his other hand over mine which clutched his escorting arm. I heard him take a deep refreshing breath and saw him looking out at the immaculate waterfall.

Thorenel: It is but nothing compared to you.

He looked down at me with only his eyes, keeping his head straight ahead, as a wider smile grew on his face. He always had a way of flattering me with his words, yet never allowed his facial expressions to give away his feelings. He was blunt yet remained mysterious. I found it very attractive.

We continued onward up a small hill where the woodlands began. Colorful trees were all throughout these woods. Soft, green grass, moss, and periodic clusters of purple lavender covered the woodland floor—that was all. The forest floor was unobstructed, clear of brush and debris. The trees were a blend of birch and evergreens. They were tall, and their limbs started high overhead. It was a smooth, gentle forest without any bushes or other vegetation. You could see only grey tree trunks and soft, green, ground covered sporadically with lavender and sprinkled with colorful leaves.

There were rays of light beaming in through the colorful trees of the woodlands. It was calm and peaceful. It was almost as if entering a whole new world. The whole forest felt warm and uplifting. It appeared shimmering and magical. I, myself, felt lighter as we continued the journey inward.

About 200 yards in, we came to an opening with a blue lake. It was surrounded by tall evergreen trees. Distant snow-capped mountains could be seen through the openings in the trees. There was a stream that flowed to the south of this lake area. I was amazed and completely mesmerized by the beauty of this place. More of the beautiful white birds flew around the sparkling lake. At a closer look, I found these birds to be white doves.

Thorenel slowed his pace to allow time for me to absorb everything. He looked down at me and chuckled to himself at the child-like expression on my face. He was happy that I was happy. There was no need for words here, we were both superbly content—simply happy in that moment.

66. Artist: Really Slow Motion
Song: Forever in my Dreams

Thorenel led us to a large, flat gray boulder which sat along the bank of the lake. He motioned for me to sit down on the boulder, and then he sat himself beside me. He looked out over the lake.

Thorenel: This is one of my favorite places to pass the time. Everything is so still and quiet here.

I saw a gleam in his eyes as he continued staring out towards the lake. His facial expression was that of contentment and complacency. He folded his hands in front of him. A few loose strands of hair fell to the sides of his face. The strands gently blew as the wind drifted through them. The glow of the crown which encircled his head brought out the lighter golden locks of hair which fell beneath it onto his shoulders. I could feel his aura. It exhibited more dominance and strength than it did the last time I was visiting Lapoi. It felt infinite. I could feel him radiating supremacy, wisdom, and vitality. He was majestic, and I couldn't take my eyes off of him. There was too much to admire about him to look away. Of course, the lake was indeed pleasing to the eyes, but Thorenel; there was just something about him. He was enchanting, hypnotizing, enrapturing. I felt myself falling short of breath.

Still looking out at the lake, Thorenel began smiling wide. He shifted his seated position forward a bit more to place his elbows on each of his knees. His hands were still folded over one another, but he brought them to meet his chin. Then, he turned his head towards me. He was looking me square in the eyes. His hands were placed on his chin in such a manner to conceal a proud smile.

Thorenel: I must admit, I am flattered by your thoughts.

I had been caught again. My thoughts had broadcasted clearly to him. Embarrassed, I quickly looked out at the lake, but Thorenel was quick to use one of his hands to gently pull my face back to look at him. Still embarrassed, I let my eyes wander the scenery behind him and to the sides of his face. I couldn't make eye contact. His hand still placed gently on the side of my face, he echoed words of comfort to me using his mind. He transmitted very slowly and clearly.

Thorenel: ***You avoid eye contact, but there is no reason to feel embarrassed. It's just me, Thorenel. You know me, and I know you. I know you just as well as you know yourself. I am yours, and you are mine. I belong to you, and you belong to me. I am a part of you, and you a part of me.***

My heart raced at his mysteriousness and his assertiveness. I was infatuated with how well he communicated with me, and how he understood my reservations so clearly. It was like he was me, in a male body that was so attractive it exceeded any possibility of finding a description through words.

He was impressive the first time I met him, but this time he was different. He carried himself differently. He seemed stronger, wiser, and more collected. There was fierceness in his eyes—like power and dominance. Everything about him, from his appearance to his persona, was divine. He was heavenly. Catching myself this time, knowing he had just read those very thoughts, all I could to do was look at the ground. He helped me relax by backing off a bit. He took a moment to look out at the lake and pull his hair back, securing it in a loose ponytail while he spoke to me.

Thorenel: Do you think that your feelings are solely your own? Do you not know that when you think or feel something, it is exactly so with me? You and I have united. We have quite literally intertwined our energies. They are unified now, feeding off and into one another. We are synchronized, you and me. Do not be ashamed of any of your thoughts and feelings because I, too, am thinking and feeling them right along with you.

67. Artist: Natanel Arnson
Song: A Hero Will Rise

I managed to fall into the comfort he provided through his words. He finished pulling his hair back. He then removed the hooded cloak from his shoulders and placed it behind him on the rock. His black tunic was laced up and loosely untied at his chest. I was so damn attracted to him. Should he ask me to do anything, I would submit to him willingly. I heard his voice interrupt my thoughts. He turned his head to look at me again.

Thorenel smirked. I heard him in my mind.

Thorenel: ***Even the most shocking of your thoughts are not yours alone.***

I managed to look into his eyes. I couldn't resist him anymore. I slowly leaned in closer to him. He mirrored me. We continued closer and closer. His hands reached up to grab my face and pull it to his. The loose strands of his hair tickled my face as the wind blew them. He carried the scent of amber on him. I could feel his warm breath just before his soft warm lips touched against mine.

We locked our lips together, pressing firmly for several intense moments as we enjoyed the shockwave of desire shooting through our bodies. I had become putty in his hands, melting into him as he continued to hold my face.

He slid one of his hands down the nape of my neck and down my entire back. He squeezed me and pulled me closer to him as his hand approached the base of my back. This sent surges of passion all over me causing the need to breathe deeper. This increased the intensity of our kiss as he responded to my deep breaths with those of his own. I could only assume he was feeling the increased passion with me. He briefly pulled away from the kiss and whispered through his breaths.

Thorenel: You are absolutely correct.

I smiled and at that, I let go. I repositioned myself to straddle his lap. I pulled my dress up enough for my knees to rest on the outsides of Thorenel's legs. Both of his hands slid to my hips pulling them passionately into his. I cupped his masculine face in my hands as we continued our kiss. Our lips opened, allowing for our tongues to wander around each other.

He tasted rustic, like the Earth, like fresh air. It gave me urges, sending surging waves down my back into my intimate regions. I began pressing my pelvis into his lap in a circular motion. He responded by moving his hips circular back against mine. He kept squeezing my body closer to his. Our tongues slid rapidly against each other as our heads swiveled and pivoted like a dance.

My hands began sliding down his neck to the front of his monstrous chest. I could feel how large and dense his muscles were through his tunic. I began squeezing his chest and arms, frantically trying to find something in which to channel my passion. I pressed my pelvic region to his even firmer. I could feel a thick hard bulge growing between his legs underneath his trousers. It pressed so perfectly between my legs. I could feel myself producing warmth in preparation for him. We were both radiating heat with one other,

Everything was happening so fast. *Was it okay for this to happen right now?* Doing so would cause me to rest in blackout for the next few days, and my journey would be significantly more difficult as I would be able to feel the ache from where Thorenel had been inside me. My mind drifted to Emalickel. I wondered where he was located. When would he return?

I moved my face down to look at Thorenel. His pupils were dilated, and his skin was flushed. He was out of breath. I wanted to feel him inside me. I yearned to feel his strength embrace my body. I enjoyed the power he radiated. I remembered from the past experience with him that engaging physically with Thorenel was absolutely stupefying. I could feel my heart racing out of my chest. I couldn't help but picture several different ways I'd enjoy for him to take me.

He held my body as he stood up from the rock. He turned around and laid me on my back before pressing his body on top of mine. Our kiss continued. He began gently sliding the straps of my dress down from my shoulders.

My mind started racing and recycling the previous thoughts about Emalickel. Thorenel buried his face into my neck and continued pressing himself to me. He wasn't receiving these thoughts from me because he was too caught-up in his own passion. His breathing intensified into short moans of yearning. It was so hard to resist him now. Despite this, I took his head and guided it to look at me.

I stopped moving my body and tried to calm myself down with deep breaths. My eyes were wide open as I locked eyes with him. Thorenel paused with a confused look on his face. After a moment, I noticed it clicked within him. He nodded understandingly. He gently lifted himself from me. He aided me up to a sitting position and began fixing my dress straps back to my shoulders while he spoke.

Thorenel: I understand.

He leaned in to kiss my forehead and embraced me in a powerful hold while resting his chin on the top of my head.

Thorenel: I understand completely.

Grabbing his cloak, he rose to a standing position. He threw the cloak across his back and positioned the hood back onto his head. He then sat back down on the rock beside me placing his arm around me.

Thorenel: I am grateful we are here together.

I relaxed my head on his chest as we continued to watch the birds fly over the lake. His breaths came steady and slow. I could feel his chest rise and fall with each breath he took. He began stroking my hair with his hand. Thorenel brought me comfort in his presence.

Something was missing, though, and it was Emalickel. I felt insecure and empty without his presence—like something was off. Then, I started drifting in thought. I couldn't help but worry about my place and purpose back on Earth and how Lapoi tied into everything. I started questioning the reality of it again.

68. Artist: Mattia Cupelli
Song: Waves

Thorenel pulled himself back, which forced me to remove my head from resting on his chest. He shook his head.

Thorenel: You still question everything—always questioning. This creates anxiety and doubt, both of which are enemies of awareness. If awareness is what you are seeking, you must extinguish your habit of worry and doubt. Replace your doubts with belief and faith. It is then you will find the answers you seek.

He turned his head to look at me again and lowered his eyebrows a bit.

Thorenel: Do you trust me?

Perplexed, I waited to see where he was going with this before answering.

Thorenel: The Lapoians. Do you know who we are? Who we really are?

He gazed at me analytically for a moment before continuing.

Thorenel: We are the elite celestials of the most high exalted God; El Elyon, Elohim, Adonai. We are the so-called angels of whom you have read about your whole life. That is who we are. We understand mortals. Appointed exclusively by God, we have watched you, trained you, and influenced you since the dawn of your creation in Millattus. This is what we do. This is our purpose—our life's work. God Himself has entrusted your well-being to the aid of our hands.

I was impressed with the strength of his confidence and his outspoken demeanor. Thorenel shifted himself on the boulder so that he was closer to me.

Thorenel: Listen to me and listen to me well. Let go of control and let God's work be done in you. Gain the mortal experience but detach yourself from the vortex of it. Do not become so absorbed in it that you forget your true inner self. Your awareness of your inner self is beginning to awaken, and that is how you are sometimes able to be here in the celestial plane. The time has come for you to remember yourself and merge it with your experiences of Earth. This is how you will expand and evolve. Find the balance between mortal and spirit. You must learn to reposition your vortex to receive the higher realms more easily and abundantly. This is done through higher vibrating emotions.

Thorenel pushed-back the hood of his cloak.

Thorenel: We are here for you. You, personally, can rest assured that you are being guided in your well-being. After all, you have physically become one in unity with the Princedoms of Millattus, Princess. Everything is always as it should be. Do not fight it anymore. Accept things as they come and let them blossom into what you will see unfold. Remember to find and focus upon the

joy in each experience. You have my word, Adrienne, my word that the true reality is within your inner self. That which you think about most, and that which you resonate with deeply, is the truth. Everything else is just for the experience, the evolution of self, the expansion of spirit.

I still questioned who I was regarding my place on Lapoi.

Me: So, what is my purpose on Lapoi?

Thorenel was quick to respond.

Thorenel: Are you happy here?

Me: Yes, I am, but I am just confused about . . .

Thorenel interrupted me and spoke bluntly.

Thorenel: There is nothing to be confused about. You confuse yourself trying to give everything a purpose. Sometimes the experience itself is the purpose.

He stood up and began walking.

Thorenel: Come with me. Turn off your mind and enjoy your spirit while we continue onward.

I understood what he was trying to say. He was trying to enlighten me, not belittle me or convince me of something. A sense of peace filled my soul, and I felt lighter inside. Thorenel was ahead of me, but he stopped to turn around. He waited for me and gave me a satisfied smile.

We began walking along the bank of the stream which exited the lake and flowed towards the south. We walked on a path parallel to the stream continuing further into the woodlands. We kept silent for a while. I was thinking about and absorbing what Thorenel had shared with me. He remained silent to let me do so.

After following the stream for about 15 minutes, it grew wider and the water began flowing faster. I couldn't get over how clean and clear the water appeared. It even carried a scent of fresh pine to it. We continued walking for about five more minutes when Thorenel held his hand out signaling for me to stop.

He took a few more steps forward before he himself slowed to a stop. He was very still. Grinning widely, he turned his head back to look at me.

Thorenel: Do you hear it?

I listened for the sound of something new or different. I could hear a deep rumbling sound in the distance. It sounded like a heard of stampeding buffalo. It reminded me of thunder, only it was constant without ceasing. It just continued rumbling. As we continued walking further, the rumbling grew louder. The stream was now a river and the speed of the river was very rough. That is when it came to me. I knew what was making the rumbling sound.

Me: The waterfall!

Thorenel smiled and nodded his head.

Thorenel: And that's where we're headed.

I was so excited! I'd seen small waterfalls in my life before, but never had I seen one this magnificent nor had I ever been at the top of one looking down. I had butterflies of excitement in my stomach as we approached. When we got to the edge of the cliff, I could barely hear Thorenel over the loud crashing of the waterfall. I followed him out to the very edge of the cliff. He stepped onto a large flat rock overlooking the edge. He turned to me and had to yell for me to hear him.

Thorenel: Are you ready?

I was confused.

Me: Ready? Ready for what?

Thorenel opened his arms.

Thorenel: To jump!

He extended his hand to me. I raised my eyebrows at him in disbelief. I looked down over the edge of the cliff. It was at least a 300-yard drop straight down. Thorenel stepped closer to me and yelled again over the raging waters.

Thorenel: Or will you still choose not to trust in me?

Why was he so hung up on trust? I sighed from anxiety. I shook my head in defeat and reached out for his hand. I was shaking tremendously from fear. My legs would barely walk. Thorenel took my hand with his, and then placed his other hand on top. Smiling, he shook his head at me.

Thorenel: You will learn, Adrienne. You will learn to trust me.

I did trust him, but I couldn't fight off my natural instincts. My heart knew Thorenel was going to protect me no matter what, but my mind said *this is suicide!*

69. Artist: Danny Rayel
Song: Rise of a Hero

Thorenel released my hand and positioned himself in front of me. He turned around so that his back was to me.

Thorenel: Get on my back. I will jump with you this time.

My mind was cluttered and clouded with fear. I wasn't even sure I was having any thoughts. Left with no other choice, I did as he said and slowly climbed onto his back. His arms tucked themselves under my legs to help keep me lifted. His demeanor was as if he were about to ride on a roller coaster at an amusement park. It was as if he were about to play a fun quest in a video game. He had no fear. Turning his head to look at me in his peripherals, I could see that he was smiling and seemed relaxed.

Thorenel: You good?

He said this in an almost joking manner. No, I wasn't good! I was terrified! It was no use in protesting, though. I knew Thorenel had his mind made up about this. Petrified, I managed to nod at him, despite my inner turmoil. Thorenel turned his head forward again. I felt him roll his shoulders a few times and heard him clear his throat. He paused for a moment and chuckled to himself.

Then, at that, he jumped over the edge. I used every muscle in my body to keep myself attached to him. I made myself into a backpack on Thorenel's back.

We fell alongside the waterfall. The water was falling with us. I watched the same drops of water fall at the same speed as us as we continued our decline. The wind ripped into my ears as we fell. My stomach felt like it was doing flips as gravity had its way. Then I looked down. We rapidly were approaching the ground. I squeezed Thorenel with my legs. I used my arms to clench his chest. I tucked my head into the back of his neck. Feeling dizzy, I closed my eyes in fear. *What if something went wrong and we hit the ground? What if I slipped from Thorenel's back? Accidents happen, so what would prevent an accident right now? One wrong move and we will splat on the ground below.*

Then, I remembered what Thorenel had said earlier. He was a celestial. This made him capable of nearly anything that could possibly be thought. His scent of amber was comforting to me. I trusted him—I truly did trust him and all his power. I could feel that he had a strong grip on me, but also knew that should something go wrong, he had the powers and abilities to quickly fix it. I submitted to him and my body relaxed into his hold.

Suddenly, I felt the rate of our fall begin to slow. Everything around us began to move in slow motion. All sounds faded, and all became silent. I no longer heard the wind whooshing through my ears, nor the sound of the waterfall violently crashing below me. The wind resistance against my body had subsided. I heard only the sound of Thorenel's thoughts. He transmitted them slowly and clearly to me.

Thorenel: ***You must always trust. Remember who we are.***

I lifted my head from his neck and opened my eyes. Thorenel was hovering midair about halfway down the waterfall. With me still on his back, he turned to face the waterfall and held his hands out in front of him with his palms facing forward. He waved them apart from one another in a motion to part the water of the waterfall. It opened like two panels of curtains. The water still flowed, but there was a gap in the flow. I could see between the split Thorenel had created in the waterfall. It looked like some kind of small cave was hidden behind it. Thorenel proceeded to fly through the parted waters.

The cave was about 15 feet deep, 20 feet wide, and 10 feet tall. There was a deep stream of water flowing out of the middle of the cave floor feeding into the waterfall. This stream was about ten feet wide and ten feet deep. Thorenel hovered himself inside the cave to the side of the stream. Then he set us down. He walked along the edge of the stream towards the cave wall. He placed his hands on his hips for a moment, and then motioned for me to come over there to him.

70. Artist: PostHaste Music (Mark Petrie)
Song: Convergence

Thorenel: There is more here than meets the eye. There are only three Lapoians who have the privilege and ability to see beyond this cave.

He leaned into my ear and spoke quietly.

Thorenel: Take notes—you are one of them, Princess.

He walked a bit further into the cave before continuing.

Thorenel: The first requirement is to conjure the element of fire.

He took a deep breath in and then blew out toward the cave wall from the right side to the left. As he did this, the walls lit up, one by one, with torches of fire which were unseen once before. They were at eye level and were spaced out along the semi-circular wall about two feet apart from one another. The power behind his breath was enough to create a breeze as it repelled against the cave wall. I could feel and smell the rustic freshness from his breath. It carried a hint of clean pine within it.

Thorenel: Next you must turn the water to ice.

He knelt down and hovered his hands above the surface of the flowing stream. After a few moments, the stream froze over completely. Thorenel stood up and proceeded to walk across it all the way back towards the cave wall.

Thorenel: You must walk across the frozen water in order to reach the back, center, and top of the cave wall.

He stopped there and turned to look at me.

Thorenel: You got that much?

I didn't understand where he was going with this, or how I would ever be able to actually do those things by myself, but I understood what he had said.

Me: Yeah. Blow fire and freeze the water to walk on it. No problem. Got it.

Thorenel knew I was being sarcastic. I heard him chuckle under his breath before turning back towards the cave wall.

Thorenel: The third requirement is that of your breath. You will exhale your breath onto the wall itself towards the top and center.

He exhaled his breath, as one would on a cold morning, onto the top middle of the cave wall. This slowly revealed a symbol of light on the cave wall. It was the same symbol which appeared on all of Lapoi's tapestries and banners. The symbol glowed brighter and brighter until it was fully manifested.

Thorenel: The final requirement is your touch.

He placed his hand directly on the glowing symbol. Suddenly, there was a rumbling sound. Thorenel removed his hand from the wall and took a small step back. The entire back wall of the cave began opening. It was a secret door. It slid downward into a crevice on the cave floor.

71. Artist: Patryk Scelina
Song: Voices of Namibia

Upon entering the dark cave, torches began lighting up all along the inner walls. The cave extended back for about ten feet before turning to the right, then curving back to the left. The stream flowed through the center of the tunnel floor. The stream was already beginning to melt again, so we had to walk on the five feet to the left or right side of the stream.

The tunnel led to a huge open circular cavern. It was the size of a grand arena. A stream flowed out of the center of the ground from a waterfall that fell from the far back wall of this enormous open cave room. A few evergreen trees were growing inside here. There were also several plateaus containing stone boulders and various flowers. In the center of the room was a 1,600-square foot plateau upon which was a pool of natural warm spring water. I could see the steam rising from it. The central stream flowed around this plateau on all sides, framing it beautifully with sparkling waters. Light was beaming in onto this plateau from a medium-sized hole in the roof of the cave room.

There were numerous tunnels forking off in all directions on three different levels of this room. There were at least 50 separate tunnels to the right and 50 to the left, and 50 on each of the four upper levels. We walked past a few of these tunnels to our right. They all looked the same. Measuring about ten feet tall and ten feet wide, they all seemed to stretch for miles deep.

Thorenel: There is a combination puzzle within this cave. You must know the exact combination in order to arrive to the ending destination. Otherwise, you will become lost in a seemingly endless maze of merging tunnels. That is, if you can even get past opening the main cave door.

In the distance, I heard the main cave door we had entered through, began to close with a rumble. Thorenel continued walking past a few more tunnels before turning into one on the right.

Thorenel: Count eight tunnels on the right and turn down the eighth tunnel.

Our footsteps echoed as we continued down the tunnel. I could still hear the waterfall faintly rumbling in the distance. I also heard the echoing drops of water and smelled the aroma of clean water, like a bathtub after it has been freshly cleaned with bleach. It felt cool in the cave, not cold, but cool and crisp.

Thorenel raised his hand to me. I saw an invisible bubble surround me. Immediately I felt warm and comfortable. He had read my mind and knew that I was slightly uncomfortable.

Thorenel: I will do whatever I can to your best interest.

We passed a few more tunnels before Thorenel turned to the left down another one.

Thorenel: Count three tunnels to the left and turn down the third tunnel.

I was trying to review everything he had said so far since passing through the waterfall outside. I didn't know how I was going to do any of it, but I figured it would be a good idea to practice memorizing it; that way, if I ever could do any of those things, I'd know what to do and in what order to do them. We continued past several tunnels. I was already lost. Thorenel turned down a tunnel to the right.

Thorenel: Count seven tunnels to the right and turn down the seventh tunnel.

We continued walking.

Thorenel: The destination is at the end of this tunnel.

We walked past at least 20 or more tunnels on either side before I finally began to see the end of the tunnel. Thorenel kept walking and didn't turn down any of the other tunnels. All I saw was a wall at the end of the tunnel. Thorenel walked to the wall and placed his hand upon it.

Thorenel: This is it.

I was not impressed. I looked all around, wide-eyed, trying to find something different or interesting about this tunnel or this cave wall.

Me: Okay? What is it? What am I looking at?

Thorenel exhibited a serious look on his face.

Thorenel: What lies behind these walls is sacred.

72. Artist: Audiomachine
Song: Radiant

Turning around to face me, he folded his hands in front of him. Without blinking an eye, he continued looking at me for a moment with a straight-faced stare. He let there be a pause of silence and stillness before continuing.

Thorenel: Are you ready?

Of course, I wasn't sure if I was ready. I didn't know what was behind those walls. I shrugged my shoulders but smiled.

Thorenel turned around and placed his hand onto the center of the back wall of the tunnel. Another trinity symbol began to appear and glow. I wondered immensely what was concealed behind that cave wall. It certainly was secure from most anything trying to intrude. The walls began to rumble and slide down into the cave floor. Thorenel turned around to face me once again with his hands folded in front of him professionally.

A room was being revealed behind the wall. From the look of the ceiling, it was about 20 feet by 20 feet. Many small orbs of light, the size of marbles, floated around the room, illuminating it in a soft glow. The orbs danced around the room in constant motion as would snowflakes in the wind. The cave door continued down until it had disappeared completely into the cave floor.

Thorenel took a deep breath and stepped to the side, revealing what was in the center of the room. It was a huge quartz boulder glowing in a beautiful shade of blue-violet. It was rectangular, about four feet tall and eight feet wide. A large orb of light formed an encasement over the entire top of the quartz. Thorenel walked over to it.

Thorenel: And this is how it is done. This is how the orders are received.

He placed one hand inside the orb of light and with the other hand he motioned for me to come closer. The orb of light began to dim. As it dimmed, Thorenel turned his head to look at me. The light faded until it was clear like a bubble.

Thorenel: Only the touch of my or your hand can penetrate this orb of protection.

There, lying on his back, on top of the quartz stone, I saw the body of Emalickel. He appeared asleep with his hands folded at his waist. He was wearing his royal beige cloak with the golden trim. The hood of his cloak was on his head covering most of his forehead. His face glowed like a radiant angel. For a brief moment, I slipped away into the image of him, absorbing the aesthetic perfection of him and forgetting about my surroundings. Every look, every smile, every touch Emalickel had ever given to me flashed into image before my mind. Then, coming back to where I was, I became frightened. I looked up at Thorenel with a worried look.

Me: Is he okay?

Thorenel gave me a reassuring smile.

Thorenel: He is perfectly fine. He is unaware of anything happening here, though. That is why he is in such a protected place. When he receives the orders, he enters a trans-hypnotic state and travels to the realm of the Dominion. That is the only way to receive the orders of God. We would be lost without this.

Me: How often does he do it? How long is he like this?

Thorenel: He comes here when he is called. He says they whisper to him, and he knows it is time to receive. He then passes the crown and the kingdom to me during the time of his absence. It usually takes three settings of Auruclerum before it is complete, and he returns to us. He has been here for two settings, so tonight he will likely be returning.

Thorenel removed his hand from the bubble around Emalickel. It began to glow in white light again, and I could no longer see Emalickel through it.

Thorenel: There are only three of us who have the ability to open this cave and dissolve Emalickel's light of protection—that is Emalickel himself; his closest brother, me . . .

He paused to shoot me a proud smirk.

Thorenel: . . . and you, Princess.

73. Artist: Kevin Ohlsson
Song: Returning Heroes

Thorenel began walking to the back of the room. The door of the room began to close.

Thorenel: This entire cave is protected with runes along the walls to keep anyone from teleporting in or out of the cave. On the floor here, where I stand, is the only way out of this cave.

He extended his arm out to me in motion for me to come to him. I went to stand next to him on a circular rune that was lit up on the floor. Thorenel stood behind me and wrapped his arms around me. I enjoyed the embrace.

Thorenel: Are you ready to travel back to the palace?

I shook my head slightly before taking a few steps to the quartz stone again. Slowly and very cautiously, I moved my hand to the protection dome around Emalickel. I wanted to see his face one more time. I knew Thorenel would tell me to stop if it wasn't safe, but I looked at him anyway for reassurance. He offered it in a nod of his head.

I slipped my hand inside. It felt like I was sticking my arm in a thick bubble, like dough or something. My arm disappeared into the light as I continued in further to my elbow. After a few more seconds of holding it there, the light began to fade. Emalickel's glowing body reappeared. I cupped his handsome face with my hand and absorbed the magnificent sight of him. I bent down to kiss his lips and then pressed my cheek to his. I missed him, but I knew I would see him soon enough. I kept my gaze on Emalickel as I slowly removed my hand.

I walked back over to Thorenel. He embraced me once again in his strong warm arms. He kissed the top of my head. Everything began fading to black for a few seconds. I could still feel Thorenel holding me. Then, when the light returned, we were looking at the front door of the palace.

Thorenel released his hold on me and took a few steps away. He looked to the sky and summoned for Seronimel and Dennoliel with his mind. I could hear his voice in my head as he allowed for me to hear his broadcast.

Thorenel: Seronimel and Dennoliel, meet me at the palace. Emalickel will be returning soon. His homecoming is to be coordinated.

I looked up at the sky in the direction Thorenel directed his sights. It was silent. Nothing was happening. No voices responded. I looked at Thorenel who appeared annoyed.

Me: Did they hear you?

Thorenel laughed.

Thorenel: All of the guards heard me. I transmitted to them all. They all play a part in Emalickel's homecoming.

We continued waiting for a few more moments before finally seeing two light-forms begin to manifest in front of the palace door. The lights grew brighter and taller until fading into Seronimel and Dennoliel.

Seronimel: We are here brother.

Dennoliel looked at Seronimel in surprise with his eyes wide. He cleared his throat before returning his focus to Thorenel and bowing his head.

Dennoliel: Brother and Prince.

Thorenel was wearing the Lapoian crown. The bearer of the crown was to be addressed as Prince of Lapoi while wearing it.

Dennoliel looked down at the ground in embarrassment.

Seronimel: Most sincere apologies... my Prince.

Thorenel bowed his head acknowledging them both.

Thorenel: You have been summoned to the palace as Emalickel will make his return at the close of Auruclerum's cycle. We have preparations to tend.

Dennoliel and Seronimel both seemed to understand what was

expected. It was evident this wasn't their first time preparing for Emalickel's return.

Dennoliel: We will begin right away.

74. Artist: Hans Zimmer
Song: Time

The three brothers began walking towards the large arched front door of the palace. It opened on its own and loudly echoed the sound of heavy metal. The doors were white and gold, but they certainly sounded like they were made of some type of heavy dense steel.

I followed behind the brothers on the way inside. Seronimel and Dennoliel wore the guardian attire. They were wearing golden-colored armor which included a gold and white cape which hung at their shoulders. Being brothers of Princedoms, they both had the distinguished beige cloaks, lined with fur, which they wore over their guardian attire. I saw movement at the opposite end of the aisle down near the thrones. It was the two huge white lions. They had risen from a sideways lying position to sit upright at attention the moment we entered through the palace door. Thorenel was delegating the different jobs and duties to be done during the ceremony. Seronimel was recording everything on a golden tablet he had conjured.

Thorenel: Choose who you wish to serve, but we will need plenty to provide wine and mead and refreshments. We will need music and entertainment in the Entertainment Hall, in the Throne Hall, the Mead Hall, and the Ballroom. We will need twenty-five assistants to tend the kitchen, five in the Billiard Lounge, ten in the Mead Hall, ten in the Dining Hall, two in the Ballroom, and fifteen floaters dispersed throughout the palace to call upon if needed.

Thorenel was walking between his brothers. They were headed down the aisle of the Throne Hall. Thorenel turned around to me and motioned for me to continue following them. He continued instructing his brothers.

Thorenel: The rest are free to enjoy themselves this evening.

They continued talking among themselves as I became absorbed in the allure of the majestic palace. The black and gold velvet tapestries were blowing on the walls from the gentle breeze coming in through the open archways behind the throne. The aisle was incredibly long. The black runner rug in the middle of the aisle was perfectly pressed and clean. Nothing here seemed to ever get dirty, tarnish, or lose its luster. Everything looked like new. Everything seemed to glow and glitter. The pinkish-white hue of Auruclerum beamed in through the eastern windows from the courtyard area and through the northern archways above the thrones. This provided a perfect balance of glow and contrast for a warm and peaceful atmosphere. Although we were about halfway down the aisle, the throne chairs were still 50 yards away.

As I looked up at the dome-shaped ceiling, I noticed how massive everything was. The archways that lined the aisle on both the ground level and on the upper level were huge with a peak arch at about 15 feet from the ground. This would make the ceiling of the Throne Hall, at least 40 or 50 feet high. I continued walking behind Thorenel as I looked up at the smooth white concrete archways, lining both sides of the aisle, towering above my head.

Suddenly, I bumped into the back of Thorenel. I had not been watching where I was going nor listening to anything they were saying. I gasped in startling surprise of the collision. Thorenel smiled trying not to laugh. The other two brothers tried to remain professional. They briefly looked at each other, then immediately down at the ground with their hands folded in front of them pressing their smiles between their lips.

Thorenel: Are you with us, or have you drifted elsewhere?

I chuckled to myself looking down in embarrassment. I had been caught. All I could do was admit defeat and smile.

Me: I drifted elsewhere.

Thorenel smirked at me. He had thought it was an amusing incident.

Thorenel: What we were talking about is you and your placement during the ceremony. Would you rather wear your crown upon Emalickel's arrival, or would you rather receive your crown from Emalickel after his arrival?

The answer was so obvious to me.

Me: I'd like to receive it from Emalickel as I did the first time I ever wore it.

Thorenel: Consider it done then. We will leave your crown where it presently resides hanging on top of your throne chair. Upon making his way up the stairs, Emalickel will surely see that you are not wearing your crown, at which point he will know to provide it to you after he has received his own crown from me.

75. Artist: Audiomachine
Song: Rebirth

I looked up at the throne chairs to see my crown. Sure enough, it rested on the back of my throne chair waiting for my return. They hadn't pushed it to the side or put it away. It sat right there for all to see. Emalickel had kept true to his word. Since the day I departed, my crown had been sitting there as a reminder that Lapoi had a Princess, and the throne chair on the right side was reserved for her return.

Thorenel was finishing up with Seronimel and Dennoliel.

Thorenel: Alright brothers, you may be dismissed. I am going to summon Romenciel and Xabiel to assign the warriors.

They each shook arms with Thorenel and bowed their heads respectfully. They then turned to me and bowed respectfully before walking away to the front door. Thorenel then turned to me and took my arm. He escorted me up the stairs to the throne chairs. The two white lions held their positions and kept their focus straight ahead. They briefly engaged eye contact with me as I smiled and acknowledged them.

Thorenel motioned for me to take a seat on my throne chair. Afterwards, he sat himself in the other.

Thorenel: How does it feel? To sit in your place again?

I looked out at the palace. From this angle it looked even larger. Everything seemed to be centered around us.

Me: It feels like a beautiful dream. Like a fairy tale.

Thorenel's face grew of satisfaction. It was different sitting next to Thorenel on the thrones than Emalickel. With Emalickel everything felt so majestic and grand. It was magical and divine. I felt dignified and noble. With Thorenel, everything felt so relaxed and casual. It was informal and mellow. I felt easygoing and laid-back. Both atmospheres, with both brothers, felt comfortable to me. I would not be able to choose which I favored more. I liked the way I felt around each of them, in their own way.

Thorenel stroked the mane of the lion beside him. Then he started playing with him, roughing him up and laughing. The lion played back just as would a dog. I admired how lively and playful Thorenel always acted. He was full of life and personality.

Thorenel: After I speak with Romenciel and Xabiel, we will go to your favorite place.

I smiled knowing he was referring to the balcony behind us. He seemed content at that, exhibiting a proud demeanor for a few moments.

76. Artist: Mark Petrie
Song: Majestic

Then he made telepathic contact with Romenciel and Xabiel.

Thorenel: Romenciel and Xabiel, Emalickel will return this evening. We need to discuss the warriors and their positions for the ceremony. Please come to the thrones for further discussion.

After only a few moments, the palace doors opened with echoes. Romenciel, as usual, exhibited the persona of a true warrior, always riding in on a horse. Xabiel had followed suit this time. They both parked their horses outside in the front courtyard and walked in by foot. They were dressed in their shirtless sparring attire—black leather trousers with knee high combat boots and a flowing red cape at their shoulders. As they paced down the center aisle towards the thrones, their capes blew from underneath their royal cloaks, lined with white fur. They didn't use teleportation and other magic skills leisurely; instead they preferred to be raw. They walked nobly as their capes blew behind them. It took them a minute to arrive at the thrones. I couldn't get over how long this aisle was—how large this whole palace was.

Once they were there, Thorenel spoke. He remained in his seat while speaking, so I did as well.

Thorenel: Emalickel will be homecoming this evening. We need to make sure the warriors are covering the entire palace, especially since our Princess is present. We will need two warriors at each station.

Xabiel conjured a golden tablet and began recording what Thorenel was saying.

Thorenel: We will need them stationed at every doorway on both sides—the front entrance, the entrance to the Throne Hall, the base of the throne stairs, the Grand Archways . . .

Thorenel kept rambling off different places of the palace. I watched as Xabiel wrote this down and Romenciel stood at attention listening to Thorenel.

Thorenel: Upstairs we need them stationed at the top of both stair-

ways—one warrior in the north and one in the south. Five are to be stationed at the entry arches of Emalickel's Private Quarters, and five at the entry arches of my Private Quarters. They need to be at the Spa Quarters, the Education Quarters, and on the upper level of the Ballroom and the Great Library. Also, keep 32 on each level of the palace to line the Throne Hall arches.

Romenciel nodded in agreement.

Romenciel: So that would be 142 warriors on the ground level and 63 on the upper level. It will be done, my Prince. I will address the warriors now. They will be on post to take their places shortly.

77. Artist: Future World Music
Song: World of Dreams

Thorenel nodded to him and leaned back in his throne chair. Romenciel and Xabiel bowed to Thorenel and then to me before turning around to walk back to their horses outside the front door of the palace. Thorenel remained silent and seated while they exited. The lions resumed their laying down positions after Romenciel and Xabiel had left.

Then, Thorenel rose from his seat and held his hand out to me. I took his hand and stood up. He walked us to the stairs behind the throne chairs. We approached the Great Northern Archways and exited out to the grand balcony. We walked across the sidewalk which traveled directly over the great pool spa. The clouds were beginning to settle across the mountain range about 50 miles in the distance. The clouds appeared warm colors of pink, coral, and lavender due to the way Auruclerum shined upon them. The vast valley below was greener than the most luxurious golf course I'd ever seen. There were no flowers in bloom this time, only vast green grass for miles out.

We sat down on a bench towards the edge of the balcony. Thorenel was still holding my hand but moved it to his lap. I looked at him once again.

He was perfection. From the glow of his bronzed skin to the light of his golden locks of hair; from his large masculine physique adorned in the attire of a king to his wise, assertive, collected demeanor; from his glacier-blue eyes, which seemed to pierce right through me upon contact, to the power and strength radiating from him behind that shadow of perfectly trimmed facial hair.

I had placed him on a pedestal, and he knew it. Flattered, he smiled proudly and looked down shying away from eye contact.

Thorenel: Again, I am flattered by your thoughts, but you do give me more credit than of what I am worthy.

I shook my head at him.

Me: You deserve more.

We locked eyes for several moments. Thorenel leaned in and kissed my forehead. He sighed before speaking.

Thorenel: We must prepare ourselves for the return of Emalickel. Let me teach you about the passing of the crown.

We headed back inside to the throne area. We practiced the ceremony of the passing of the crown, so I would know what to do when the time came. Laughter from Thorenel and me filled the echoing Throne Hall as we enjoyed cutting up with each other and goofing off. He was a lot of fun; not quite as serious and professional as Emalickel.

The light of Auruclerum began to fade and warriors and guards began entering the palace. I noticed the lions were sitting upright at attention again. Thorenel began to pet one of the lions nearest to him again. He knew I was curious about them.

78. Artist: Audiomachine
Song: The Dreammaker

Thorenel: The lions, they rise any time there is another presence

in the palace besides Emalickel, you, or myself. If a presence not of Millattus were to enter the palace, the lions sound a great roar transmitting to every being on Lapoi. They will then tactfully back the presence into a corner roaring them into submission. Otherwise, they attack until takedown, or if one of us instructs them to do so. They understand our commands and will do anything we say within their capabilities. They are our loyal companions. They will never hurt us nor turn on us.

We heard a throat clear. Thorenel was being summoned by Dennoliel at the foot of the stairs. Dennoliel motioned with his head that he needed Thorenel.

Thorenel: It looks like we have begun preparations for this evening. I will likely be occupied until the gathering begins. You are free to come along with me, but remember, this is your palace too. Go and do as you please, wherever you please. Just stay within the parameters of the palace so the warriors will be nearby.

He took my hand and brought it to his lips giving it a gentle kiss. Then, he smiled at me as if to say, "I love you" before turning to walk down the throne stairs. His red velvety cape moved royally behind him as he walked.

I sat down on the floor next to the white lion on my side. I began to pet him. I leaned my head onto his side and drifted away. I was smiling in thoughts of excitement, anticipating Emalickel's return. The lion breathed slow deep breaths. My head moved with his side as he inhaled and exhaled. He was very soft and warm.

Since Thorenel and the other celestials were occupied on the ceremony preparations and Emalickel was not there, I decided to wander the palace and take my mind off the seemingly long wait. I headed towards the arched windows which lined the Throne Hall behind the aisle archways in the east. I could see the landscaped courtyard area. There were benches to sit upon near sparkling great fountains. Flower beds lined the paved walkways. I noticed a grand open room to my left and began roaming around that way. From there, I continued into many other different grand rooms on the ground floor.

79. Artist: Adrian Von Zeigler
Song: Song of Brotherhood

Night fell, and the palace became packed with the beings of Lapoi. Upbeat music was playing. It was a blend of Celtic, Renaissance, and Viking music. It was being played in several of the rooms on the ground level. I was looking for Thorenel, as I hadn't seen him since he started tending to the preparations. I wondered where he was. That's when I heard his voice in my head.

Thorenel: ***There you are. Come to the Mead Hall. Go down the throne stairs and turn left. It's through the Great Hall all the way back. You'll hear the commotion. I have an empty chair beside me—it is waiting for you.***

When I got to the Mead Hall, I noticed Thorenel was sitting across the room drinking from a tankard. He was in a chair which sat upon a slightly raised platform. There was another chair on this platform next to his. He saw me, placed his tankard on the table beside him, and stood up like a gentleman, with his hands folded down in front of him, as a solider would stand. He smiled and motioned for me to sit in the chair beside him.

There was dancing, drinking, laughing, and loud conversations carrying on throughout the Mead Hall. It was a fun and light atmosphere. When I arrived to Thorenel, he spoke to me over the noise.

Thorenel: And this is my favorite place in all the palace! So full of energy and life!

I stayed in there for what seemed like an hour. It was fun to watch everyone. We could see everything from where our chairs were located. Different songs played, and many were dancing and laughing while others came to us to share stories of adventure. There were group step dances in which we participated a few times. Most of us huddled together in the middle of the Mead Hall floor, but there were many who chose a table to dance upon. Other tables were occupied by those gorging themselves in drinking and feasting. They were all drinking from tankards and acting carefree. Spills were happening left and right, but nobody seemed to care. It was a room filled, wall-to-wall, with relaxed and joyful presences. Every face was smiling and laughing. Everyone was either eating, drinking, or dancing—some were doing all three!

During one of the songs, Xabiel requested to see Thorenel. Kissing my hand, Thorenel politely excused himself and headed out of the Mead Hall with Xabiel. I decided to go to the balcony to see what the night sky looked like on Lapoi.

80. Artist: Brian Tyler
Song: Thor, Son of Odin

When I got out there, all I could hear was the faint sound of music and laughing in the distance within the palace. I could feel a cool sensation in the night air. I wasn't cold, but there definitely was a slight chill in the air without Auruclerum's light.

Suddenly, I felt a breeze stronger than all the rest. A slow whisper came along with the breeze. It sounded like the voice of Emalickel mixed with the whisper of the wind. First it sounded like a sigh, and then it formed words. I heard it as if it were passing by me in the wind.

Emalickel: I have missed you.

The next thing I heard was the sound of Thorenel's voice from inside the palace. He was calling in a loud authoritative voice.

Thorenel: He has arrived! Emalickel has returned! All make way to the Throne Hall! Take your positions! He is here!

I headed back into the Throne Hall from the Grand Balcony. I began walking down the stairs to the ground level. The lions had risen. Celestials, wearing different attire and colored garments, were feeding in from all directions through all the arches. They were all conversing. I was unsure where to go, so I stood on the ground, to the side of the stairs. There were so many celestials, it was hard to see individual faces.

Everyone was still settling in the busy room when I felt a pair of warm and calm hands gently place themselves on my shoulders. I turned my head to see who it was. It was Thorenel. He still wore the crown of Lapoi. He knew I was becoming overwhelmed. His touch alone sent energy waves of calm and peace through my body.

He placed his arm around my back and guided me back up the stairs.

Thorenel: We will take our places up here, Princess.

He showed me to my throne chair, and we took our seats. I looked out at everyone who was gathering and suddenly felt a churning of nerves deep in the pit of my stomach. I was really nervous, not only about the ceremony and all the attention, but about seeing Emalickel again. It had been six Earth-years since I had last seen him, and he was about to make his presence right there in front of me—in the physical.

81. Artist: Thomas Bergerson
Song: Colors of Love

The giant front arched doors began to open with its majestic echo. I saw Emalickel's figure standing at attention while he waited for the doors to open completely. He slowly removed the hood of his cloak from his head. Then, he stepped inside. A ray of glowing light illuminated him. He took steady steps along the black aisle rug keeping his gaze straight ahead.

The palace was packed with cheering celestials. They had conjured some kind of golden glitter to throw into the air. As Emalickel walked past them, they would bow to him. A Lapoian bow was subtle; bowing celestials would fold their hands to their chest and slightly bend both knees together while their heads looked downward and nodded once.

Emalickel continued walking. He was wearing loose-fitting black pants trimmed in gold and a black tunic. Around his waist was a white belt with a golden Celtic trinity symbol in the middle. His black boots were hard to see under his pant legs. He wore his red velvety cape under his cloak. The hem of his cloak gently glided along the floor behind him as he progressed down the center aisle towards the thrones.

The celestials were cheering his name repeatedly. It amazed me how much respect they had for him. They were all so ecstatic for his return. I looked briefly over at Thorenel. He remained professional on the throne chair, but I could tell he, too, seemed happy to see his brother again. Even he, who was about to relinquish his crown to pass back down to Emalickel, had great respect for the eldest Princedom brother. He was looking out at Emalickel and smiling peacefully. He noticed I was looking at him and acknowledged me by glancing over at me with a smile and a wink. He then returned his focus to Emalickel's grand entrance.

As Emalickel got closer I could see he was making eye contact directly at me. It was as if he saw nobody else in the room. His focus was right on me. His smile grew wider, and I could begin to see his bright white teeth peeking through. Everything in the room suddenly became dimmer, slower, and quieter. I could faintly hear an angelic choir humming harmonious joyful notes as he continued closer. He stood out in the glow of light which continued to illuminate him. He continued walking down the aisle, approaching closer and closer. I became more and more nervous, the closer he got. I was taken away at the beautiful image of him. I tried to control my facial expression, but it was all I could do to breathe as he came even closer. His presence made my legs grow weak, and it made my heart tremble. His energy was sovereign. I was infatuated with him.

When he finally arrived at the foot of the stairs, he stopped. Thorenel and I stood up in unison. We had practiced this earlier. Emalickel continued looking at me for a moment. He winked at me and held his bright smile for even a moment longer. Then, he turned his head to look at Thorenel. Thorenel motioned for Emalickel to come up the stairs. Emalickel took his time bringing himself up each of the nine steps.

Once Emalickel arrived at the top of the stairs, Thorenel removed the Lapoian Crown from his own head and held it with both hands. The crown was presented to the celestials in the Throne Hall as Thorenel spoke loudly.

Thorenel: The Crown of Lapoi represents supremacy among the entire realm of Millattus. May he who bears this crown, adorn it with great honor in their title as the Prince of Lapoi. May all who come into his presence, embellish him with great respect and admiration.

Thorenel turned back to Emalickel with the crown. Emalickel kneeled to Thorenel. Thorenel gently placed the crown onto Emalickel head. Emalickel then returned to a standing position. At this, Thorenel knelt on one knee to Emalickel. Emalickel placed his hand on Thorenel's right shoulder signaling acknowledgement. Thorenel then rose and bowed his head to Emalickel before turning to descend gracefully down the stairs. He took his place at the foot of the stairs, off to the side. This completed the ceremony. The celestials roared deeply chanting in unison.

Celestials: Prince Emalickel! Prince Emalickel!

The celestials were clapping and cheering, but Emalickel held up his hand signaling for them to stop. He turned to me. He stepped closer and reached for the crown on the back of my throne chair. He held it with both his hands waiting for me. He gazed at me deeply, smiling at me with so much love within his twinkling aqua eyes. I remembered he previously told me not to bow before him, so I simply tilted me head forward for him. When I felt him gently place my crown onto my head, I had forgotten how heavy and solid it felt. Emalickel placed his hands on my shoulders and brought his face in closer to mine. He whispered very quietly to me, so nobody would hear.

Emalickel: One glimpse of you, and I lose myself. I forget where I am and who I am.

His lustful gaze toggled between my eyes as if searching for a place to focus his passion. He was breathing hard, which in turn made me breath hard. I smiled at him, not knowing what else to do. Then, he snapped out of it and took my hand into his. He squeezed my hand and I could feel his passion radiating through me. He raised our clasped hands together in the air and presented me loud and clear.

Emalickel: Lapoi, your Princess has returned!

The celestials all began clapping and cheering loudly again. I scanned the entire Throne Hall with my eyes absorbing the scene. The entire hall now grew into illumination. I saw the glitter being thrown into the air and heard random shouts and whistles of celebration. When I glanced down in Thorenel's direction I could see that he, too, was clapping and smiling proudly at me.

When the roar decreased and came to an end. Emalickel addressed the celestials.

Emalickel: Tomorrow evening, I shall provide the orders in which I received. Until then, let us celebrate the glory of tonight!

82. Artist: Brunuhville
Song: Dragonland

Emalickel pointed towards the instrumental celestials who were gathered at the base of the stairs to our left. They began to play. The instruments consisted of violins, cellos, accordions, mandolins, flutes, bass drums, and vocalists. Everyone began to move and shuffle, filling the aisle, dancing and laughing in celebration. Some celestials made their way into the Mead Hall while others dispersed into the Entertainment Hall. They also filled the Throne Hall on both the upper floors and the entire ground level all between archways. They began socializing among one another.

A female approached the thrones with Romenciel and Xabiel. She was wearing a beige and gold hooded cloak, like the royal cloak worn by the brothers. Until this point the only celestials that I had seen wearing the cloaks were the brothers. I saw Emalickel look at me briefly before speaking to the cloaked female.

Emalickel: Zamadriel! What a pleasure to see you this evening! Have you been formally introduced to our Princess?

Zamadriel spoke kindly.

Zamadriel: I know of her very well but have not been formally introduced.

Emalickel: Well, let us go to the balcony so we can all become more acquainted.

He held out his arm to escort me. We turned to go up the stairs behind the thrones leading to the Grand Balcony. I looked back and saw that Thorenel was coming up the stairs behind Zamadriel, Romenciel, and Xabiel. When we got outside, we all continued walking across the spa pool towards the balcony's edge. We all stood looking out at the Valley of Dillectus for a moment. Emalickel spoke, moving over to Zamadriel.

Emalickel: Princess, this is Zamadriel.

She respectfully bowed her head to me.

Emalickel: Zamadriel is our sister.

I didn't know they had a sister.

Emalickel: She is our sister through brotherhood. Zamadriel is one with Romenciel and Xabiel, as you are one with Thorenel and me.

Emalickel walked to lean onto the balcony rail. He looked out again at the mountains in the distance. The other brothers stood to the side.

Emalickel: Each partnership is balanced with a chosen female. Like you, Zamadriel came from the mortal plane. Her energy captivated my brothers, who then sought-after her as I once sought-after you.

I had questions but could tell Emalickel still had more to say. He began walking around the balcony with his hands behind his back. I knew he could hear my questions and would deliver the answers to me in a nice neat package, if I would just let him continue. He was looking down at his feet as he walked.

Emalickel: As you know, everything was created with balance—darkness and light. The conscious beings of creation must also be in balance. Although celestials and mortals are not to blend with each other on the mortal plane, as many have wrongfully done, we are to keep ourselves balanced through the energies often referred to as the feminine energy. Especially the celestials in higher-status positions, like my brothers and I, are in need of finding that balancing energy.

Emalickel turned and walked towards me with a gentle smile on his face.

Emalickel: This desired feminine energy exists only in the mortal plane. This is because the mortal plane is where the contrast exists. It is where duality exists. The mortal females encompass the feminine energy. We are to wait for that energy to awaken before seeking its companionship. That can take eons. This is

because, although we are allowed to influence awakenings through inspiration, synchronicities, and symbolisms, we are not allowed to make manifestations in our celestial bodies to contact mortals unless ordered by God. Awakenings can take an extensive amount of time because mortals tend to lack in faith and often have doubts. They must "see it to believe it" and even then, they try to find justifications for things that are unusual.

He walked over to Zamadriel and then behind her as she faced me.

Emalickel: Zamadriel was once a part of the mortal plane. She came from Grahst, and like you, she once passed between planes in her astral body, and has recently become into her full awakening. She now permanently resides with Romenciel and Xabiel at the Warrior Temple in Karnequlus. Upon your full awakening, you will reside permanently with Thorenel and me, here at the Palace of Lapoi.

I was quiet as I was trying to process everything.

Zamadriel: You look as I did when Romenciel first had this talk with me. I was confused and overwhelmed with new information to sort and process. Rest yourself. You will see everything in time. It will all be revealed, and you will then understand everything completely.

83. Artist: Stephen D. Lemaire
Song: Voyage in Time

Emalickel came to my side.

Emalickel: I do not wish to overwhelm you, but I do feel there is something you must know. I can feel a sense of unseen discomfort from you pertaining to your future in Lapoi. I wish to suppress your discomfort by providing you information regarding the matter which I presume is causing the unease. In regards to your creation from the Earth, the one you call your daughter, be at ease

with her fate. She is well-protected and will certainly be taken care of with the upmost priority. I hope you are ready for what I am about to say.

Slightly smiling, Emalickel paused to make sure he had my full attention. He turned my body at the shoulders to face him more squarely before continuing.

Emalickel: Seronimel and Dennoliel—they have chosen her. She has energy unique in form, just like her mother. They are hopelessly attracted to her soul, as I am to yours. They will begin contact with her when she completes her prerequisite experiences and becomes ready for her awakening.

I became excited and was thoroughly impressed with how boldly Emalickel addressed some hidden internal disturbances of mine. I knew something was bothering me, but even I did not know what exactly was causing the anxiety. Emalickel did. Not to my surprise, he nailed it. His abilities and perceptions were beyond extraordinary.

Me: Will she come here? Will she see me? Will she stay here?

Emalickel smiled, knowing I was pleased and excited by this news.

Emalickel: She must choose Seronimel and Dennoliel for herself. They do have an advantage to winning her heart—after all, her Earthly mother is the Princess here. Eventually, she will discover this truth during one of her visits in the future. Should she choose Seronimel and Dennoliel, she will continue her awakening on the Earth until she permanently resides at the Guardian Mansion in Terpetrus with them.

Seronimel and Dennoliel were the brothers in charge of the Guards of Lapoi. They seemed younger than the other brothers, but also seemed to be soft-hearted, kind, and genuine. The warriors all seemed rough around the edges, but guards were softer. The guard brothers were a profound option for her. I truly was excited to hear this news. I had been subconsciously wondering about her fate.

Emalickel: I hope it is well that I have revealed this much to you. I am only trying to satisfy your intense passion for growing knowledge and deeper understanding. Zamadriel is right, you shall see everything when you are fully awakened. I hope you are not confused or overwhelmed with this additional information. All will become clear to you in time.

84. Artist: Brunuhville
Song: Medieval Legends

Xabiel walked closer to Zamadriel. He put out a James Dean cool-guy vibe as he leaned his back casually on the rail of the balcony.

Xabiel: Zamadriel started her awakening shortly after your last visit to Lapoi when I had tried to capture your interest. Remember that, Princess?

He turned his head to glance at me lustfully before continuing.

Xabiel: The only reason Zamadriel is fully awakened in such a short time is because she cannot resist me and has received a steady stream of my energy, thus evolving her much more rapidly than normal.

Zamadriel smiled, rolled her eyes, and shook her head at him. He returned the look with a wink. I saw a few of the brothers roll their eyes at Xabiel. He was a middle brother and the most arrogant of the six Princedom brothers. When Emalickel was around, he always cut Xabiel down to size.

Emalickel: Although your energy may have contributed to her awakening, Xabiel, the real reason she has evolved faster is because she is from Grahst. The structure of their matter enables them to be more receptive to knowledge and less resistant to doubt. It is the way they are wired.

Thorenel had gone to stand next to Emalickel and looked out from the balcony with him. Xabiel grew a mischievous smirk on his face.

He turned his head to look in the direction of Emalickel and Thorenel. Xabiel chuckled to himself.

Xabiel: At least I refrained from childish grumbling when the law of celestial-pairs came into play in the relationship. I certainly accepted it a little better than those in higher positions.

Xabiel was looking directly at Emalickel with an arrogant expression. Emalickel whipped himself around and walked right up to Xabiel's face.

Emalickel: You waste my time, Xabiel, but I do feel a strong desire to put you in your place, so I will say this. If it were possible for a celestial to find balance in the number of two, then I would be the one to discover it. Unlike you, instead of becoming a slave to my physical urges, I am a challenger to all the possibilities. You see, Xabiel that is why I am superior to you. That is why I am Prince of this kingdom. That is why I am able to do all the things I can do. That, my dear brother, is what distinguishes my power and my status from that of yours. May you not forget your place should you choose to address me in such a belittling manner in the future.

Emalickel stood there staring challengingly at Xabiel, his jaw muscles clenching. Until now, Romenciel had been quietly roaming around the balcony, but he quickly chimed in on the conversation before Xabiel could talk back to Emalickel and regret it.

Romenciel: You know Xabiel, I played a part in her awakening as well, brother. And I actually tried to do it by providing her knowledge and enlightenment instead of relying on the brute force of my energy molecules.

Xabiel looked the other way, rolling his eyes in the process. He muttered sarcastically under his breath and mocked Romenciel.

Xabiel: I'm Romenciel, the Knight in Shining Armor of Lapoi. I do everything right. I am so dignified. I am better than everyone else.

Zamadriel attempted to interrupt the quarrel.

Zamadriel: Well I am happy to have you both as mine own. I would not be able to choose between the two of you. I am glad I did not have to make such a choice.

Another celestial walked with determination out to the balcony area where we were all standing. He brought himself in front of Emalickel and bowed.

Celestial: I beg your pardon, my Prince...

The celestial turned towards me and bowed.

Celestial: Princess.

He turned back to Emalickel.

Celestial: They are ready for your party's presence in the Entertainment Hall.

Emalickel nodded his head at the celestial acknowledging that he had heard. The celestial quickly bowed again to us both before going back inside.

Emalickel: Come, brothers and sisters. Let us make our way to the entertainment!

85. Artist: Olexandr Ignatov
Song: Emotions

The pairs of brothers, each took one of the arms of their mate. Emalickel took my right arm and Thorenel took my left. They escorted us back over the bridge of the spa pool.

I was surprised to meet Zamadriel. I had no idea Romenciel and Xabiel had united with a female since my last visit to Lapoi. They had mentioned she was a mortal of Grahst, but I wondered where females came from before becoming mortal. I knew that males were former celestials but was still unclear of the origins of females. Emalickel was the first to address my thoughts.

Emalickel: As the mortal project began on Earth, the male mortals desired female counterparts to act as companions and to procreate. God sent female volunteers, from the realm of Jesserion, to inhabit the mortal planes of Millattus. Jesserion is one of the nine realms in the Third Sphere. It is our ally, inhabited only by divine female forms who are extraordinarily wise, powerful, and independent.

Thorenel joined in.

Thorenel: They are one of the strongest realms in the Third Sphere of existence. Their Princedoms and warriors are feared among the other realms. Not even the darkest of realms think of intruding on the females of Jesserion.

Emalickel resumed what he was saying.

Emalickel: The female volunteers from Jesserion were sent to Earth, Fynne, and Grahst to accompany males and participate in the mortal experience. Upon full-awakening, all mortal females will return back to Jesserion and resume their divine positions. However, if they have found unity with a pair of male celestials in Millattus, the female will carry her divinity into Lapoi with her pair of celestial brothers.

Thorenel added a bit of humor.

Thorenel: So now you understand why females are so different from males. Not only do you have a different physical format, but you think and behave so different from males. Your Jesserion wisdom, power, and independence still emit, even on the mortal planes. Females literally come from a different realm. You are all aliens to Millattus!

Emalickel smiled and rolled his eyes at his younger brother's juvenile demeanor.

We had just arrived inside and were making our way down the first set of stairs behind the thrones. I felt Thorenel tug at my arm. When I looked up at him he was looking down at me with a smile. He mouthed the word, "beautiful" while shaking his head in disbelief. His eyes squinted in desire. That seemed to be his thing, mouthing the word "beautiful" at me. I smiled back at him in appreciation. When I looked to my right I saw Emalickel. He was looking at me already but was chewing somewhat nervously on his lower lip.

86. Artist: Future World Music
Song: Anthem of the World

I wondered what he was thinking about. He appeared to be hesitant, like he wanted to tell me something, but wasn't sure if he should. I decided to try and pull it from him—whatever it was.

Me: What is it? What are you wanting to say?

He continued hesitating before taking a deep breath of preparation.

Emalickel: Would you like to know your real name?

Me: Real name? Is it not Adrienne?

Emalickel: Variations of your real name have been given to you on the Earth through the whispers of the guards during each of your lifetimes. Each time, your parents heard the whispers slightly differently, giving you names such as Andrea, Alexandra, Adriana, Arianna, and Adrienne.

I was intrigued.

Emalickel: Your name, your real name, here from Lapoi is —Hadriannel.

I couldn't help but smile. I felt the sensation of tickles deep within my gut. The sound of my Lapoian name gave me the same feeling as love at first sight. I felt giddy. I also felt silly with a paralyzed smile plastered on my face. Although I tried not to make eye contact with Emalickel, I could see him, in my peripheral vision, looking at me in satisfaction.

Emalickel: I am pleased to see that you are pleased.

Up ahead, I noticed Romenciel was smiling. Usually serious and stern, Romenciel only smiled on occasion. He carried that warrior persona, always keeping a watchful eye on his surroundings. It was a privilege to see him smile, for when he did, his smile was always genuine and bright. When he smiled, his eyes squinted, creating laugh lines on the outer edges. His teeth were pearly white. They shined beneath his facial hair which was slightly fuller than any of the other brothers.

He and Emalickel were similar in personality. The two of them carried a good vibration together.

Romenciel briefly removed himself from the hand of Zamadriel to wait for Emalickel, Thorenel, and me to catch up to him. He placed his arm around Emalickel and playfully patted his back and roughed him up a bit—just like an older brother. Romenciel spoke through his wide grin.

Romenciel: Our Prince and Princess are both pleased! Tonight's festivities are going to be well-remembered!

87. Artist: Adrian Von Zeigler
Song: For the King

Having made our way through the Throne Hall, which was still packed with celestials conversing and laughing with one another, we turned the corner to the right and entered the Entertainment Hall. Seronimel and Dennoliel, who had been engaging in friendly conversation with a group of guards, met us outside the Entertainment Hall door so they could walk in with us.

Inside, there was upbeat Celtic-like music playing. All the circular tables and chairs were full, except for one 15-foot rectangular table. It was positioned along the back wall, under the arched windows which looked out at the Valley of Dillectus. Like the chairs in the Mead Hall, this table sat up on a small platform. There was real food and mead around all the tables. I saw breads, fruits, and cheeses.

Romenciel, Zamadriel, and Xabiel entered first. They were followed by Dennoliel and Seronimel. Emalickel, Thorenel, and I followed behind Dennoliel and Seronimel.

I remember looking at Seronimel and Dennoliel as they walked in front of us. As with all the brothers, they were both very masculine. With the blood of Emalickel, facial structures of models, and the bodies of warriors, I could grant them my approval to peruse my offspring. Not that they would need my approval, but at least I could rest easy knowing my girl would be in good hands. They both noticed me giving them a once-over in approval. In unison, they both nodded their heads to me and smiled a satisfied smile.

We all made our way back to take our seats at the table. As warriors, Romenciel and Xabiel sat on the ends. The rest of us sat in the remaining chairs which were all on one long side looking out towards the rest of the room. Everyone moved to the sides, so that Emalickel and I could sit down first. Our backs were to the extravagant wall of arched windows. From left to right we sat: Romenciel on the left end, Zamadriel, Dennoliel, Emalickel, myself, Thorenel, Seronimel, and Xabiel on the right end.

Before she sat down in her chair, Zamadriel leaned into my space and kindly whispered.

Zamadriel: We all envy you—all the females. What a fairy tale you live having this magnificent palace, with your handsome Princedoms, and access to all the powers which will someday blossom to you. I am proud; I am honored, to be able to call myself your sister.

She bowed her head to me before proceeding to her seat.

The celestial who was ahead of the ceremony announced our arrival and led the room in prayer giving gratitude to God.

After the prayer, the music picked back up and the Head of Ceremony gave the word for us to eat, drink, and be merry. Some people got up and started dancing. Others engaged in loud joyful conversations, filling the room with voices and laughter. I noticed many females, probably making up one third of the room, with various guard and warrior celestials.

Everyone at our table began digging into the food. Assistants were on either end of our table waiting to be needed. Thorenel, Xabiel, and Seronimel began chugging their mead and were finished before most of us noticed. We looked up when they all slammed their empty tankards on the table and wiped their mouths with their arms almost in perfect unison.

Romenciel: Are you having some sort of contest?

Thorenel laughed out loud.

Thorenel: No, brother, we are simply consumed with thirst for mead! It has been too long.

Romenciel: It has merely been since the last festivities.

Thorenel jokingly teased at Romenciel.

Thorenel: Do you have wax in your ears!?! Like I said, it has been too long!

Disregarding Romenciel's comments altogether, Xabiel shouted at the assistants.

Xabiel: Do provide us with more!

Emalickel bumped my arm with his elbow. He raised his tankard. I knew he was signaling for me to follow suit. I raised my tankard. The entire room, one by one, began to raise their tankards with us until everyone had theirs in the air. Conversations stopped, but the music continued. Emalickel addressed his celestials.

Emalickel: May there continue to be many blessing bestowed upon Millattus as there has always been. We shall be forever grateful.

May we eternally please our Father in Heaven and may His will continue to be done with ease.

88. Artist: Tunes of Fantasy (Florian Bur)
Song: White Angel

All in the room shouted the words "so may it be!" before drinking their mead. We indulged in our food and continued to have a few drinks. Thorenel leaned over me and spoke to Emalickel.

Thorenel: My Prince, may I ask our Hadriannel for this dance?

Emalickel nodded in approval to him.

Thorenel then leaned in with a flirty smirk to ask me himself like a true gentleman.

Thorenel: Princess, may I escort you in this dance?

I smiled and agreed. Thorenel took my hand in his to the floor.

The evening progressed and carried on for an extensive amount of time. The palace was busy, and it was packed with celestials going every direction. It was one giant, full-blown party. Different music was being played in different rooms. There were celestials in the Courtyard, the Ballroom, the Billiards and Lounge Hall playing card games and pool. They were everywhere in the palace except for three places. Those three places were Thorenel's Private Chambers, Emalickel's Private Chambers, and anywhere above the stairs to the thrones. Everyone knew those places were strictly forbidden unless by personal invite, and they were well guarded by some of Romenciel and Xabiel's finest warriors.

After several hours, I found myself watching a poker game in the Billiard and Lounge Hall. I was standing with Emalickel and Romenciel. Thorenel was in his favorite room, the Mead Hall next door, drinking with Seronimel and Dennoliel. Suddenly, I felt my eyes grow heavy. I tried to fight it as none of the celestials grew tired except for every few weeks. I felt petty and weak and wanted to resist the urge to crawl into a soft bed and close my eyes.

Emalickel: Let me take you up upstairs, beloved. You need to rest.

Emalickel was looking down at me. I blinked my eyes a few times, still trying to fight it.

Emalickel: This is not a question or an option.

Me: What about the party?

Emalickel: I will tend to the party after I know you are at rest.

He held out his arm for me to clutch. I could barely keep my eyes open. When we had made our way through the crowd, across the Throne Hall, and arrived to the stairs on the opposite side of the aisle, I felt Emalickel place his entire arm under my arm to aid me up the stairs. There were so many steps. When we finally reached the top, we walked past several more archways on our right which over-looked the giant Throne Hall. We walked back until we came to several archways on our left which were heavily guarded with warriors. Emalickel steered us in this direction. We continued down another hall filled with windows which looked out at the Western Courtyard.

Finally, we had arrived to some arched doorways. Emalickel opened one of them. I was too tired to pay attention to which one. We walked through a living room area, then a kitchen area, then across another hallway, into another arched doorway. I recognized the room we entered next. It was the room I had woken up in on my first visit to Lapoi.

Too tired to say anything or react in any way, I headed toward where I knew his bed was. Emalickel turned down the covers for me. He placed his hand on my chest and closed his eyes. A bright light engulfed me, and then faded. I was wearing a satin white nightgown which came to just above my knees.

Emalickel: I want you to be comfortable and rest for as long as you wish.

He helped me to crawl into the bed. It was most certainly the most comfortable place I had ever placed my body to rest in all my existence. I remember thinking about how soft his sheets were, how perfect the cool temperature of his bed felt against my skin, how happy I was that he brought me to lay in it.

Emalickel: This is not my bed, Hadriannel. This is our bed.

He lay down beside me and stroked my hair. Outside the large archways to his balcony, I could see the light of Auruclerum still emitted dim light rays like that of soft candle light. It was peeking in between the white chiffon drapery. The light of both moons, one larger than the other, beamed down on all the glory of the land below and on the mountain peaks in the distance. A white owl perched itself of the stone railing of the balcony, seeming to admire the scenery below. Emalickel slowly leaned into me for a kiss. His lips were so soft and supple, so warm and inviting. If only I could wake up. I wanted to enjoy the splendor him. Then he whispered to me.

Emalickel: I would refuse you. I insist you need your rest.

He once again had read my mind. Shooting him one last satisfied smile. I decided to give in and submit to the heaviness of sleep for that evening.

89. Artist: Mattia Cupelli
Song: Mooncatcher

The next day came, and the light of Auruclerum was peeking in through the veils of the archways from the balcony. I rolled over in the white sheets and noticed I was alone in the bed. Emalickel had either not slept that night, or I slept so long that he had already awoken. I slipped out of bed.

Still wearing my satin nightgown and bare feet, I made my way to the balcony to greet the beauty of Lapoi. The allure and vastness of the land still amazed me. Taking a deep breath in of the crisp wintergreen air, I smiled in gratitude and satisfaction. Everything was so still and quiet. I wondered where everyone was.

I made my way back into the bedroom from the balcony, through the hallway, passed through the kitchen and the living room, and opened the door to the palace hallway. The courtyard windows were in front of me as I stepped out into the hallway and looked through the windows overlooking the western courtyard area. Nobody was in the courtyard below. I did hear voices echoing around the walls. I turned left to follow the hallway, past a warrior who, along with five others, guarded the archways of Emalickel's Private Quarters. As I passed under the archway, I excused myself through more celestials to peer over a rail overlooking the Throne Hall. It was filled with celestials, including on the upper floor where I was wandering.

Emalickel was sitting in his throne chair with a golden tablet in his hands. He was wearing a long sleeve dark-brown gown with a bronze belt around his waist and gold-colored designed fabric around the sleeves and chest area. He appeared to be reading something from the tablet while another celestial was speaking to him. Emalickel seemed intensely focused on what he was reading and hearing.

I saw Thorenel wearing his cloak, but it was pushed behind his shoulders like a cape. He had on a long sleeve dark-red velvety gown trimmed with gold fabric around the sleeves and neck area. The gown came down to his knees. He wore a bronze belt at his waist too. His pants were loose, black trousers trimmed in gold, and they could be seen coming out from the base of his gown at his knees. He wore black boots, but his pant legs covered them. He was standing in his spot at the western foot of the throne stairs.

Emalickel suddenly looked up, right at me. He lowered the tablet and stood up. Thorenel saw Emalickel and turned around to see what he was looking at. All the celestials were looking at me now. They were all staring. At once, Thorenel's face lit up as he cleared his throat and spoke.

Thorenel: Please continue, my Prince, I will excuse myself to tend to the Princess.

Thorenel started to walk my way when Emalickel held out his tablet to Thorenel.

Emalickel: No, brother. Please, tend to the orders for me.

Seeming a bit dispirited, Thorenel proceeded up the stairs towards the throne. He took the tablet from Emalickel and sat down in the throne chair. Emalickel never took his eyes from me.

Then, his body faded from where he was standing and reappeared upstairs directly in front of me. He smiled and held out both hands as he walked a few more feet to me. All the celestials were still watching us. Emalickel placed his hands on my hips and gripped me closer. All was silent. We gazed at each other for a moment before Emalickel's facial expression grew confused. He turned around and looked down over the upper balcony rail at Thorenel. He, too, was staring at us.

Emalickel: Celestials, are we at the expense of your entertainment?

Startled, everyone immediately came out of their trances, and turned back around. Thorenel cleared his throat quite vocally, almost as if irritated, before I heard him ask the celestial to continue where he had left off with Emalickel. Emalickel spoke to me in a playful voice.

Emalickel: I cannot say I blame them for staring.

He was looking at my body when he said this, not my face. I looked down and realized I was still wearing the night gown! My jaw dropped in surprise. I couldn't believe I had walked out into the crowd of the palace wearing my night gown. I simply had forgotten. Emalickel guided me aside from the crowd until we were standing in the archway of his Private Quarters. He smiled and shook his head before placing his hands on my chest.

A bright orb of light engulfed me, and then faded. I was wearing a full, sleeveless, golden, glittering, gown that tied into a halter style around the neck. A royal cloak was draped across my shoulders to grazed the floor.

Emalickel: Have you seen the entire palace?

Although I had explored many rooms the day before, I had not seen all there was to see.

Me: Not all of it.

Emalickel: Well after today, you shall say you have seen all of it.

He took me by the arm and began walking back towards his private quarters which were on the Northwest corner of the palace. We continued down the hallway. The windows overlooking the western courtyard were to our left. Emalickel opened the first door on the right and allowed for me to walk inside.

Emalickel: This is my personal Trophy Room.

The room was filled with beautiful glowing artifacts, statues, jewels, and trophy boxes with armor, garments, and weaponry. Tapestries hung from the northern and southern walls of the trophy room. Two open archways were in the Northwest corner.

Emalickel: These are things I collected in my experiences over the eons. Each item holds its own story. Someday, I will share each of them with you.

90. Artist: Mattia Cupelli
Song: Waves

He motioned for me to continue through the open archways ahead. They exited to a perpendicular hallway. I looked right and saw a closed arched door.

Emalickel: That is a bathroom.

There was a brief silence. I was trying really hard not to laugh. This was not an answer I had expected. I was also confused because I didn't think celestials had to eat, drink, sleep, or... use the bathroom. Emalickel's tone became playful.

Emalickel: As you witnessed last night, we do eat and drink for pleasure. Where do you think the biproduct of all that goes? We are powerful beings, but we cannot defy the laws of biology.

To our left the hallway extended with several open archways on both sides. Straight ahead, to the north, was a room with bookshelves, couches and tables with chairs, and a fluffy white centrally located rug. Two giant windows were on the northern wall overlooking the Valley of Dillectus and mountains. On the western wall were three more archways leading into a dining room.

Emalickel: Yes, that room is the Dining Room. The other one, straight across here overlooking the mountains, is my Study Chambers.

Both rooms seemed to measure about 40-feet by 40-feet. They were huge and extravagant. They were colored shades of tan, white, and gold. Everything was so bright and also so clean.

Me: Everything is so perfect and put into place. It all matches and is decorated so beautifully!

Emalickel: All the thanks to our palace caretakers. They stay here and work in shifts. It is what they love to do. They reside in the Residential Halls upstairs.

We continued back down the hallway. On the right another archway opened to the Dining Room, but across from that, on the left was an archway that led to another 40-foot by 40-foot room.

Emalickel: That is the King Room.

This room was similar to what I would refer to as a "man-cave." It had entertainment seating, a pool table, a card table, a kitchen and bar area, and a large screen hung down on the eastern wall. Music was even playing from speakers in the walls.

Me: What is the screen for?

Emalickel: Do you not think we enjoy gaming and entertainment? We can play or watch anything on this screen!

Me: Video games?

Emalickel: Everything.

Me: Skyrim?

Emalickel smiled proudly and chuckled lightly to himself.

Emalickel: I knew you were going to ask that. As I know you enjoy that game of Earth so deeply. Rest assured it is one of priority within my chambers.

There was a closed arched doorway on the southern wall.

Emalickel: That door simply leads out into the palace hallway where the courtyard windows are.

A set of open archways were on the western wall. We walked through them into another perpendicular hallway. Looking left, a door was at the end of the hall.

Emalickel: It, too, leads to the palace hallway.

To our right, at the end of the hallway was another archway leading into the Dining Room. Straight ahead of us were three archways which lead into another large room. This room contained white couches, a giant ottoman, a fireplace, end tables with orchid plants, and a large white-fur area rug.

Emalickel: This is the Living Room.

There were windows on the western wall looking out at the woodlands in the distance. On the northern wall were three more open archways leading to a 20-foot by 40-foot kitchen area. I had never seen such state of the art appliances and counters. Everything was sleek and shiny. Another archway was on the northern wall. Emalickel led us through. We came to a small perpendicular hallway. To our right was another archway leading to the Dining Room and to our left was a closed archway door. Emalickel went to open the door.

Emalickel: This room is quite familiar to you as you have slept in it a few times now.

We made our way back to the palace hallway and turned left towards the Throne Hall. Once we had come through, Emalickel walked us across an archway which bridged the western and eastern sides of the upper palace. It went right over the main central Throne Hall aisle below. The eastern half of the palace was a mirror image of the western. Emalickel pointed towards the Northeast corner.

Emalickel: And that area is Thorenel's Private Chambers. It is a mirror of mine.

Once across the walkway, we turned right towards a grand white staircase. Emalickel had an overly excited look on his face. I knew he was about to say something comical. He held out his arms and spoke in an exaggerated powerful tone.

Emalickel: And these, my dear Princess, prepare thyself! These are the Eastern Stairs! They lead up, and they lead down! And, well, that is their purpose. The end.

I shook my head and chuckled at him. He was always so serious, so it felt good to see this playful side of him.

We walked down the stairs, to a landing, and then back up some more stairs on the other side of the landing. Extending to the right of the landing were more stairs going down to the ground level of the Throne Hall. We stayed on the upper level and proceeded south down a huge hallway lined with about five 10-foot archways to our right which overlooked the Throne Hall. To our left were five windows overlooking the Eastern Courtyard. These windows were lined up with the archways and were just as large.

All the way back was a 15-foot archway leading out to a perpendicular hallway lined with windows. Turning left down this hallway led to the upper floor of the Great Library. It was the first door on the right. The second door on the right was the Education Quarters where celestials can read, train, and practice energy manipulation—or what I would call magic. Across the hall from the Great Library and the Education Quarters were several windows overlooking the Eastern Courtyard from a different angle.

We turned around to walk down to the opposite end of the hall, to the West. It mirrored the eastern side, except the rooms were for different purposes. Down on the opposite end of the hallway, the first door on the left was the balcony level of the Chapel. The second door on the left was the huge Spa Quarters. It was about 50-yards by 50-yards and was walled-off to form different rooms containing things such as hot tubs, sauna, a fountain, a hair dresser, yoga studio, meditation rooms with essential oils, crystals, massage rooms, and more pampering-like things.

There were extravagant stairs on both ends of this hallway. Emalickel and I went down the ones nearest to us on the Southwest corner of the palace. There were two sides to choose from to go down the stairs, then a landing area, and another perpendicular staircase to enter the front hall on the main level of the palace.

The front rooms on the ground level mirrored the front rooms of the upper level. The first door on the right, directly under the Spa Quarters, was a Residence Hall for the residing palace celestials. The ground level of the Chapel was the next door on the right. The middle section of the palace had windows looking out from the front of the palace at the southern scene of the ocean. Afterwards, the next door on the right was the ground level of the Great Library. Finally, at the eastern end of the front hall was another Residence Hall. It was directly under the Education Quarters of the upper level. The Residence Halls had about ten condo-like rooms within them branching off from a central hallway.

Emalickel: There are more Residence Halls on both the third and fourth floors of the palace which collectively contain 120 condos to further house our guests and residents.

91. Artist: Audiomachine
Song: The Fire Within

Emalickel did not want to interrupt the meeting in the Throne Hall, so he teleported us to the Billiard and Lounge, located on the main level at the northeast corner of the palace. I remembered it from the night before. There were two archways on the southern wall of this room which led directly to the Mead Hall which I had also remembered from the previous night. The Mead Hall had a door on its southern wall which led out to the Eastern Courtyard. There was another door on the western wall which led to the Great Hall which was about 50-feet by 100-feet.

Upon walking into the Great Hall from the Mead Hall, to our left was a closed arched doorway also leading out to the Eastern Courtyard and to our right was a closed arched doorway leading to the 75-foot by 150-foot Ballroom.

In the Ballroom, the entire northern wall was lined with glorious windows looking north out at the Valley of Dillectus and mountain range. The upper level of the Ballroom was encircled by a balcony overlooking the main level. The northern wall of the upper level also had windows. There was another closed door on the same southern wall as we entered, but Emalickel didn't open it.

Emalickel: That door opens to the Throne Hall just behind the archways beside the throne stairs. That is all of the eastern side. Let me take us to the northwestern side.

He placed his hands on my shoulders and all went dark for a

moment. When the light came back, we were standing in a 30-foot by 50-foot room filled with wines and meads.

Emalickel: This is the Wine Cellar.

This room was stocked with drinking sprits from ceiling to floor on shelves of gold. The bottles were all plain, clear, glass and void of labels. There were wooden barrels of mead stacked in the corners and all along any empty places on the walls. There were also a few of these barrels resting near the door. There were no windows in the room and only one door.

That door led to another room of the same size filled with all kinds of food and refrigerators. This room also had only one door. Walking through that door led us to the extravagant palace kitchen. It was even more extravagant than the huge one in Emalickel and Thorenel's Private Quarters. The kitchen was lined with windows on the northern wall. I saw the familiar view of the valley and mountains from these windows.

The last place he showed me was the Dining Hall. We arrived there by exiting the kitchen through an arched door on the eastern wall. We walked through a short hallway which ended with three giant open archways. These archways led to the beautiful Dining Hall. Like the Ballroom, the Dining Hall had an upper balcony area with smaller tables. On the ground floor there were countless rectangular tables. This room was equal in size to the Ballroom. Nearly every room in the entire palace had a gold and diamond chandelier handing from the ceiling.

The tour of the palace took nearly the entire day. It was enormous! I truly was astonished at the magnificence of the entire structure. There was no doubt it was of a divine creation.

92. Artist: Wardruna
Song: Solringen

Thorenel had finished the meeting of the orders. He found Emalickel and me as we walked out of the Dining Hall at the end of our palace tour. The two of them started talking about the orders, which I couldn't follow because they were using terminology I didn't understand. I continued gazing out in awe of the palace when I heard Emalickel's voice address me in a somber tone.

Emalickel: We should take you to the Spa Quarters. You will be pampered in every way tonight before your return to Earth.

Me: Return? But I have only been here a few days!

Emalickel: Yes, but you have seen and learned all which was ordered for this visit. Your visit this time was not intended to be as long as last time. Every celestial in the land is gathering in the valley tonight. We have been instructed to spawn another surge of light-energy to the Earth and begin another leap in awakening as we did in the Earth-year 2012. You must return to the Earth and resume your journey there as it is of upmost importance to your spiritual evolution.

Me: Will I get to come back again?

Emalickel: I am uncertain, at this time, whether you will return to Lapoi during your experience on Earth. I will be informed when it is time for your return, but I can not say when that will be. I can say this, you will one day return for certain, and one day you will reside here permanently.

One of Emalickel's assistants interrupted with a respectful bow. He informed Emalickel that Xabiel had sent for assistance with the warriors in some matter. Thorenel extended his hand to me.

Thorenel: May I escort you to the Spa Quarters?

I wanted to stay in Lapoi for longer. My heart started to feel empty as I thought about having to leave this beautiful majestic place once again and possibly not return for the rest of my Earth-life. Thorenel squeezed my hand.

Thorenel: Do not ache, beloved. Everything will be well. We will be right here anxiously waiting for you whenever you return—be it 5 years, 70 years, or 500 years.

I smiled at him, but it was forced. I wanted to stay, and I certainly did not want to wait, even five years, before I was able to see them all again.

When we arrived at the spa quarters, the assisting celestials took me from Thorenel and escorted me inside. The assistants were so charming. Dressed in white robes and eager to help, they seemed to take pride in their work and enjoyed what they did with a passion. I was first pampered to a full massage with hot stones in a large room with a hot tub. I relaxed in the hot tub for a very long time. They then dressed me in a fine, full length, cream-colored, diamond jeweled, flowing ball gown. My hair had been done with flowing curls and was pinned in a loose style, accented with tiny jewels. The celestials used their light-energy to brighten my skin and smooth it out.

Thorenel came into the spa after a while.

Thorenel: And how was it my…

He stopped with a look of stun on his face.

Thorenel: …my magnificent, ravishing, divine Princess?

It did feel really good and I did feel a little better.

Me: It really was helpful. I feel a little better.

Thorenel: We knew that would help and planned it accordingly. I had no idea your appearance would take my breath and heart away as you have done.

Thorenel extended his arm once again to me.

Thorenel: Come. . . . everyone has arrived in the valley now. Shall we make our way there?

We walked away from the Spa Quarters, headed for the Western

Stairs of the Throne Hall. My stomach sank. I was sad, nervous, and unsettled. Doubts circled my mind, and I felt like running away to hide in the cave. I saw Thorenel shaking his head at me.

Thorenel: No, do not do that. You are right on track in your fate on the Earth. You have done so well in your progress. Look at all you have done! You cannot bail now—I will not let you. As much as I will miss you during your departure, you must go back. You will go back. If you go to that cave, or anywhere else for that matter, we will be sure to find you.

Knowing he was right I had no choice but to face it. We headed down the stairs of the West side of the Throne Hall. I caught a glimpse of the valley. It was completely full of celestials. I also saw the brothers standing on the balcony with Emalickel. Wearing their royal cloaks with the golden symbol on the back, they stood away from the balcony railing, near the pool. Emalickel was talking to them about something. Thorenel and I entered the aisle of the Throne Hall and walked on the black runner rug. We headed for the stairs behind the thrones.

Emalickel saw us approaching. He broke away from his brothers to meet me at the top of the stairs. His face lit up and his eyes seemed to sparkle when he saw me. The lions were in a lying position and stayed that way as I slowly walked up the stairs with Thorenel. At the top, Emalickel adjusted my crown before extending his arm out to escort me.

I released Thorenel and went with Emalickel. Thorenel went ahead of us to stand with the rest of his brothers on the balcony. They all stood in a horizontal line about 15 feet from the balcony rail. As they formed this line, music started to play. Emalickel squeezed my arm hard.

Emalickel: You are going to be alright, my Princess.

At that, we walked out. We crossed over the bridge of the pool and towards the edge of the balcony's stone railing. The celestials roared in celebration. We positioned ourselves in front of the brothers and looked out at the celestials in the valley. Emalickel was scanning the valley repeatedly.

Emalickel: We are missing one of the guards.

I wasn't even going to ask how he could tell if one were missing. He never ceased to amaze me with his abilities.

A deep thud sounded in the distance followed by a celestial's voice.

Celestial: My Prince, my sincerest apologies. The mortal came out of his body during surgery, and I had to convince him to go back inside. He was a stubborn one.

Emalickel: You speak the truth, Zaezel. I understand. We are glad you are here. As you all know, tonight is a special night. We have been instructed in our orders to send another surge of light to the Earth.

93. Artist: Annie Lennox
Song: Into the West

Emalickel began walking along the balcony behind the rail.

Emalickel: You all know how this is done and why it is done. We are to do this every five years until the mortals have reached a bronze age of enlightenment. They are beginning to accept the energy, so we will continue our purge of it into them.

He walked over to me.

Emalickel: Your Princess will depart tonight. She, too, shall receive this light and continue her expansion on the Earth. We all have our places and purposes in creation and this is the time in which we shall send hope to the mortals—the guards walking among them, with them, as a part of them. Let us share our celestial energy.

Emalickel stepped up to the center part of the rail, and somewhat leaned over the rail. He held up his hands in the air with his palms facing each other.

Emalickel: Celestials of Millattus, if you can hear, let me know what you hear!

They held up their hands mirroring Emalickel. They roared out in unison, "Faith!" The brothers on the balcony were also doing this behind Emalickel as he continued.

Emalickel: If you can see, let me know what you see!

All the celestials yelled, "Hope!" as orbs of light began to build between their palms. The land lit up as during a sunrise. The brothers and Emalickel lit up the balcony with their orbs. They held the orbs between their palms as they continued building to the size of beach balls. The celestials in the valley had orbs the size of soccer balls. Emalickel spoke again.

Emalickel: If you can feel, let me know what you feel!

All the celestials yelled, "Love!"

Emalickel: Share it then. Release it to the mortals. Celestials . . . light the sky!

The orbs all began floating into the air. They rose like balloons floating away into the atmosphere. There were millions of them, perhaps billions. The sky was lit beautifully as they slowly drifted upward. The celestials lowered their hands and folded them in front of their hips. Emalickel, however, kept his hands up. He waved them in the air. All the orbs followed in the same directions he would move his hands. He swayed them left and the orbs would all move left; then he swayed them right, and they all moved right. When they moved they looked like shooting stars streaking across the sky. He continued waving them and mixing up the orbs like a giant soup until they all gathered into a cluster together. Emalickel chanted some phrase in the celestial language. I couldn't understand it. Then, he pushed his hands in an upward motion and the giant orb exited the atmosphere of Lapoi.

Emalickel turned around to me. He smiled, but I could see a hint of somberness in his expression. He started walking in my direction until he was behind me. I followed him with only my eyes for as far as I could. When I heard him stop behind me, I fixed my eyes ahead again and closed them while taking a deep breath. I knew what he was about to do.

Emalickel: It is time.

I dropped my head and slowly turned around to him. Drawing a large circle in the air with his finger, Emalickel formed a portal. I could see the inside of my car as if behind the steering wheel. I turned around again to see the Valley of Dillectus once more. I wanted to absorb as much as I could before returning to Earth. It was like I was trying to take a picture in my mind to look at later. Visions from my experiences on Lapoi recycled in my mind like the preview to a movie. It was interrupted by the sound of Emalickel's voice behind me again.

Emalickel: The time has come for your return to Earth... Adrienne.

I slowly turned around. One step at a time I brought myself to face the portal. I looked at each of the brothers. They were standing behind Emalickel, shoulder to shoulder, facing me with their arms folded down in front of them. As they watched me, their demeanor seemed calm and content. I tried to smile kindly to them.

94. Artist: Brunuhville
Song: The Elven Prophesy

Thorenel stepped forward. He was smiling at me reassuringly. He came up to me and stared into my eyes for a moment. It was as if he were trying to take a mental picture. It reminded me to do the same back at him. I took a mental picture so that I would always remember what those glowing glacier-blue eyes looked like as they rested upon that perfectly sculptured face, framed by long, angelic, golden locks of wavy hair. His eyes were so clear, clean, and reflective that I could see myself within them. I noticed how depressed I looked and forced myself to smile once again.

Thorenel: You do not have to pretend with me. I already know what you are feeling. I wish I could offer you more comfort than my words, but that is all I have to offer. Everything will be done. You will be complete. You are only departing to complete a quest called life, and then you will return here, and you will not have to leave again.

He pulled me into him with force for a passionate, tight embrace. It felt so very comforting in his arms. I felt his chin resting on the top of my head. Then, he pressed his lips there and took in the scent of my hair with a deep breath. He slowly pulled away and held my arms for another moment of eye contact before turning to take his place back in the line of brothers. I felt empty again.

Then, I turned to look at Emalickel. He reached up with both hands and slowly and gently removed the crown from my head.

Emalickel: I will put this safely in its place where it shall stay until your return, Princess of Lapoi.

I felt my eyes pooling up with tears, so I closed them. I took a step towards Emalickel until I felt the embrace of his comforting arms and the heat from his radiant body against mine. I was about to collapse in sorrow. Then Emalickel kissed my forehead.

When he did this, a wave of peace came over me. I felt strong and brave. I no longer felt anxious and sad. I was ready to complete my expansion on the Earth. I felt inspired to experience more on the Earth before coming back to Lapoi. Excited, I began stepping into the portal. I looked back at the Valley of Dillectus and the rainbow-hued skyline of Lapoi one last time as I put the other foot in.

That's when something unexpected happened. There was a loud

rumble, much louder than that of thunder. Confused, everyone looked upward into the sky. A large twinkling light, like that of a huge star, was approaching and descending high above the balcony. The brothers rushed to surround Emalickel. I heard Thorenel ask Emalickel.

Thorenel: Is that who I think it is, brother...?

Romenciel whispered aloud to himself.

Romenciel: Immanuel.

Then I heard Emalickel say loud enough for his brothers to hear.

Emalickel: Something big is about to take place, brothers. Prepare yourselves for what is to come.

He rushed to the edge of the balcony. The orb was almost there. It was extremely bright and about ten feet in diameter. Emalickel addressed the millions of celestials in the valley below.

Emalickel: Celestials! Take to your knees! The King has arrived!

Everyone, including Emalickel, dropped to one knee with their face looking downward. The orb started to fade in brightness, revealing the figure of a man who floated above the balcony. I felt an overwhelming feeling of comfort and joy as I felt myself slip back into the realm of Earth. Images of Earth, evolution, and major historical events rushed through my mind. It was like I was seeing everything, in chronological order, that had ever taken place in the history of Earth.

I was at a stop light. My car was stopped. I slowly turned my rearview mirror to see myself. I looked for a minute and gathered myself to become oriented. It was like I had been spaced out for an extended period of time and was snapping out of it. Thinking about everything that I had seen, it took only moments before I started developing doubts of the reality of it all. Had I really just experienced that or was it my imagination? I remembered what Emalickel had said about imagining things. He said that it is always real—whether I imagined it because it is real or if it is real because I have imagined it, either way it certainly does exist. I felt those powerful feelings of hope and faith. I looked at myself in the rearview mirror once more before turning it to look out the back window. I started to smile with excitement and spoke out loud.

Me: I'm going to start writing this stuff down!

95. Artist: Thomas Bergerson
Song: Empire of Angels

I still had thirty minutes of driving before arriving to the mountain. I felt the need to review everything and sort it out in my mind. I was overwhelmed with information and felt anxious about it. I actually thought out loud.

Ok, so God created everything including our Universe. The Universe has billions of galaxies. Nine of those galaxies host conscious life. In each of those nine galaxies there are three mortal planets and one giant celestial planet located near the center of these galaxies. The celestial planet oversees the mortal planets. Celestial beings inhabit the celestial planet while mortal begins inhabit the mortal planets.

The celestial beings came first in creation, then the mortals. The male mortals are actually celestials from Lapoi who chose to temporarily experience mortality. The female mortals are from one of the other nine galaxies, called Jesserion, who volunteered to join the males in the mortal experience. The mortal experience expands their consciousness and evolves their spirit. Through the mortal experience, celestials are able to feel emotions and contrast, thus providing enrichment of the self.

The celestial beings who remain on the celestial planet hold positions including Princedoms, Warriors, and Guards. There are two Princedoms on each of the nine celestial planets who are in charge of overseeing their entire galaxy. They are to receive orders passed down from God and execute those orders among their Warriors and Guards.

The Guards are the celestials who directly interact with mortals of the mortal planets. They can sometimes physically manifest. When an angel is seen on a mortal planet, it is usually a guard. The warriors are the celestials who protect the galaxy. They can also affect and influence the mortal planets according to God's will. Both the warriors and the guards carry out the orders of God's will as it was passed down from Him to the Dominions to the Princedoms, and then to the guards and warriors.

God has His own agenda for each galaxy and each planet. Our galaxy is called Millattus. The celestial planet of Millattus is called Lapoi. The three mortal planets within Millattus are called Earth, Fynne, and Grahst. The Princedoms in charge of Millattus are Emalickel and Thorenel.

There are three galaxies of the nine that are inhabited completely by negative beings. Within those galaxies, both the celestials and the mortals are corrupted. They were created for balance in the universal experience. They have the same titles, positions, and expectations as the other galaxies, but they do not always do as they are supposed to do. They are power-hungry, intruding on the other galaxies to appease their egos and develop a sense of power.

They try to control the mortals of other galaxies by influencing them to make decisions which will cause fear-like emotions to mass numbers of mortal beings. I'd be willing to bet they especially target higher-ranking officials such as within the governments worldwide. They feed off of fear and cause whatever havoc they can to instill emotions associated with fear such as worry, anxiety, sadness, anger, frustration, jealousy, and stress. It makes them feel in control and also takes away from the progress and accomplishments of the celestials of the target galaxy.

The Bible speaks of angels and demons, and I wonder if this is where it all derives from. The angels are from our very own Lapoi and the demons come from one of the three negative galaxies. There is an ongoing celestial battle going on between our Lapoian Warriors and the warriors of the negative galaxies.

There are also countless stories of alien abductions by beings with large dark eyes who carry a negative aura and do experiments on mortals. I wonder if these beings are from one of the three negative galaxies. There are also stories of aliens who look similar to us in appearance, often glowing in light, and seem to be helping in various ways. I wonder if these are actually the celestials of Lapoi.

And what about that big bright orb that everyone knelt to? Romenciel had referred to the orb as Immanuel and Emalickel had referred to it as, "The King." Could that be in reference to Jesus Christ? If so, what was He doing? What was He about to share with the celestials? Emalickel said it meant something big is about to happen, but what could it be?

I realized that everything started to make sense. All the unexplained files of the Earth somehow fit into this story. All of the major religions of the world somehow are integrated into this story. This goes to show that nobody has been completely wrong and nobody has been completely right. Although I felt clear about what has been and how everything fits together, I felt very unclear about where we were all going and what the future would hold—not only for Earth, but for the entire collective universe of creation.

96. Artist: Thomas Bergerson
Song: Two Hearts

The red light turned green. I pressed the gas pedal and began moving forward. I realized that is all I could do—move forward. I didn't know what would take place on the road ahead, but it was senseless to drive worrying about what may or could happen ahead. I realized that this is how one must approach life. We must live for the experience, including the good and the bad. The experience will expand us and take us to where we evolve, doing what we are supposed to be doing.

Emalickel had said it best; for every road block, there will always be a detour which steers to the road meant to be traveled. God ensures His will is carried out as it should be. No entities have any power over Him, as He created The All with perfection from the beginning. We must trust in Him completely and know that He is truly the One in which we are all extensions. We must always have faith in Him and in His will. We must always have hope to evolve from our experiences given by Him.

Most importantly, though, we must always reach for the emotions of love—happiness, joy, peace, contentment, excitement, gratefulness, appreciation, and passion. This will keep us in our light, repulsing any negative energy. This will evolve our souls and spirits. Love will ensure our mortal purpose has been fulfilled to its fullest extent so that we will evolve to the next level, exhibiting Christ Consciousness.

We must always remember love, as it is the most important emotion. It creates, it spreads, and it offers light against the darkness. No amount of darkness can make a light become dim, but one little candle can light an entire room from darkness. Love is truly the bearer of all things and we shall remember it always. May the guards watch over us, the warriors protect us, and the Princedoms see to God's will. Remember, God is within you, a part you, experiencing with you as you are a direct extension of Him. He is with us all, every single thing in existence, always and eternally.

VERSES

"Consider it all joy, my brethren, when you encounter various trials, knowing that the testing of your faith produces endurance. And let endurance have its perfect result, so that you may be perfect and complete, lacking in nothing." James 1:2-4

"By faith we understand that the worlds were prepared by the word of God, so that what is seen was not made out of things which are visible." Hebrews 11:3

"But if it is by the finger of God that I cast out demons, then the Kingdom of God has come upon you." Luke 11:20

"For the Kingdom of God is not just a lot of talk; it is living by God's power." 1 Corinthians 4:20

He determines the number of the stars; He gives to all of them their names. Great is our Lord, and abundant in power; His understanding is beyond measure." Psalm 147:4-5

"The Son radiates God's own glory and expresses the very character of God, and he sustains everything by the mighty power of His command." Hebrews 1:3

"Now all glory to God, who is able, through His mighty power at work within us, to accomplish infinitely more than we might ask or think." Ephesians 3:20

"Our struggle is not against any flesh and blood, but against the rulers, against the powers, against the world forces of this darkness, against the spiritual forces of wickedness in the heavenly places." Ephesians 6:12

"I have told you these things so that in me you will have peace. In this world you will have trouble. But take heart! I have overcome the world." John 16:33

"Be still and know that I am God. I will be exalted among the nations. I will be exalted in the earth." Psalm 46:10.

APPENDIX A

PRONUNCIATION KEY

Key

a - apple, alligator
ā - ape, acorn
ä - father, ah
ə - about, circus, gallop
ē - eat, bee
e - elephant, egg
i - igloo, indigo, iguana
ō - oats, toe, boat
û - heard, urge, term
ōō - boot
th - this, that, the
ô - ore, for, hoarse
ö - ought, caught, pot

Names/Characters:

- Emalickel (ē·**mal**·i·kel)
- Thorenel (**thôr**·e·nel
- Xabiel (eks·**ā**·bē·ul)
- Romenciel (rō·**min**·sē·el)
- Dennoliel (de·**nä**·lē·el)
- Seronimel (se·**rä**·ne·mel)
- Zamadriel (zə·**mä**·drē·el)
- Hadriannel (hə·**drä**·nē·el)
- Barthaldeo (bär·***th*ôl**·dē·ō)
- Jamaleo (jä·**mä**·lē·ō)
- Zaezel (**zā**·zul)
- Immanuel (i·**man**·yōō·ul)

Places/Locations:

- Millattus (mi·**la**·tus)
- Lapoi (lə·**pöi**)
- Fynne (fin)
- Grahst (gräst)
- Terpetrus (tûr·**pet**·rus)
- Dillectus (di·**lek**·tus)
- Karnequlus (kär·**nek**·yōō·lus)
- Haffelnia (ha·**fel**·nē·ə)
- Jesserion (je·**sir**·ē·än)

APPENDIX B

MUSIC PLAYLIST CREDITS

1. Artist: Audiomachine
Song: Existence (Extended)
Album: Existence (2013)
Available: Amazon Music, iTunes

2. Artist: Future World Music
Song: New Beginnings
Album: Reign of Vengeance (2011)
Available: Amazon Music, iTunes

3. Artist: Nordwise
Song: Evolve II
Available: www.nordwise.com

4. Artist: Symphony of Specters (Charles Evans)
Song: Things Worth Fighting For
Available: Sound Cloud

5. Artist: Audiomachine
Song: Spirit of the Stallion

Album: The Platinum Series IV: Labyrinth (2010)
Available: search.audiomachine.com

6. Artist: Really Slow Motion (Cesc Vilà)
Song: Suns and Stars
Album: Elevation (2014)
Available: Amazon Music, iTunes

7. Artist: Audiomachine
Song: Age of Innocence
Album: Tree of Life (2013)
Available: Amazon Music, iTunes

8. Artist: We are all Astronauts
Song: Ether
Album: Lambo - Original Soundtrack (2018)
Available: Amazon Music

9. Artist: Patrick Doyle
Song: Can You See Jane?
Album: Thor (OMPS - 2011)
Available: Amazon Music

10. Artist: PostHaste Music (Mark Petrie)
Song: Omega Point
Album: Titan Approaching (2016)
Available: Amazon Music, iTunes

11. Artist: Mark Petrie
Song: Where We Are
Album: Atonement (2017)
Available: iTunes

12. Artist: Mark Petrie
Song: High Stakes

Album: Binary (2011)
Available: iTunes

13. Artist: Epic Score (Gabriel Shadid)
Song: This is Our Land
Album: Epic Action and Adventure Vol 5 (2010)
Available: iTunes

14. Artist: Howard Shore
Song: The Bridge to Khazad Dum (Extended)
Album: Lord of the Rings: Fellowship of the Ring (OMPS)
Available: Amazon Music

15. Artist: Hans Zimmer
Song: Chevaliers De Sangreal
Album: The Da Vinci Code
Available: Amazon Music

16. Artist: Really Slow Motion
Song: You Will Be This Legend
Album: Of Mist and Magic (2014)
Available: Amazon Music, iTunes

17. Artist: Tunes of Fantasy (Florian Bur)
Song: White Angel
Album: Dream Once Again (2013)
Available: Amazon Music, iTunes

18. Artist: Thomas Bergerson
Song: Immortal
Album: Illusions (2011)
Available: Amazon Music, iTunes

19. Artist: PostHaste Music (Mark Petrie)
Song: Convergence

Album: PHM Presents: The Best of Mark Petrie (2014)
Available: Amazon Music, iTunes

20. Artist: Audiomachine
Song: The New Earth
Album: Epica (2012)
Available: Amazon Music, iTunes

21. Artist: Mark Petrie
Song: Majestic
Album: Binary (2017)
Available: Amazon Music

22. Artist: Audiomachine
Song: Godspeed
Album: Magnus: B-Sides
Available: Amazon Music, iTunes

23. Artist: Audiomachine
Song: Hell's Battalion
Album: Chronicles (2012)
Available: Amazon Music, iTunes

24. Artist: Patrick Doyle
Song: Ride to Observatory
Album: Thor (OMPS - 2011)
Available: Amazon Music, iTunes

25. Artist: Thomas Bergerson
Song: Colors of Love
Album: Sun (2014)
Available: Amazon Music, iTunes

26. Artist: Epic Soul Factory (Cesc Vilà & Fran Soto)
Song: Everdream

Album: Sigma (2015)
Available: Amazon Music, iTunes

27. Artist: Patryk Scelina
Song: Voices of Namibia
Album: Original Soundtrack (2016)
Available: Amazon Music, iTunes

28. Artist: Audiomachine
Song: Transcendence
Album: Epica (2012)
Available: Amazon Music, iTunes

29. Artist: Adrian Von Zeigler
Song: Home of Heroes
Album: Moonsong (2016)
Available: Amazon Music, iTunes

30. Artist: Audiomachine (Ivan Torrent)
Song: Wars of Faith (Extended Remix)
Album: Magnus (2015)
Available: Amazon Music, iTunes

31. Artist: Epic Score (Aleksandar Dimitrijevic)
Song: Waiting for Gods
Album: Epic Action & Adventure Vol. 14 (2012)
Available: Amazon Music, iTunes

32. Artist: Adrian Von Zeigler
Song: Angel of Death
Album: Starchaser (2012)
Available: Amazon Music, iTunes

33. Artist: Adrian Von Zeigler
Song: Fallen

Album: Queen of Thornes (2014)
Available: Amazon Music, iTunes

34. Artist: Audiomachine
Song: Akkadian Empire
Album: Chronicles (2012)
Available: Amazon Music, iTunes

35. Artist: Audiomachine
Song: Sand of Time
Album: Chronicles (2012)
Available: Amazon Music, iTunes

36. Artist: Audiomachine
Song: Guardians at the Gate
Album: Chronicles (2012)
Available: Amazon Music, iTunes

37. Artist: Epic Score (Aaron Sapp)
Song: You Were Born for This
Album: Epic Action & Adventure Vol. 10 (2011)
Available: Amazon Music, iTunes

38. Artist: Epic Score (Aleksander Dimitrijevic)
Song: They Fought as Legends
Album: Epic Action & Adventure Vol. 11 (2011)
Available: Amazon Music, iTunes

39. Artist: Epic Score
Song: You Must Overcome
Album: Epic Action & Adventure Vol. 13 (2012)
Available: Amazon Music, iTunes

40. Artist: Epic Score (Edward Bradshaw)
Song: Prepare for the Onslaught

Album: Epic Action & Adventure Vol. 14 (2012)
Available: Amazon Music, iTunes

41.Artist: Howard Shore
Song: The Bridge to Khazad Dum (Extended)
Album: Lord of the Rings: Fellowship of the Ring (OMPS)
Available: Amazon Music

42. Artist: Tunes of Fantasy (Florian Bur)
Song: White Angel
Album: Dream Once Again (2013)
Available: Amazon Music, iTunes

43. Artist: Audiomachine (Ivan Torrent)
Song: Wars of Faith (Extended Remix)
Album: Magnus (2015)
Available: Amazon Music, iTunes

44. Artist: PostHaste Music (Mark Petrie)
Song: Convergence
Album: PHM Presents: The Best of Mark Petrie (2014)
Available: Amazon Music, iTunes

45. Artist: Hans Zimmer
Song: Time
Album: Inception (OMPS - 2010)
Available: Amazon Music, iTunes

46. Artist: Eurielle
Song: Je t'Adore
Album: Arcadia (2015)
Available: Amazon Music, iTunes

47. Artist: Mattia Cupelli
Song: Waves

Album: Waves (2017)
Available: Amazon Music, iTunes

48. Artist: Audiomachine
Song: No Matter What
Album: Life (2017)
Available: Amazon Music, iTunes

49. Artist: Audiomachine (Ivan Torrent)
Song: Wars of Faith (Extended Remix)
Album: Magnus (2015)
Available: Amazon Music, iTunes

50. Artist: Kevin Ohlsson
Song: Returning Heroes
Available: Sound Cloud

51. Artist: Mattia Cupelli
Song: Mooncatcher
Album: Waves (2017)
Available: Amazon Music, iTunes

52. Artist: Steve Jablonsky
Song: My Name is Lincoln
Album: The Island (OMPS - 2015)
Available: Amazon Music, iTunes

53. Artist: Two Steps from Hell
Song: Miracles
Album: Miracles (200)
Available: Amazon Music, iTunes

54. Artist: Really Slow Motion
Song: You Will Be This Legend
Album: Of Mist and Magic (2014)

Available: Amazon Music, iTunes

55. Artist: Future World Music
Song: Anthem of the World
Album: A Hero Will Rise (2012)
Available: Amazon Music, iTunes

56. Artist: Really Slow Motion (Dylan C. Jones)
Song: End of An Era
Album: Spectrum (Industry Release)
Available: hdsoundi.com, Amazon Music, iTunes

57. Artist: Brunuhville
Song: Spirit of the Wild
Album: Age of Wonders (2016)
Available: Amazon Music, iTunes

58. Artist: Brunuhville
Song: Celestial Temple
Album: Age of Wonders (2016)
Available: Amazon Music, iTunes

59. Artist: M83
Song: Starwaves
Album: Oblivion (OMPS - 2013)
Available: Amazon Music, iTunes

60. Artist: Anne Lennox
Song: Into the West
Album: Lord of the Rings: Return of the King (OMPS)
Available: Amazon Music, iTunes

61. Artist: Epic Soul Factory (Cesc Vilà & Fran Soto)
Song: Riding the Light
Album: Sigma (2015)

Available: Amazon Music, iTunes

62. Artist: Audiomachine
Song: Homecoming
Album: Tree of Life (2013)
Available: Amazon Music, iTunes

63. Artist: Audiomachine
Song: The Fire Within
Album: Tree of Life (2013)
Available: Amazon Music, iTunes

64. Artist: Audiomachine
Song: Across the Horizon
Album: Tree of Life (2013)
Available: Amazon Music, iTunes

65. Artist: Audiomachine
Song: Leaving the Nest
Album: Tree of Life (2013)
Available: Amazon Music, iTunes

66. Artist: Really Slow Motion
Song: Forever in my Dreams
Album: Solitude (Industry Release)
Available:

67. Artist: Natanel Arnson
Song: A Hero Will Rise
Available: Sound Cloud

68. Artist: Mattia Cupelli
Song: Waves
Album: Waves (2017)
Available: Amazon Music, iTunes

69. Artist: Danny Rayel
Song: Rise of a Hero
Available: Sound Cloud

70. Artist: PostHaste Music (Mark Petrie)
Song: Convergence
Album: PHM Presents: The Best of Mark Petrie (2014)
Available: Amazon Music, iTunes

71. Artist: Patryk Scelina
Song: Voices of Namibia
Album: Original Soundtrack (2016)
Available: Amazon Music, iTunes

72. Artist: Audiomachine
Song: Radiant
Album: Life (2017)
Available: Amazon Music, iTunes

73. Artist: Kevin Ohlsson
Song: Returning Heroes
Available: Sound Cloud

74. Artist: Hans Zimmer
Song: Time
Album: Inception (OMPS - 2010)
Available: Amazon Music, iTunes

75. Artist: Audiomachine
Song: Rebirth
Album: Tree of Life (2013)
Available: Amazon Music, iTunes

76. Artist: Mark Petrie
Song: Majestic

Album: Binary (2017)
Available: Amazon Music

77. Artist: Future World Music
Song: World of Dreams
Album: A Hero Will Rise (2012)
Available: Amazon Music, iTunes

78. Artist: Audiomachine
Song: The Dreammaker
Album: Life (2017)
Available: Amazon Music, iTunes

79. Artist: Adrian Von Zeigler
Song: Song of Brotherhood
Album: Starchaser (2012)
Available: Amazon Music, iTunes

80. Artist: Brian Tyler
Song: Thor, Son of Odin
Album: Thor: The Dark World (OMPS - 2013)
Available: Amazon Music

81. Artist: Thomas Bergerson
Song: Colors of Love
Album: Sun (2014)
Available: Amazon Music, iTunes

82. Artist: Brunuhville
Song: Dragonland
Album: Tales from the Lost Kingdom (2012)
Available: Amazon Music, iTunes

83. Artist: Stephen D. Lemaire
Song: Voyage in Time

Album: Eclipitum (2015)
Available: Amazon Music, iTunes

84. Artist: Brunuhville
Song: Medieval Legends
Album: Anima (2012)
Available: Amazon Music, iTunes

85. Artist: Olexandr Ignatov
Song: Emotions
Album: Piano Scenes (2018)
Available: Amazon Music, iTunes

86. Artist: Future World Music
Song: Anthem of the World
Album: A Hero Will Rise (2012)
Available: Amazon Music, iTunes

87. Artist: Adrian Von Zeigler
Song: For the King
Album: Starchaser (2012)
Available: Amazon Music, iTunes

88. Artist: Tunes of Fantasy (Florian Bur)
Song: White Angel
Album: Dream Once Again (2013)
Available: Amazon Music, iTunes

89. Artist: Mattia Cupelli
Song: Mooncatcher
Album: Waves (2017)
Available: Amazon Music, iTunes

90. Artist: Mattia Cupelli
Song: Waves

Album: Waves (2017)
Available: Amazon Music, iTunes

91. Artist: Audiomachine
Song: The Fire Within
Album: Tree of Life (2013)
Available: Amazon Musi, iTunes

92. Artist: Wardruna
Song: Solringen
Album: Runaljod-Yggdrasil (2013)
Available: Amazon Music, iTunes

93. Artist: Annie Lennox
Song: Into the West
Album: Lord of the Rings: Return of the King (OMPS)
Available: Amazon Music, iTunes

94. Artist: Brunuhville
Song: The Elven Prophesy
Album: Northwind (2015)
Available: Amazon Music, iTunes

95. Artist: Thomas Bergerson
Song: Empire of Angels
Album: Sun (2014)
Available: Amazon Music, iTunes

96. Artist: Thomas Bergerson
Song: Two Hearts
Album: Sun (2014)
Available: Amazon Music, iTunes

APPENDIX C

VISUAL AIDS

The following pages are rough-sketches, drawn by the author, to help the reader obtain a clearer vision of certain parts of the Palace of Lapoi.

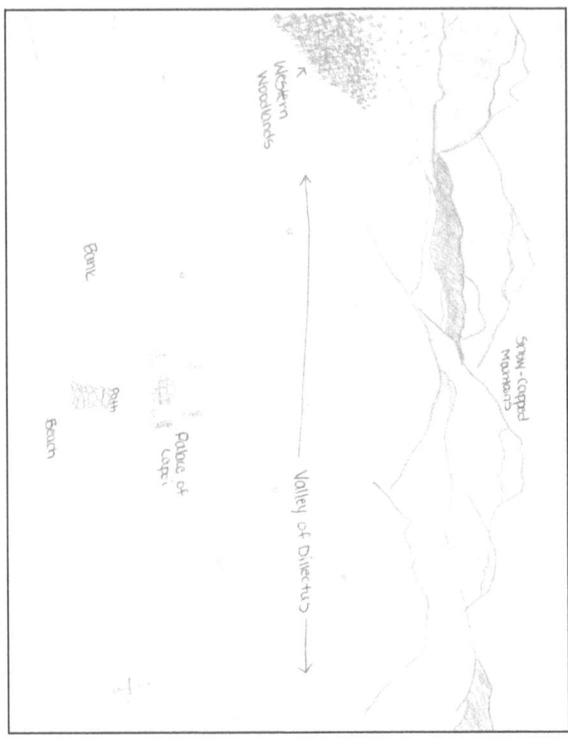

Aerial view of the Palace of Lapoi and its surrounding land

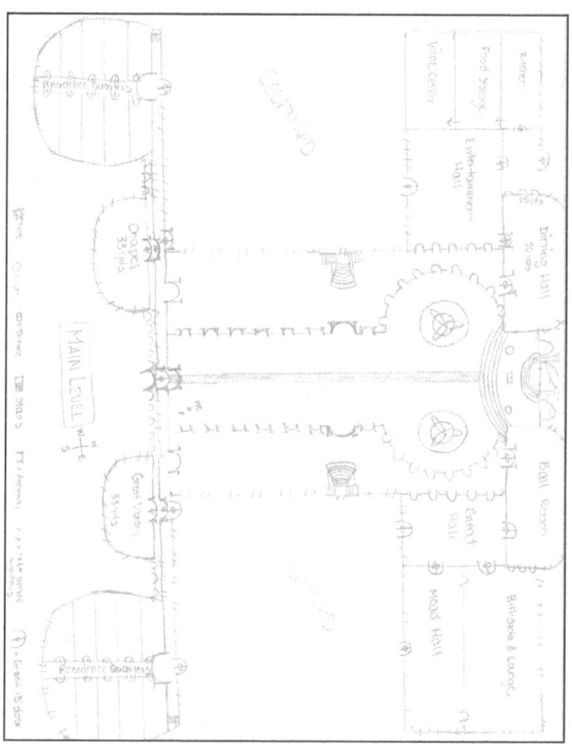

Blueprint for palace main level

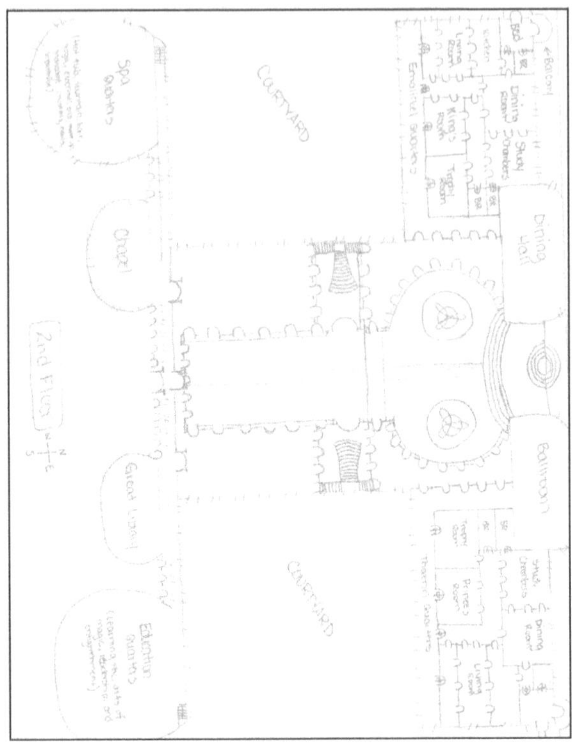

Blueprint for palace second level

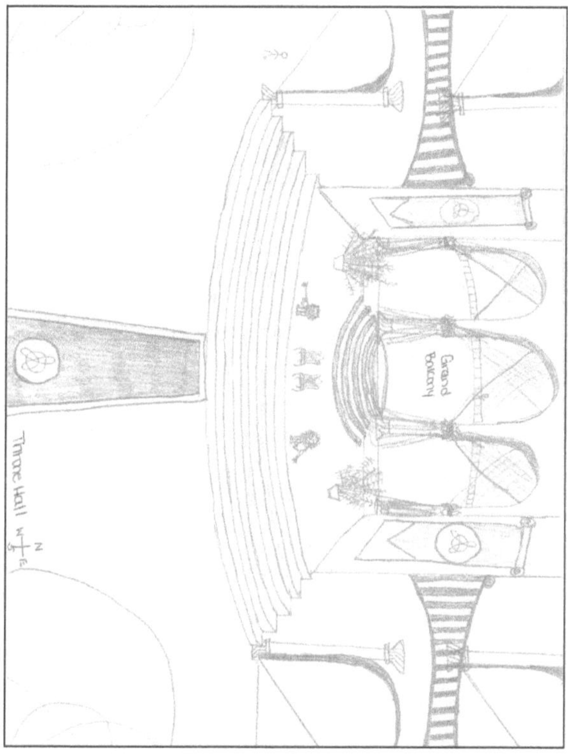

Palace Throne Hall (facing thrones from the central aisle)

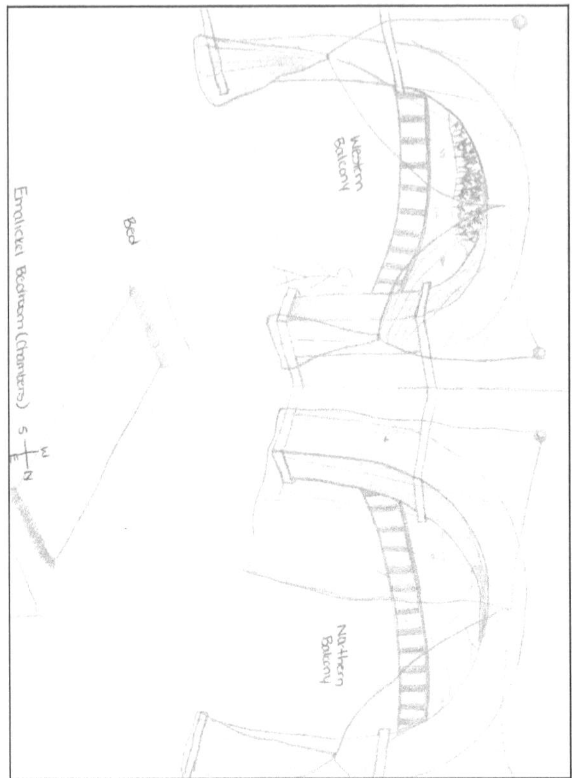

Emalickel's Bedroom Chambers

ABOUT THE AUTHOR

A. M. TRUE became an author unintentionally. Her first novel, *Emalickel: The Celestials are Real*, was written over a period of five years after a very vivid dream she experienced. During that time, she had been avidly recording her dreams for memory recall. The first novel was one such recording. Initially, she kept this dream private, known only by those closest to her. In 2018, she decided to make it public.

Born in 1984 in the United States, True enjoys living a quiet, simple life in the rural country. She has a profound love and respect for life, nature, and animals. A deep thinker and dreamer, she enjoys moments of quiet and serenity. Aside from a few select shows, she does not watch television, but prefers expanding her mind in topics of science, history, and spirituality. During the school year, she works as an elementary teacher. In her free time she enjoys archery, home improvement, landscaping, playing Elder Scrolls V: Skyrim on PlayStation 4, and listening to music. She also has played the cello, piano, and guitar. Her favorite types of music include Celtic/traditional Irish, cinematic scores, classic rock, and the music of the 1960's.

A. M. True still regularly recalls and records her dreams. Who knows what she will share next?

facebook.com/authoramtrue

instagram.com/authoramtrue

amazon.com/author/amtrue

www.ingramcontent.com/pod-product-compliance
Lightning Source LLC
Chambersburg PA
CBHW060805310726
48980CB00002B/246
* 9 7 8 0 5 7 8 5 3 6 2 7 9 *